WHEN IN

Dublin

TRACY AVERY

Heuston Press

Copyright © 2026 by Tracy Avery

All rights reserved.

No part of this publication may be reproduced, distributed, or transmitted in any form or by any means, including photocopying, recording, or other electronic or mechanical methods, without the prior written permission of the publisher, except as permitted by U.S. copyright law. For permission requests, contact the author at www.TracyAvery.com.

This is a work of fiction. Names, characters, businesses, places, events, locales, and incidents are either the products of the author's imagination or used in a fictitious manner. Any resemblance to actual persons, living or dead, or actual events is purely coincidental.

Book Cover and Illustration by Andy Bridge

ISBN: 978-1-970967-00-5 (paperback)
ISBN: 978-1-970967-01-2 (hardcover)
First edition 2026

For anyone who has ever felt like they didn't
have a passion or a place in the world . . .
you do.

A Note to Readers

Reader expectations are an important part of the reading experience, and I wanted to take a moment to share a little context before you begin *When in Dublin*. While this story contains some romance and many familiar romantic elements, at its heart, it is a work of women's fiction. Jess's journey is ultimately one of self-discovery and growth. If you enjoy stories that combine travel, humor, romance, and self-discovery, I hope this one resonates with you.

Thank you so much for being here, and I hope you enjoy the journey.

1

THEY SAY WHEN ONE door closes, another one opens—but standing frozen in front of the turquoise door, I wondered how long I'd have to wait.

It was the same unmistakable shade as the one I almost walked through with him, back when our future still felt inevitable. Even after two years, that door occupied more real estate in my mind than I cared to admit.

I could still picture the life I'd once rehearsed in my head. Coming home from work, sorting through junk mail as I kicked off my heels and caught a whiff of whatever he'd made for dinner. Friends tapping the brass knocker for one of his impromptu gatherings. A honeymoon on some island, him in a ridiculous souvenir hat, carrying me over the threshold like we were in a movie. I'd even imagined us wrestling a too-big crib box through the doorway, laughing as we failed miserably.

But that future, once so vivid and tangible, had unraveled. And I didn't know if it was *him* I missed . . . or the turquoise door we never ended up opening together.

But *this* turquoise door though? It would be mine alone. The mail would be addressed only to me. Dinner parties only if I'd planned them far in advance. No romantic threshold crossings, no crib. According to my original plan, I should have been married by twenty-eight and with that birthday less than two months away, I was determined not to miss another major life milestone in the plan. If I couldn't check the relationship box, then I'd check the homeownership one—even if buying a house alone wasn't part of the plan.

"You could always repaint it, you know? Something cheerful. Maybe yellow?" Mom shielded her eyes from the sun as we stepped onto the herringbone brick porch.

"Yellow?" I repeated, judgment dripping from each syllable while fishing my notebook from my black leather tote. Inside it, I'd printed out the full listing sheet and a checklist of requirements, complete with scoring rubrics.

"You hate yellow," I added.

She hummed but didn't deny it.

"I just can't believe the sellers didn't paint it something more neutral. A front door sets a first impression. It's like choosing not to wear a belt. Or earrings."

"I think the turquoise gives it character, but I know you'll paint everything black or white," she said.

I went to give her a look, but she was already peeking through the window, mumbling to herself approvingly.

The house was a cozy South Tampa bungalow in a neighborhood known for its ideal location and sky-high prices. Along a street lined with multimillion-dollar homes, tucked behind mature willow trees, sat this three bedroom, two bath gem. With modern upgrades and an actual garage, it checked every box, despite its lackluster exterior. I'd nearly disqualified it on the door alone, which even I knew was insane. My realtor practically dragged me to see it twice before. And now, for our third viewing in a week, I was bringing my mom with us for backup.

"It only scored a seventy-eight," I muttered, tapping the pen to my chin.

"Out of a hundred?" Mom asked.

"Yes. My spreadsheet penalized it heavily for curb appeal."

She shook her head and smiled like she couldn't decide whether to be impressed or concerned.

"You've been house hunting for a year, Jess." Her eyes darted to the realtor pulling into the driveway. "Maybe it's time to trust your gut instead of your models and spreadsheets?" She was, of course, right. I'd been touring houses for well over a year; color coding spreadsheets, tracking comps and stalking every new listing like it was my side hustle.

"People who trust their gut are the same people who spend $300 at Target when they only went for sunscreen. This is a $600,000 invest-ment. I'm not looking to my digestive system for input."

Never one for any sort of confrontation, she lifted her hands in sur-render as the realtor hurried up the walkway, jiggling the keys and apol-ogizing for being late. But she wasn't late, we had arrived fifteen minutes early.

The truth was, buying a house wasn't *just* about the plan or even the fact that everyone around me seemed to have already purchased a home. It was also because in consulting, being on the Partner track meant showing stability in the community. Candidates for the Partner track owned homes and didn't look like they were going anywhere. And I wasn't. Tampa was all I'd ever known, and I wanted to lay down roots. Even my college was only forty minutes from my parents' house, so Sunday dinners at home had been religion since freshman year.

Inside, light spilled across the classic beige and white staging furniture which mimicked my own style and complemented the fresh linen air freshener. The staging served its purpose because I could really picture myself living there.

"Geesh, this furniture is so sterile. Reminds me of a waiting room," Mom said under her breath before wandering toward the kitchen.

A squeal pierced the air and echoed through the room. I braced for a rat to come tearing into the living room.

"Oh my goodness gracious," she gushed. "This island is *huge*. Three times the size of ours."

"Well, your house was built in the eighties. You two could have a big island if you ever remodeled."

She smiled faintly. "Our house works just fine for us."

They were still in the home they raised us in, and Mom always said it'd be the home she'd die in. A beautiful sentiment once I got past the morbidity of it. Dad always said that the true measure of parenting was whether your grown kids still wanted to spend time with you. And my brothers and I did.

During late-night study sessions and the brutal workweeks of the first few years at work, Mom would leave containers of homemade food outside my door. I wanted to be able to do that one day too. To have kids that wanted to stay in the city they were raised in, where I could see them and support them without suffocating. But at twenty-seven, with no romantic prospects in sight, I needed to prioritize goals that didn't depend on anyone else. The husband and kids would have to come later.

"You know," Mom said softly, "you don't have to prove anything to anyone. You don't need to check arbitrary boxes before you're thirty."

"I like plans." I shrugged. "It's not about turning thirty soon, it's about controlling what I can. Plus, it's a smart investment."

She smiled knowingly. "I know. Even as a kid, you'd stay up all night to make sure you hit your reading goals for those monthly book challenges. And you'd make color coded activity sheets."

"And look how perfect I turned out." I flashed a toothy smile.

"You sure did."

Our footsteps clicked against the polished hardwood in a way that felt like I'd already moved in. The realtor had listed off replacement dates for the HVAC and roof—details I'd already memorized—as my fingers glided along the thin molding accentuating the hallway. A waft of cedar drifted out of the surprisingly spacious linen closet.

The primary bedroom wasn't staged, so I filled it in myself. My bed centered between the windows and a reading chair tucked into the corner, even though I'd probably spend more time with memos and presentations than novels.

"I can see you here," Mom whispered, reading my mind. "It feels grounded. Sensible. Like something you could manage on your own." She smiled, her gaze dropping to the floor—the telltale sign she was holding back. A trait she'd passed down to me.

I couldn't tell if she meant it as a compliment or a jab. She's the type that probably thinks it's weird for a single woman to buy a house with a yard and garage but would never say it aloud.

I flipped on the light in the en suite bathroom knowing exactly what it'd reveal: bright white tile, brushed gold fixtures, and a faint scent of Lysol. When I first viewed the house earlier in the week, the modern, white primary bath was a huge tipping point for me.

My navy silk blouse and high-waisted black pants reflected sharply in the mirror, a stark contrast against the brightness of the room. Other managers at my firm dressed more casually, but I dressed for the job I wanted. And the job I wanted was to be a consulting Partner.

I was too young to be a full-fledged Partner, but the plan was to make Associate Partner in the next two years before turning thirty. A few years after that: make Partner, have kids in my mid-thirties, and work toward a senior leadership role at my firm by forty. A clean and orderly plan.

After the realtor showed us the backyard complete with a shed and the laundry room with a tiny mudroom, she delivered the blow. "Just a heads up—the sellers have received two strong offers. They're asking for the highest and best by 8 p.m. tonight."

My pulse raced. Pressure decisions violated every personal rule I had. But this wasn't on whim. It was the result of dozens of open houses, countless hours of research, and my personal rating system that now showed the house with the turquoise door as the most logical investment. Still, my eyes ping-ponged between Mom and the realtor, hoping one of them would say something to reaffirm my decision to go for the house. If I hesitated now, it wouldn't be because I needed more time—it'd be because I was afraid to commit to the life I'd planned.

And I wasn't afraid.

"I want this house," I said, confidently. "I have a competitive number in mind."

With my annual performance review the next day and knowing my billable hours for the year were the highest in my class, I was expecting a bonus that would allow me to bid beyond my initial budget.

Her eyes lit up, probably delighted at the prospect that our yearlong search might be coming to an end. "Fantastic. I'll notify the seller's agent that they can expect an offer from us tonight. Let's go to my office and draw up the paperwork." She slammed the case of her electronic planner shut.

Accomplishment and nausea swirled inside my stomach.

Inside my Acura, the Florida sun pressed down with such intensity, I wanted to tear off my black pants like a savage. Sweat was piling in every nook and cranny, and I blasted the air conditioner so hard it drowned out the music. My fingers gripped tighter around the wheel as I drew in a deep breath.

You can do this. You *are* doing this. Alone.

And if my offer was accepted, at least step one was simple.

Paint the door black.

2

My concentration was locked on the dual monitors as I toggled between a client presentation and the latest cash flow model. Keeping my eyes on the screens, I reached into the drawer and pulled out my red pen. Black was for making the to-do lists and red was for crossing things off. With the anxiety of the day looming, I needed to be productive and stay on top of every detail.

From the corner of my eye, something bright red began to cackle—followed by loud chatter at a pitch that could attract stray cats.

Raya.

Swiveling in my chair, I saw her holding court three cubicles down. The red turned out to be a perfectly tailored, knee-length dress that was surely custom-made for her body. Her long blonde hair was swept into a loose, low ponytail that showed off the delicate layers of gold around her neck. Effortless and chic. I became acutely aware of my cream-colored blouse and wide-leg taupe pants complete with a matching belt and kitten-heel pumps—the same outfit from yesterday, even the same brands, just in different colors. Professional and timeless.

Raya breezed up to my cubical, trailing Coco Mademoiselle, the same scent she'd worn since new hire training in Atlanta when we were hotel roommates. We'd basically spent the following almost six years trying to one up each other.

"Hey Jess! Happy corporate reaping day," she said, way too bubbly. "May your rating be ever in your favor."

Forcing a tight smile and shooting both pointer fingers at her, I replied, "Good one. I hope yours went well too."

"Oh, fantastic." She waved a hand. "Annual reviews are like New Year's. A chance to reflect, reset and manifest bigger client projects." Did she really give me a wink? "I'm sure you'll be fine. Don't even think about when you froze during that Empire Technologies pitch. I'm sure everyone has totally forgotten about it by now."

"Right." I said. "Thanks?"

Raya never froze. Never stumbled, never scrambled, never searched for the right words. She made the job look easy, largely because she didn't do the parts that weren't. Never one to log seventy hour workweeks, master new tech, or build decks no one asked for—that was my lane. And she loved to remind me of it.

Her eyes scanned the area before leaning in, lowering her voice. "You know I'm not one for gossip, but . . ."

After rolling my eyes, I braced.

". . . people have been whispering about how slammed you look lately. Just be careful. You know the partners hate it when someone looks overwhelmed."

My nails dragged down my neck. "I'm not overwhelmed."

"Of course not," she said, smiling like a mannequin. "I told them you've always had that, like, really intense energy about you."

"Who's *them*?"

"Oh, you know, just people from our intake." She flicked her wrist as if swatting a fly away. "Don't even think about it. But hey—I gotta run.

I'm covering a budget meeting for Kent while he's stuck in performance reviews." She jerked both thumbs toward each shoulder. "Team player right here."

She double tapped my monitor and disappeared.

Team player, my ass. What she *was,* however, was strategic. An opportunity seeker and credit taker.

Still, I couldn't help wondering if Raya would even be in the office if she wasn't covering a meeting. Most treated annual performance reviews casually, dialing in from home or their client site. Not me. My parents always said that important conversations happened in person, and there was nothing more important than the conversation about Associate Partner.

Sure, I knew making Associate Partner meant being put into a fishbowl for three to four years. Everyone would watch and rate my every move. At that stage, it's not about brilliance but endurance. Who could grind through the long hours, smile through the pressure, and sell the most work while focusing on the client relationship? That part—the schmoozy dinners, the clubhouse tickets, the networking—never came naturally to me.

The rest of it, I did by the book; took every training, used every new tool, built models that sang and danced, and could pull together an interactive deck in my sleep. I do okay at group events, chiming in and laughing at all the right moments, but ask me to make a presentation, and I become an intern again, um-ing my way through slides. One-on-one conversations often went sideways the moment they veered from the technical. Golf? No clue. Kids? Couldn't tell you the difference between a five-year-old and a seven-year-old to save my life. Vacations? Unless childhood camping counted, I had nothing.

Work had swallowed everything else, leaving my social skills out to rust.

A calendar alert flashed, reminding me of the meeting in fifteen minutes as if I could forget. *Kent Taylor—10:30 a.m.*

Exhaling, I rolled my shoulders back.

Head up, shoulders back. Look confident, be confident.

I'd rehearsed different versions of the meeting all week, making sure I could always steer the conversation back toward the Partner track so that Kent couldn't wiggle around and hide under vague corporate-speak. I'd left too many performance reviews buoyed by phrases such as "team player" and "good trajectory" only to realize days later that it translated to: she's a reliable set of hands, so staff her where we need bodies.

Not this time. This time I'd leave with bullet points, milestones, and an actual roadmap to Associate Partner within two years.

Kent was the Partner mentor assigned to me by HR—young, personable, and proof that hard work could pay off even if you weren't the most charismatic guy in the room.

Among my dad's many sayings, one of them was, "If you're not early, you're late." So, at 10:28 a.m., I wiped my clammy palms on my ironed trousers and knocked on Kent's door.

"Come in," he said, pecking at the keyboard with his pointer fingers.

I stepped inside, notebook clutched so tightly the muscles in my forearm pulsed.

Head up, shoulders back. Look confident, be confident.

Not one for small talk, he flipped opened a manila folder and launched in. "Jessica, you've had a strong year."

I nodded knowingly.

"Your clients like you, your teams like you, your work product is technical and thorough. And you're consistently in the top tier for utilization."

I waited for the "but." There's always a "but."

"But," he continued, reading my mind, "at your level, everyone works hard. Everyone is hitting targets and keeping multiple balls in the air. If you want to stand out, you need something bold. Working tons of overtime alone won't cut it."

My throat tightened. Staring at the grain of his desk for longer than was comfortable, I feared my body was giving too much away. "That's exactly what I'm looking for. Something bold." I cleared my voice. "So, what's out there?"

He flashed a "funny you should ask" look and leaned in, almost conspiratorially. "There's something hot off the press," he said in a low voice. "A Fortune 100 client is planning to expand into Ireland. Think acquisitions and consolidation nightmares. They'll need models to help decide what stays and what goes. With your skill set, you'd be a natural fit."

My heart and stomach were racing one another. It was exactly the kind of project that could catapult me into serious consideration for Associate Partner. "Wow. That sounds . . . big."

"It is," he agreed. "There was an email sent out last night to all the partners nation-wide asking for top talent recommendations. One-rated individuals that could be on the ground in Ireland for about a year. The Tampa partners agreed to put you forth, offering you first right of refusal."

"So . . . I'm one-rated?"

He half laughed, half huffed. "Yes. Congratulations."

One-rated. It buzzed through me like the champagne bubbles I'd have to celebrate, hopefully with my best friend Lindsay, and not alone. Being one-rated meant not only that my bonus would cover the amount I went over on the house for, but that I was the top of my class.

But as the high faded, and clarity came into focus, I fixated on another part.

On the ground in Ireland for about a year.

A relocation? To another country?

The ink hadn't even dried on the paperwork for the house. The sellers accepted my offer, so I was under contract. Plus, I'd never been outside of Florida save for the onboarding week in Atlanta and a trip to Chicago with my ex.

"As I was saying," Kent continued, "it's high visibility. Everyone will be watching. We'll have support from the local Dublin office, and we're even pulling from London for the EU cross-border compliance work, so it'll be a global team."

I absorbed every word, soaking up the opportunity to really jump on the Partner track.

"And the best part?" He cocked his head. "Townsend himself will be overseeing it."

I sat straighter. "Townsend? As in Crawford Townsend? The Managing Partner of the entire company?"

"The one and only."

Townsend wasn't just a Senior Partner; he was *the* Partner. The face of every town hall, the signature on every company-wide email, the kingmaker, or, Partner maker to be more precise. He was practically royalty in the consulting world.

"I . . . I didn't realize he still did client work."

"He doesn't, but this one's too big. The client demanded the best, and for the fees they're paying, they'll get him."

I swallowed hard and pushed my hair behind my ear. "Could I commute? Or would I need to be there the whole time?"

"The client was very clear about boots on the ground."

Shit.

A full year. Abroad. I couldn't even place where Ireland was on a map. Sheep, Guinness, and rain was the extent of my associations with it. Words crowded in my mouth, but none of them would come out.

"I know you're not exactly keen on travel," Kent said gently, "but I'm going to be direct. This will fast-track your career. Impress Townsend and you could make Associate Partner as early as next year. These chances don't come often."

"I understand. I . . . um . . . I just need some time to process." I scolded myself for saying "um".

"Of course." He tapped his pen on the desk. "Take the weekend to think about it, but I'll need an answer by Monday. The team will need to be mobilized in Ireland in a few weeks."

He began typing again, making it clear the meeting had concluded.

As I reached the door, I paused. "Would anyone else from our office be going? Or would I know anyone on the team?"

"As of now, you're our first choice."

The first choice. One-rated.

For a moment, I was on top of the world, soaring far above Raya and her perfectly tailored, red dress.

But if I turned it down, they might ask her instead. And Raya never missed an opportunity, especially not one that involved trendy European pantsuits and proximity to Townsend.

I couldn't let that happen.

But I also couldn't move to Ireland.

3

I REPLAYED THE CONVERSATION with Kent a hundred times over the days that followed my performance review. By the time Sunday rolled around, the day before I had to give him my answer, I couldn't get out of my own head.

The weekend passed without leaving my apartment, not even for Sunday dinner at my parent's house. Instead, I put on eighties rock, a salmon DNA mask and channeled my nervous energy into deep cleaning. After scrubbing every surface and appliance, bleaching the toilet and reorganizing every closet and pantry, I moved to the things I did every weekend even when I'm not in crisis mode: laundry, ironing, and meal prep.

Identical glass containers cooled in neat rows on the counter. The week's menu consisted of baked chicken, brown rice, roasted vegetables, and turkey meatballs with chickpea pasta. Five lunches, five dinners for the five workdays ahead. Order. Peace.

On Saturdays, I usually went wild and picked up a Greek salad topped with gyro meat from Wright's Deli after spin class. Sometimes I'd meet my best friend Lindsay for dinner if neither of us had plans. But she almost always had plans, especially the past month when she started dating a gorgeous surgeon named Jason.

I tried to be like that, but since my breakup with Brad two years earlier, I'd only had two short-lived boyfriends and a few awkward first dates. One of the boyfriends seemed permanently stuck in college; his weekends were devoted to keg parties and tailgates. It was fun until it wasn't. I quickly found myself declining party invitations "due to work" when mostly, I just didn't want to drink myself into an oblivion. The other guy I ran from the moment he revealed he was an amateur ventriloquist and showed me sketches for a doll with long brown hair, amber eyes, and freckles scattered across the cheeks—exactly like me.

On the coffee table, my laptop was open to a deck I was pulling together on information about Helix, the client expanding into Ireland and throwing a wrench into my plans. The expansion would be informally referred to as Project Roadrunner.

I performed research on their product offerings and financial performance in between loads of laundry, rolling meatballs, and ironing my six work outfits for the week. The sixth is a backup, just in case.

The routine gave me comfort and a sense of control. It always had. Especially as I weighed the pros and cons of Ireland. I wanted nothing more than Townsend's attention and his backing when it came time for promotions. I knew how those discussions went—it was about who had the loudest advocates.

Some people leveraged connections. Exhibit A: Raya. Her father knew half of Tampa and was on a first name basis with most of our firm's clients. Others volunteered for committees, charmed clients, built reputations as natural leaders. And then there were the people like Kent and me. The doers. The first in and last out.

But moving to Ireland to have a shot at promotion? It scared me, not just because it was another country, but because it was away from my life and the systems I'd built to keep myself steady. Away from my family, friends, my car, and my routine.

Sure, thanks to the internet and competitive airlines, the world had gotten smaller, and international travel was becoming commonplace for a lot of people, but not for me.

Growing up, family vacations meant Florida beaches and camping at Silver Springs, never anything out of state, and I never felt like I'd missed out on anything. From my very limited experience of domestic travel as an adult, it made me anxious, *not* excited. The flying, the hotels, the disrupted routine. My body physically rebelling with headaches, insomnia, and constipation when things felt unfamiliar. Needless to say, I never caught the travel bug.

When I told Mom about Lindsay going to Paris for a semester to study abroad for her fashion marketing degree, she was utterly confused why she couldn't just look at pictures or watch videos. When Brad started planning a trip for us to Barcelona to see the architecture and walk the Camino, my dad said he shouldn't bother as we could hike anywhere in America. The planning for that trip ended when our almost five year relationship did, so there was no Barcelona, no passport.

But this thing in Ireland wasn't just a trip; it was a *year* of working, living, trying to socialize. It meant another year without a house to call my own. Another year frozen while everyone around me marched on toward engagements and pregnancies, and . . . life.

The only appealing part of the assignment was working with Townsend and beating Raya to the punch. Was that really enough to upend everything?

My realtor had emailed a link to the payment portal for my home inspection the next day. I'd just clicked in when I heard a knock at the door, immediately followed by Lindsay barging in, her long, auburn hair bursting in like an exclamation point.

I shot her a "what the hell?" look, to which she replied, "I'm making spicy dirty martinis, and we're going to eat sushi and decide whether you're going to Ireland or not."

I'd called her on the way home from the office the day of my annual review to tell her about Ireland, but she was tied up with a work event, so I was surprised to see her.

"Um, hi to you too," I said, shutting the front door she'd left open. "I'm glad you think vodka and sodium overload will help me make a life altering decision."

"Would you prefer a PowerPoint presentation?"

I gestured to the deck open on my coffee table. "Already done."

She rolled her green eyes while slicing jalapenos, surveying my apartment. Pressed outfits hung on the doorframes, the lined up meals, the ironing board still out.

"You know, you really don't make it easy to argue for spontaneity when your apartment looks like this."

"I like order."

"No. You like control," she said.

I didn't disagree. She handed me a martini with a toothpick speared through two queen size olives and a jalapeno slice. I didn't like to drink liquor on nights before a workday, but it felt like a time to make an exception.

We clinked rims.

It was a tradition since college—martinis for decisions, for celebrations, for bad days, and good ones. Thanks to Lindsay, whenever we drank in college it was always premium cocktails and not cheap beer.

"Don't take this the wrong way, but . . . why are you here? Don't you have plans with Jason?"

"Don't you worry your smart, little head." She bopped my nose as if I were a toddler. "I'm right where I should be."

She sat cross-legged on the couch with her martini balanced in one hand while opening a set of takeout chopsticks with the other.

"Okay. Talk to me. Like, actually talk to me, not the bullet point version you do at work."

I exhaled slowly through my nose and walked her through the offer and what working with Townsend would mean for my career.

She nodded along, absorbing.

"But . . . a year?" I said. "It's *so* long. And Ireland? I had to Google to see where it was. It's an island next to the UK in case you didn't know."

"Jessie, you'll be fine," she assured.

"I don't even have a passport."

"Then get one expedited," she said with a tone that screamed "duh."

"I wish it were that simple. I'm under contract on a house! Literally weeks out from closing."

Lindsay thought. "Okay, that part sucks. I'm not going to pretend it doesn't."

I raised the corners of my lips to say "thanks."

"But," she continued. "It's a once in a lifetime opportunity."

"See, that's the part that makes me feel boxed in. Like if I don't do this, I'm throwing everything away."

Lindsay opened her mouth, then closed it. Then took a sip of her drink.

"Okay," she said. "I'm going to say something, and it might not land perfectly."

I paused mid-dip, my volcano roll hovering over the soy sauce. "Oh good."

"I just mean," Lindsay said, dropping into an even tone; her serious voice, "you've been doing everything right your whole life. Every step, every plan. And it's worked, you're good at it. But sometimes I wonder if you've been so busy staying on track that you haven't stopped to ask whether the track still fits."

I looked down at the speared salad bobbing in my martini glass. "Yeah, it fits."

"But does it excite you? The promotion, the house?" Lindsay asked. "Or does it just feel safe?"

"I don't need excitement. Excitement is overrated," I said. "I need stability, I need my family. I need my dad close by to hang TVs and change the oil in my car."

"You don't need your parents' help. If I can do it, so can you."

Realizing how my close-knit family was one of the only luxuries I had that she did not, I opted to sip my martini instead of responding. Being an only child with a distant mother, no cousins, no aunts or uncles, and no grandparents, Lindsay couldn't know what it was like to have a built-in support system close by.

She broke the silence. "It's Ireland! Go see some cliffs, see some sheep, see some big burly Irish . . . you know." Her hands gestured around an imaginary cylinder. "You can even pop over to Paris, my old stomping grounds. Travel Europe, live a little, and come back firmly on the Partner track."

"I'm not like you. I don't want to travel Europe, certainly not by myself." I pushed the tiny orange balls of roe off a piece of sushi.

"So don't. You could just get to know Dublin; that will be adventure enough."

"You sure have an answer for everything, don't you?" I asked.

"Okay, fine. Let's play devil's advocate, shall we?" She set her martini on the coffee table and repositioned on the sofa. "Let's say you don't go. What happens next?"

"Well, from what Kent was describing, I'd need to look for a different assignment to set myself apart."

"And what if *that* opportunity involves you having to move somewhere else? Like some freezing cold, remote, industrial town?"

"Presumably it'd be in the US, so I'd fly back every Thursday night."

"Yes, yes, I see how flying and renting a Kia Rio every week just to come back to Florida for laundry is a far superior choice."

"Most assignments don't require being out of town for more than a few months. This Ireland one is unique," I explained.

"Okay, so what happens if there isn't a better opportunity this year? And whoever takes this spot in Dublin makes Associate Partner and you get passed up? What's your next move?"

I pulled my mouth to the side, thinking. "I'd hope one comes up so that I don't fall behind."

"Hope? Your plan is to hope? Now, *that* doesn't sound like you."

"Well, I guess at a certain point, I'd have to leave McAfee and go to a different consulting firm." Leaving to go to a competitor would surely burn bridges. "Or I'd need to change paths all together."

"Exactly. Jess, don't you see? Ireland isn't the more *spontaneous* option, it's the *safer* option."

I bit my lip and looked away.

"You know I'm right," she added.

"I guess I thought I'd feel a lightning bolt, ya know? Like, yes, do the bold thing and knock Raya out of the running. Or the opposite . . . like an absolute no, I'm not going. But neither option feels right."

"That's because you're scared." She placed her hand on my knee. "And that's normal. I'd be more worried if you weren't. I just don't want to see you miss out because you're scared."

Just then, my phone buzzed.

"It's my real estate agent—making sure I've got everything sorted for the inspection tomorrow."

Lindsay stared for a beat before snatching my phone and turning her back to me. She hunched over the screen while I tried to get it back.

"Lindsay! Give me my phone back this instant!"

She read aloud as she typed. "Something has come up. I'm actually moving to Ireland, so I have to withdraw my offer. I apologize for any inconvenience. Thank you."

"Don't you dare!" I said, not recognizing my own voice.

She handed the phone back to me.

I stared at the drafted message.

"Do you really even want this house or is it just another milestone?"

"Easy for you to say; you bought your townhouse two years ago."

"Yeah, because I got money when Howard died. I couldn't buy it on my own." It's not that she disliked her mother's late third husband; she just didn't know him well.

"Raya bought a house last year, and we have the same job."

"Her parents are loaded," she countered.

"Well, most of the people we knew in college are married, some are having kids. I'm pretty sure they all have houses too."

She shot me a confused look. "Name three of them."

"Big Jim," I answered.

"The huge guy that lived above us and was always shirtless and eating Taco Bell? *He* is married with kids?" she asked.

"Not quite. But I saw on social media he *was* at a bachelor party. And now that you mention it, I think he was eating a crunch wrap in one of the photos."

"Jess, you're going to be twenty-eight this year. You're hardly an old maid. Houses will always be here, they're really not that special. Living abroad and kicking ass at your job *is*."

Her eyes dropped to the phone in my hands and back at me.

She was right. Again.

"I'll come visit while you're there," she added.

I stared at the blue arrow next to the drafted text message and thought of a year in a different country. Even though I didn't want to go, maybe the alternative *was* worse.

Tired of overanalyzing, I let myself ride the wave of excitement and nausea that came with making a big decision.

And I tapped the arrow.

The message that would change my life had been sent.

4

MONDAY MORNING FOUND ME alone in the office yet again. My heel tapped Morse code against the dark grey carpet until sitting became impossible. Maybe it was the two cups of mediocre breakroom coffee or maybe it was the fact that I was about to finalize the biggest career decision of my life in a matter of minutes? Likely both.

A faint tremor pulsed in my hand as I drained the last sip of coffee and stared out at the skyline. Tampa mornings always looked crisp, but now the cloudless, baby blue sky bordered on artificial as the sunlight bounced off the mirrored glass of the surrounding buildings. I'd always appreciated our downtown; it wasn't bustling, certainly not outside of normal work hours, but that was the feature, not a bug.

Our office offered no indication that my life was about to change. Industrial carpets, rectangular panels of fluorescent lighting, and rows of cubicles interrupted only by the occasional focus booth. My desk was tidy. No photos, trinkets, or plants. Just a few neatly stacked folders and a small old fashioned calendar to supplement my digital one.

On my third trip to the coffee machine, Kent walked into the break-room midcall. He lifted a finger, signaling for me to wait. For sure, he'd be asking about Ireland.

He ended the call, shoving the phone into the pocket of his khakis.

"So," he said, loading a coffee packet into the machine. "Have you made a decision?"

I nodded, steadying my voice despite my stomach doing somersaults like it was auditioning for Cirque du Soleil. "I've thought it through," I said slowly, "and I'd like to accept the project in Ireland."

For a split second, his eyebrows twitched. It was so quick that it'd be unnoticeable to most, but I caught it.

"Fantastic," he said, sliding seamlessly into professional enthusiasm. "The partners will be glad to hear it. And frankly, you'll do great. You've got the technical chops and the drive. You'll compliment the team nicely."

I smiled as my eyes fell. There was something in the way he said "you'll do great" that sounded less definitive than I'd expected.

"The team?" I asked, careful to keep my tone light. "Do you have more information about who is going besides Townsend?"

Kent hesitated. "Someone from the Boston office and possibly New York. A few international folks. Oh—and Raya."

I blinked hard and slow.

"Uh, wh-what?"

"She heard about the project through the grapevine on Friday and apparently sent Townsend's secretary a box of cookies. Got herself a virtual meeting that same day."

Of course she did.

I laughed nervously. "I guess the squeaky wheel *does* get the grease?"

So I wasn't going to be the only one from our office? I was going to have to fight Raya for Townsend's attention? I could see it crystal clear—me drowning in research while Raya tossed buzzwords around like a frisbee and stole the spotlight.

Kent brought his cup to the counter to add at least five mini creamers. "But you're both going," he added. "Two senior consultants with complementary skill sets will only make the project stronger."

I forced a nod. "Complementary. Right."

He continued, oblivious to there being any tension between Raya and I. "You've got two weeks to wrap up and handover your assignments, pack and sort out your affairs. Then you'll have one week of corporate housing in Dublin while you look for something permanent and get settled. Three weeks from today, you'll be working out of the Dublin office."

Three weeks? Shit, I'd need a passport. There was no way a government agency could turn something around in three months let alone three weeks. My stomach tightened.

"Understood," I said.

Kent added three sugar packets to his cup, stirring with a little wooden stick. "I really think this will be good for you, Jess. You've been in the same place for a while. This will be a chance to really stretch."

"Looking forward to it."

We exited the breakroom together and as if on cue, the elevator dinged and out stepped Raya. An emerald blouse framed her shoulders and an orange ribbon formed a bow around her half ponytail.

You've got to be kidding me. Irish colors?

She saw me and smirked. "Well, well. Looks like we're going to be teammates abroad." Her voice carried loud enough for the nearby associates to hear.

"Don't I have the luck of the Irish?" I muttered.

Taking zero hints, she launched into her plans for renting out her house and refreshing her wardrobe before the move. Then casually, she asked, "Do you want to grab lunch and brainstorm?"

"Sure, I only just started some initial research on Helix, but I already—"

"No, silly. We'll learn all that stuff when we're there. I meant like . . . fun stuff. Where to shop, where to go out, the best European trips to take over bank holidays. The important things."

"Oh, right." It was uncharacteristic of Raya to invite me to lunch and even under the circumstances, I didn't trust it. "Maybe another time, I need to expedite a passport."

She froze. "You don't have a passport?" I pressed my lips together as my face went hot. Her thumbs tapped her phone screen a mile a minute. "I've got a guy."

Of course she had a passport guy.

"An old sorority sister's husband, he works for the State Department, he's fab. Submit the application tonight, and he'll push it through. You'll have it in a week, trust me."

"Wow, thanks, Raya. That's really . . . helpful."

Kent reappeared, likely went back for more cream and sugar. As he entered earshot, Raya announced loudly, "We'll get you a passport, Jess. I'll make sure of it!"

That, on the other hand, is not helpful.

"Jessica, you didn't think to mention you didn't have a passport? This could really delay your work visa." He sounded like my dad whenever he was disappointed.

"Don't worry, I'll handle it," Raya pounced. "I have some connections at the State Department that I'd be glad to leverage. I'm used to crisis management."

Kent appeared grateful. "Okay. But if it's not posted by Friday, let us know immediately."

"Yes, sir," I said.

As he walked away with his cup of sweet cream, Raya leaned in. "Rough start, huh? I'm sure it will get better." She flashed a menacing grin before disappearing down the hall, her stupid orange ribbon bobbing.

I wasn't naturally competitive, wasn't a charmer like her and didn't have any buddies in the government I could call for favors. I'd built my career by staying in my lane, keeping my head down and quietly outworking everyone. But there was no way in hell I was going to let Raya Reynolds outrun me on the Partner track.

5

These might come back in style someday.

I tossed the pair of black, lace-up Victorian boots into my keep pile. If nothing else, they'd come in handy at Halloween—the only time I'd worn them in the five years I'd owned them.

"Jessie, you've been going through your closet all day, and you haven't even filled one box for donation?" Lindsay sat cross-legged on the bedroom floor, selectively eating one kernel of popcorn at a time.

"I'm sentimental," I defended.

"No, you're a borderline hoarder. An organized hoarder, but still . . . a hoarder."

The thought of throwing something away I might later want or need made my chest tighten. Every purchase was intentional. Even the witch boots. I'd bought them to complete a *Hocus Pocus* costume but still weighed the pros and cons for two days before pulling the trigger.

I shrugged hopefully. "Who knows, I might develop a whole new fashion sense living in Europe?"

"Doubtful. Despite all the free samples and discounts I get, you still wear the same boring, monochrome pieces you've had since college."

"College wasn't that long ago," I protested.

Lindsay raised an accusatory eyebrow.

It felt like yesterday we were rooming with two other girls in our off-campus apartment, but our six year graduation anniversary was in May, just months away.

I shot her a side-eye and grabbed a stack of carefully folded shirts from the closet shelf. "Remember this?" I held the grey-washed t-shirt by the shoulders as it unfolded to reveal the iconic red tongue and lips logo splashed across the chest.

"How could I forget? You wore it for most of that week-long hurricane party senior year." She set the empty popcorn bowl on the bedside table and went to rummage under my bathroom sink. "I'll never forget the power was out in the whole apartment complex but yet there you were . . . studying. By candlelight."

"Yeah, and you snatched my notebook and threatened to burn it if I didn't go to that party with you." She always gets her way. "And then I did my first keg stand that night."

"I don't know what's more unbelievable . . . that it took you till senior year to finally do a keg stand or that you were still home before midnight."

"I was out long enough to meet Brad. Remember? He held my legs."

"Ah, yes. Nothing says budding romance quite like inverted beer chugging." The clanking of tiny glass bottles under the sink drowned out some of the sarcasm.

It wasn't the most romantic meet-cute, but it was ours.

The moment my feet hit the ground after my debut keg stand, Brad was there, steadying me. "You crushed it!" he yelled over the music, raising both palms for a high ten. Still buzzing from the adrenaline rush, I smacked my hands to his, and he pulled me in for a too-tight bear hug like we were old friends. A few people whooped and cheered, but the volume had been turned down when I looked at him for the first time. His crooked little smile with a singular dimple made my stomach flip. He pointed to my shirt.

"What's your favorite Stones album?" he asked.

I blinked rapidly. "Uh—the band?"

He tilted his head like a confused puppy processing a new word. "Uh, yeah. The band whose shirt you're wearing." He pointed again. "The giant mouth."

My cheeks burned. My parents were big on music, but somehow The Rolling Stones never made the rotation, so I knew the band, of course, but not the songs. "Oh, right. I know I'm wearing their shirt, I just . . . I don't actually listen to them." I braced for the teasing that never came.

He laughed. Not in a mean way, but in a way that felt like Sunday dinners at home. "Well then, I'm going to turn you into a fan. It's practically my obligation now, and I won't stop until I've succeeded."

From that night on, we were inseparable.

Until I separated us.

I clutched the shirt in my lap. Lindsay emerged from the bathroom with a handful of nail polish bottles, eyeing me.

"You're not packing that, are you?"

I hesitated. "It's just a shirt. It won't take up much room. Plus, I'll wear it to bed."

"No, you won't. You only wear matching sets," she said, dropping beside me. "You're holding on to a memory."

I traced the cracked mouth logo with my thumb. "I liked who I was that night," I said, quietly.

That girl felt like a ghost. No, the memory of one. Tipsy at a party, doing keg stands and flirting instead of studying. No real plan beyond graduating and getting a decent job at the career fair.

"You don't need an old, raggedy shirt to connect with her again. You'll see her in Ireland."

I folded it slowly and placed it in the donation pile under Lindsay's watchful eye.

"That a girl. You're one shirt closer to *maybe* filling a plastic grocery bag," she said before returning to the bathroom to paint her nails.

Going through my work clothes took all of about two minutes because there wasn't anything to donate. Since starting my career, I've essentially worn a uniform. Each day, a combination of high-waisted pants, a blouse or cardigan, a belt, and either kitten heels or loafers. I own each component in black, navy, tan and cream. If I want to shake things up, there's one work appropriate dress and one royal blue top. Every Sunday evening, after dinner at my parents' house, I line up my outfits for the week and steam each piece so it's ready to go.

"Do you like this?" Lindsay leaned back so I could see her foot perched on the vanity. "It's the only actual color I could find buried under all of the nudes and pale pinks."

"I *like* nudes and pale pinks," I protested.

Her bottom lip pouted. "Oh Jessie, you are so predictable."

"I *like* to be predictable," we said in unison before dissolving into laughter.

When I first met Lindsay, I pegged her as only into designer brands funded by Daddy's credit card. You couldn't blame me—on move in day, she stuck out a perfectly manicured limp wristed hand and proudly declared she was majoring in an MRS degree.

Our first month as roommates was chaos. She left half eaten yogurt cups everywhere, cranked the thermostat down to arctic levels, and fell asleep to *Gilmore Girls* at full volume. I spent weeks rehearsing the most diplomatic confrontation speech in the mirror like it was going to be broadcast on national television. When I finally approached her in our cramped kitchen and delivered my lines, she simply asked, "How many times did you practice that?" while holding in a laugh.

I froze. Then told the truth. "At least twenty."

She burst out laughing, and I joined in. That was the moment we stopped being assigned roommates and started being friends.

"I can't move to Ireland tomorrow, Linds," I said, wiping tears of laughter from my eyes. "It's all happening too fast. I haven't found an apartment, I haven't done any client research. I don't have a plan."

"Maybe that's the point?"

I bit my lip. "When I come back, I'll be almost twenty-nine, single, and homeless."

"Homeless?" She countered.

"Yes, without a home . . . that I own."

She rolled her eyes as if to say, "not that again." "The good news is that the early-to-mid thirties are the first divorce wave. So, there's that."

I smacked both hands over my face.

"What? It's working for me. Jason got divorced in his early thirties, and now I get to reap the benefits." She was right about that; Jason was pretty darn perfect.

I removed my hands and stared up at her, standing next to the bed where I lay.

"But seriously, so what if you're single and renting at thirty? Stop inventing expiration dates; they're only recommendations, after all."

I made a face. I'd never eat anything on or past its expiration date. Not even the "best by" date.

She plopped down on the bed and on my hair. After yanking it from under her leg, she combed it with her fingers and began braiding. "What if you find someone there? A big, sexy Irish man who works a dairy farm by day and plays at a pub by night. Maybe you'll buy a cottage in the countryside and raise sheep and babies with funny accents—the babies, not the sheep."

I flinched as she pulled too hard. "You think I'm going to find a cheesy stereotype while I'm away?"

"I think you're going to find exactly what you look for. Not what you plan for." She secured the French braid with the hair tie around her wrist. "You have corporate housing for a week, you'll get up to speed on the new client quickly. Stop overthinking."

I hate when anyone says that to me. Even when I deserve it. Internally, I rolled my eyes. Externally, a small smile. "If nothing else, I'll forever have a good fun fact to share for icebreakers," I said.

Her face scrunched, searching for clarification.

"One time at work, we had to go round-the-horn and share a fun fact about ourselves. The guy before me had hiked Mount Kilimanjaro. Everyone was so impressed and asked him all these questions. Meanwhile, I sat there, sweating profusely, wondering what I could possibly say. When all eyes turned to me, I panicked and flapped my hyperextended arms like a bird, saying, "I can do *this*.""

"NO. YOU. DID. NOT."

My head dropped. "I don't have a fun fact. I'm not a fun person and certainly not interesting."

"Nonsense. Your first keg stand lasted well over ten seconds. That's impressive." She slapped my knee and stood. "Okay, enough of this. I know you said no send-off gifts but too bad." She waddled out of my room, careful not to smudge her freshly painted toes, and returned with two oversized gift bags. The first had a pink ribbon tied in a perfect bow to secure the handles together; Lindsay's signature gift wrapping touch. Inside was an Emporio Armani trench coat. Classic beige and more money than I would have spent on myself, even with her discount.

The handwriting on the tag of the second bag looked like a serial killer's—undeniably my mom's. Inside were black Hunter rain boots. It was touching that they had organized to give quintessential rainy weather pieces. I tried them both on and posed for Lindsay.

"Your mom wanted to get the green ones . . . said something about it being a happier color? But I knew you'd want black, so I told her that green rain boots in Ireland felt cliché."

"But the dairy farmer slash pub musician isn't cliché?"

She shook her head, slowly mouthing, "Nope."

"Thank you for these. And thank you for being here. Thank you for everything."

While she went to the kitchen to cut the tags, I pulled the Rolling Stones shirt out of the donation pile and wedged it between two other shirts in my suitcase.

***

Lindsay stayed the night, which I suspected was less about convenience and more about making sure I didn't bail. She curled into a tiny ball under a throw blanket and fell asleep halfway through *P.S. I Love You* while I stared at my suitcases, willing an email to appear. Something along the lines of *"Due to budget constraints, the project will now need to be done from Tampa."*

Rent was paid through the end of March, and my parents agreed to stop by after I left to move the remaining boxes and furniture into storage. They'd also keep my car in their garage and triage my mail to determine what should be sent to Ireland and what was junk. I offered to pay them a secretarial fee, but they refused. That didn't stop Dad from teasing that he'd be logging his hours.

I hadn't had time to thoroughly research Dublin rentals, but from what I could gather, places went on and off the market so quickly that any research would be in vain. Most came fully furnished with kitchenware, appliances, furniture, and sometimes even linens. That part made packing much easier, but walking away from everything I owned with just two suitcases and a carry-on felt unnatural. As if it were a yearlong vacation.

My parents arrived at 10 a.m., a full forty minutes earlier than we'd agreed. They'd be driving Lindsay and me to the airport so the three of them could see me off. With the extra time to spare, we had a leisurely brunch at a new spot in South Tampa that was meant to be all the rage.

"Sixteen dollars for avocado toast?" Dad scoffed as he scanned the menu.

"Don't be dramatic, honey," Mom said, sliding her reading glasses down her nose. "Oh look, they have duck confit hash, isn't that interesting? Or crab and mango benedict, now *that's* interesting."

It was Mom's thing, to read the entire menu aloud as if seriously considering every item, only to order two eggs over easy, hash browns with extra onions, and dry toast with grape jelly. She only liked the appearance of being spontaneous.

The waiter hovered with a carafe of coffee while Lindsay interrogated him about egg substitutions, cooking oils, portion sizes, and whether the bacon was crispy or floppy. The poor guy looked like he wanted to quit. In the end, she went with an egg-white omelet, black coffee, and a plate of allegedly crispy bacon.

It was comfortingly familiar. Dad complaining, Mom being a hype woman, and Lindsay being a pain in the ass. My chest ached knowing I was leaving it.

Mom and Dad quizzed Lindsay about her job as a buyer for Saks while I picked at my overpriced avocado toast and imagined what would happen if I didn't get on the plane. I considered escape routes and plausible excuses. Could I fake a medical emergency severe enough to cancel but minor enough that no one from the office would come visit? Maybe appendicitis or a severe allergic reaction? Would purposely getting hit by a car do the trick? That one was less appealing given the uncontrollable injuries, possible insurance fraud, and the undeniable fact that it was an insane idea.

I pictured calling Kent and saying I'd changed my mind. Was there a world where I'd score points for honesty? Unlikely. Backing out at the last minute would kill any shot at making Associate Partner. Worse, everyone in the Tampa office would think I was a flake. And they'd be right.

I inhaled deeply.

This will launch your career. This will fast-track your promotion. This should be fun and exciting. Just do it.

At the airport, I checked my bags and watched them disappear down the conveyor belt, briefly considering running after them. The goodbyes were both something I wanted to skip and something I didn't want to end. Dad pulled me into an awkward side hug. "You got this, kiddo. And if you don't, it's only a year. You can put up with anything for a year. Get in, kick ass, come home."

"Words to live by if I ever heard any," I sniffled.

Mom held on way too long, rambling instructions like I was twelve. "Call us when you arrive at the corporate housing. Dress in layers. Don't walk alone at night. And don't go to bed with wet hair."

"Aluminum in the microwave, plastic in the oven, right?" I said.

She nudged my shoulder and let out a half laugh through glassy eyes. "Oh, and remember . . . nothing good happens—"

"After midnight," we said together. Lindsay was right. I am predictable, and it's obvious where I get it from.

Lindsay hugged me so tight it hurt. "Oh, Jessie, boo-boo, you'll be fantastic." She pulled away to look at me. "Don't chicken out. Whenever you're feeling nervous, try labeling it as excitement. Apparently they're the same emotion, the brain just interprets them differently."

I nodded, although I wasn't entirely sure what she meant.

By the time I reached TSA PreCheck, my throat was a solid knot, and dread pressed heavier with every step. What I hated most wasn't that I was moving to another country—it was the fact that I hated it. Most people in the same position would be thrilled for the opportunity to live abroad, but not me. I was an ungrateful, nervous brat.

The thought made me laugh out loud. It hadn't been ten minutes since Lindsay's advice, and her words were already echoing in my head. Maybe the nerves *were* actually excitement in disguise? Doubtful, but maybe.

I tried re-labeling the feeling, but my brain wouldn't cooperate.

A family of five stood ahead of me in line. The navy uniforms and blue latex gloves waved people through; reciting instructions about laptops, liquids, shoes and clearing out pockets.

When it was my turn, I glanced back.

There they were. Three lunatics waving and jumping like I was boarding a spaceship. It was ridiculous and perfect and exactly what I needed.

You *can* do this. You *have* to do this.

With one last wave goodbye, I slipped off my New Balances and walked through the scanner in my socks.

At the gate, I pulled out my notebook to make a list, something that usually calmed me. I wrote down tasks for the first week:

- *Register for PPS number*

- *Set up local bank account*

- *Get SIM card/get a local phone number*

- *Schedule apartment viewings*

- *Figure out commute route*

- *Finish researching Helix*

- *Get meal prep containers*

But drawing the little squares for the bullet points didn't soothe me. My knees bounced so hard I could barely read what I'd written. With my head in my hands, I listened to the flight announcements.

This wasn't excitement; it was hell.

I shoved the notebook away and stared down the long terminal.

My mind was made up. I was going to call Kent. I'd apologize for bailing, try to diplomatically join a competitor, lose a year off the Partner track but save my sanity. I could easily slide back into my old apartment and resume the house hunt.

It didn't feel like failure, it felt like relief.

A good plan. No, a great plan.

I grabbed the handle of my carry-on and beelined to the exit. Freedom.

The intercom crackled. "Attention passengers on Flight AA31524 to Dublin. We will now begin boarding."

Shit.

Shit.

No matter how much I didn't want to go, I knew Lindsay was right.

Going was the easier option.

So I chickened out of my chicken out.

And turned around.

6

THE DOOR TO THE seventh flat slammed behind me with a thud. I froze in the dim entryway, waiting for my eyes to adjust to the gloomy converted attic space. A stale smell hung heavy in the air, likely from the old carpeting layered with decades of tenants and poor air circulation. The outdated kitchenette didn't look suitable for making a sandwich, let alone a week's worth of meal prep.

In the bathroom, the angled ceiling dipped so low that at five foot nine, I'd have to slouch just to wash my hands at the pedestal sink. Not to mention there was nowhere to set any products.

How could anyone get ready in that cell?

I didn't need to check out the bedroom, but it felt obligatory. The bed bounced under my hand with the ease of a sit-up ball.

"There's a washer-dryer unit downstairs that you would share, for a fee, with the other tenant," the landlord boasted. I almost laughed out loud but recalling that the previous six places didn't have access to one, it was in fact a huge selling point.

It was day four of my seven day corporate housing allowance, and no closer to finding a place to call home sweet home. I had three days to find a suitable apartment, sign the lease, vacate the temporary place, and settle into the new one before starting work with Townsend on Monday.

The Dublin rental market was brutal. Anything even remotely modern and central was astronomically priced, even if you were part of a couple splitting the bill. From what I'd gathered—partly from Googling and partly from landlords themselves—most people in my situation crammed into flats with two, three, even four other roommates. I'd done that in college with Lindsay and two other girls, and then I'd lived with Brad for a few years after. But after two years of having my own space, there was no way I could go back to tiptoeing around other people's cereal bowls or worrying if the TV was too loud. This meant I'd either have to balloon my budget or seriously lower my expectations. Most likely, a bit of both. My rent budget was respectable back home, but it wasn't stretching as far in Dublin.

You idiot, I scolded. *You gave up an amazing South Tampa bungalow, albeit with a turquoise door, for this?*

Outside, the sky began leaking again. I pulled the hood of the trench coat from Lindsay over my head in an attempt to protect the blowout I'd managed to maintain since landing. The blue dot on the Google Maps app jolted around as I wiped the droplets and entered the address of the next place.

The neighborhood was called Ranelagh, which blog after blog described as "lively but livable," scattered with charming pubs and plenty of brunch options.

The landlord was already waiting for me when I arrived; a man named Fergus with salt-and-pepper hair and tight pants, who dished out a startling double cheek kiss with his "Hello."

"She's small but mighty," he said, gesturing to the redbrick building behind him.

Six apartments were stacked neatly, two per floor, at the end of a postcard street lined with Georgian doors in every bright and beautiful color of the rainbow. Bikes leaned against stoops; one even had a black cat perched on the seat and potted plants hung outside the vibrant doors. I wished my potential apartment came with one of those iconic doors, but I'd settle for simply being on the idyllic street.

Fergus jiggled the keys as he said hello to a neighbor who was returning home as he led the way to the entrance, which was actually in the back of the building. He pointed out the courtyard and one parking space that I wouldn't need before mumbling something about roof access.

Inside, the apartment was indeed small but pleasantly bright and clean. A ridiculous couch covered in pink lilies and green leaves squatted in the living room. Sitting on it didn't feel gross and there wasn't a trace of must; to my pleasant surprise, it smelled of a sweet fabric detergent.

The refrigerator was tiny and shoved under the counter next to the . . . washer-dryer unit. *Inside* the apartment? Not a communal machine? That alone was reason to sign the lease right then and there.

I stared out the kitchen window at the cobbled street. The man across the street pedaled with what looked to be an instrument case strapped to his back. I'd hoped landing in Dublin would ignite some excitement or feel transformative in some way, but it hadn't. Instead it felt disjointed. Off. The lingering jet lag probably wasn't helping.

With three days left and only one more viewing lined up that I knew wouldn't be as good as the Ranelagh one, it was pointless to make a checklist.

"I'll take it," I blurted, shocking myself.

Fergus clapped twice, delighted. "Brilliant! Let's get you some keys."

Relieved to have found a suitable place, I couldn't help thinking again about the turquoise door back at home and how I'd traded it for a loud, floral loveseat.

We signed the paperwork at the tiny dining table with mismatched chairs, and then Fergus walked with me to the nearest ATM so I could take out cash for the deposit. Since it was going to take another week to get my Irish bank account set up, it had to come from my US one. I nearly died seeing the astronomical foreign transaction fee it tacked on, but since Fergus was waiting a few feet away, I fought the urge to scream at the machine, or cry. I couldn't wait to get the keys and start doing what I went to Ireland to do: impress Townsend, and set myself up for promotion.

Walking back to the corporate apartment one last time, I forced myself to take in my surroundings. A gaggle of smokers shuffled outside of a pub, the lively music and chatter from within escaped when one of them opened the door to go back inside. A butcher lowered his metal shutters with a rattle that rang through my body. The window bar of a café was lined with people still sipping espresso even at 6 p.m.

Dublin was damp, expensive, and not great for my hair, but it was also undeniably alive. None of this had been in the plan. But yet, it was a plan already in motion, and whether I liked it or not, I was moving with it.

7

"Are you kidding me?" I screamed at the blue Peugeot after it sped through a puddle, leaving the hems of my pants completely soaked. I'd planned to be in early to make sure I beat Townsend. If I went back to change my pants, I'd be in after 9 a.m., so wet ankles and squishy loafers were going to have to do.

After moving my things from corporate housing over to the new flat, I had spent the rest of the first week jumping through the hoops of Irish bureaucracy. Everything was inefficient. Opening a bank account had dragged on, and after a full week of trying, it was still in progress. The bank insisted my letter of employment had to be on company letterhead to be dubbed official. Okay, fine. A bit humorous, but I get it; rules are rules. The humor soon turned to annoyance when the second letter was also rejected. Apparently, it wasn't addressed to a specific bank branch, which was another ridiculous rule. The third attempt was almost another failure because the signature from HR on my employment letter used blue ink instead of black. The woman assisting me must have sensed I was about to lose my shit because she waived it, citing an act of good faith. It took all my energy to appear grateful and not roll my eyes. I should finally get a bank card by the end of the second week—apparently they are created in the UK and shipped over. In the meantime, I had paid a small fortune in currency fees and commissions to use my US card.

After dropping my things off at my desk, I made sure to walk by Townsend's office on the way to the ladies room. I lifted my loafers to the low velocity hand dryer and swung my leg back and forth to get the pants too, praying no one would walk in and see me like that.

Back at my desk, I rearranged my notes, cleared down emails, and refreshed my calendar even though the team kickoff was already set for 9 a.m. Someone hovered over my workstation.

Ugh. Raya, looking like she belonged on the cover of *Forbes*.

"Jessica!" She greeted me like we were old friends. "Isn't this amazing? Gosh, we are just the luckiest." An awkward silence. "So, how has the move gone so far?"

The polite smile was second nature now. "It's going. Getting the PPS number and a bank account took forever, but I know you know the feeling."

"I'm sorry it was so difficult for you," she said, clutching her coffee with a fresh manicure. "I have a friend in London who just moved to Cork last year. Her boyfriend's best friend knows someone at Immigration or the Embassy. I don't really know the details, but he was able to get it sorted for me on my first day."

Of *course* she had a friend of a friend in Irish Immigration that took care of everything for her. Of *course* she knew someone that could expedite my passport and make herself look good in front of Kent. Of *course* she looked amazing and probably didn't experience jet lag. Of *course* she hadn't been splashed by a toy car on her way in.

"Th-that's . . . great," I managed. "And what about housing? Did you manage to find something acceptable?" I don't know why I decided to torture myself. Of *course* she managed to find a perfect apartment.

"Oh my god, I'm obsessed with our flat," she said, eyes and hands wide.

"Our?"

"Yeah, Aoife. I met her through my friend from London. She has this incredible flat in Ballsbridge—super modern inside, but still chock full of character. And oh my god, it has the *cutest* yellow Georgian door that reminds me of the Florida sunshine." She smoothed an invisible wrinkle from the lapel of her red tweed blazer. "Anyway, she works for a local marketing firm—runs digital campaigns or something and travels a lot for work—so it made sense for her to have a flatmate for the year. She's been taking me out, showing me around. Such an amazing city, don't you think?"

"Yeah, it's great." Another forced smile. "Hey, I'm gonna grab some tea before this meeting. I'll see you in the conference room." I bolted before she had a chance to invite herself. I needed a minute to collect myself before we kicked off Project Roadrunner and the real work started.

I'd already had a coffee at home and didn't want to have a second one, but also needed something warm and something to do, so tea it was.

While waiting for the water in the microwave, a booming voice startled me.

"Hiya! How ye gettin' on?" The boisterous greeting came from a head of dark, wild curls dressed in layers of statement pieces. A flower-patterned blouse that was alarmingly similar to my new sofa peeked through the green tweed jacket she paired with a flowing blue skirt. Grey tights, black ankle boots, and a chunky necklace completed the busy outfit. I made a mental note to tell Lindsay about her boots that resembled my witch ones. Maybe they *were* in style?

"Uh . . . I'm good, thank you for asking." I extended my hand. "I'm Jessica. It's so nice to meet you."

"Oh, sweetest god! You are actually *so* American." She laughed loudly, shaking my hand with a limp grip. "I'm Orla."

"Guilty as charged," I said, playfully. "You're on Roadrunner too, aren't you?"

"Yeah, I just found out about it last week—supposed to help with stakeholder communications and anything that needs to get filed with the Companies House. I'm basically a glorified secretary which I don't mind."

She looked me up and down. "So how ye finding it? Where ye living?" Orla spoke a mile a minute, and I tried my best to keep up. Her accent was as thick as the foundation on her porcelain skin.

"I really like it so far," I lied. "It's only been a week, but everyone seems friendly and I just moved into my apartment over the weekend." I didn't think it was appropriate to mention my frustrations, homesickness, or how my Irish apartment was a massive downgrade in every way except for the outrageous rent.

"Ooh, lovely! Who ye living with?"

The microwave dinged, and I pulled my cup out. "Nobody. I'm on my own."

"Ah, fair play to ye. See now, that wouldn't be common here." Her gaze shifted between the microwave and a metal jug that I assumed was coffee. "Emm . . . is the kettle broken?"

"That thing?" I pointed at the jug. "I have no clue."

"Do you not know what a kettle is?" She looked utterly scandalized.

"Ohhh, it's an electric kettle." I jokingly smacked my palm to my forehead. The only kettle I'd ever seen in real life was at my grandma's house, and it was the stovetop kind. "I use the microwave for everything. It saves time." One of those electric kettles came with my furnished apartment, but I put it in the storage closet not knowing what to do with it.

Orla must've sensed my embarrassment. "Well, I'd say hot tea wouldn't be big in America, but in Ireland we are simply *mad* for it. Here, let me show you." She dumped my microwaved water in the sink and filled the kettle with water from the faucet. I took note as she placed it on the base, pushed the button down, and retrieved a pint-sized container of milk from the fridge. "Right so, come here . . . a proper cuppa must be made with *boiling* water and Barry's tea bags." She showed off the red box like it was a trophy. "It's very important that you use Barry's and not Lyons. The Dubs prefer Lyons, but it's absolute shite, so it is."

When the kettle clicked, she continued, "Always pour the boiling water over the bag, never drop the bag into the water. Let it steep for at least two full minutes and don't forget to stir it counterclockwise twenty-seven times before taking the bag out." Using the string, she wrapped the bag tightly around the back of the spoon before tossing it in the trash. "Milk first, then sugar. Honey only if you're sick."

Was she serious?

Trying to remember her personal ritual for tea making, I took more mental notes: buy the tea in the red box, boil water, only make tea if I have at least ten minutes to spare.

As I tried to absorb everything Orla had said, a small man entered the room. He barely reached my shoulder and yet, somehow, still managed to look down at me.

"Bloody hell, are you going on about Barry's tea again? Quit wasting precious time and calories and do espresso," he snapped at Orla in a way that only a friend would.

Without missing a beat, she barked back, "Now go on and drink your bitter piss, and I'll teach our American friend here how to make a cuppa tea—no microwaves necessary."

He gave me a slow, exaggerated once-over. "Microwaved tea? What's next, scones from Starbucks?"

I managed a slight smile. "Hi, I'm Jess, uh, Jessica, uh, Jessie's fine. Or J-dog or whatever you want." I held out my hand despite wanting it to cover my face.

He looked sympathetic. "Christ, love. Breathe. You're making *me* nervous."

"Sorry, first day jitters."

Why am I so awkward?

"Jess, this is Simon. From London. With the complex to prove it," Orla said.

Confused, I asked, "If he's from London, how do you two know each other?"

"I'm over all the time. Less now that most of the Brexit malarky has been sorted, but there was a time when Coppers practically rolled out the red carpet for me," he said.

A split second of confusion likely showed on my face causing Orla to chime in, "Coppers is a bit of a rite of passage. You're not a true Dub till you've gone there at 2 a.m."

I awkwardly laughed, thinking how the chances of me arriving somewhere at 2 a.m. were incredibly slim.

"I volunteer to pop that cherry for ya, love," Simon said as he shot back an espresso, and my face reacted again. "Relax, you're safe with me," he added with a wink.

They were undeniably strange, but from the looks of it, they were the only people on Project Roadrunner that were around my age and also *not* Raya, so if I wanted any office buddies, they'd be it.

As we stood in an uncomfortable silence, Townsend emerged from his office that was adjacent from the breakroom and smacked his hands together once. "All right, Roadrunners, into the war room."

We gathered in a glass-walled conference room that looked out over a patch of grey sky, the signature color scheme based off my first week. Townsend was already sketching something on the whiteboard when I took my seat. Raya snagged the chair closest to him.

"As you know," Townsend began, "we've been tasked with optimizing the integration strategy for Helix Renewables as they expand into the Irish and UK markets. I want this team to be cross-functional and hungry. This is a proving ground for all of us."

He looked directly at Raya as he said it, which I tried not to interpret.

We went "around the horn" and gave introductions. Two tax specialists from our New York office and a guy from Boston who is apparently some sort of "company culture guru" kicked it off. Then there was Simon, who I'd already met, and based on his intro, had a lot of experience with the Irish and UK trade regulations. There were a handful of employees from the local Irish office as well, including Orla.

Townsend assigned a few initial work streams and deadlines. As expected, I was assigned to the market entry strategy team given models were my bread and butter. The company was a green energy equipment supplier, so I'd be analyzing the Irish sites to help management determine which ones should be acquired or sold and which had the most growth potential. I'd done some pricing models and scenario analysis before, but never to that scale with that many factors and inputs.

Raya's assignment was also a no-brainer. She'd be a client-facing lead in charge of building relationships with the local site managers and liaising the communications between them and the execs to help ensure a smooth integration. Given her connections and overall presence, it was the perfect role for her.

But I needed to focus on myself. I'd have plenty of client-facing opportunities and could show Townsend a range of strengths, but I'd never get to if I fixated on Raya. If I worked hard and stayed the course, I'd shine.

After the introductions and initial assignments were doled out, Townsend opened a slide deck called "Helix Irish Market Prioritization – Preliminary Outlook."

"We're grouping our initial focus into four core markets—Greater Dublin, Cork, Galway, and Limerick. Each region's opportunity profile looks different, so we're not treating them equally. Every recommendation we make needs to have hard data and market comps to back it up."

He scanned the room. "Use the next two weeks to build directional recommendations. Simple questions: what's worth investing in? What isn't? And why?"

I already had some ideas but wasn't ready to share.

"Jessica," he said, turning toward me. "I heard you'd been looking at the financial due diligence reports. Anything jump out yet?"

Adjusting in my seat; my heart raced.

It felt like minutes but was more likely seconds before clearing my throat to buy even more time. "Yes. I've done a preliminary ranking using a weighted scoring model across four key performance indicators: revenue per square meter, labor retention, permitting efficiency, and manager productivity. So far, Greater Dublin is outperforming across the board, but there's nuance. Galway, for example, scores lower overall, but one of the suburban locations has the highest three year compound growth in the portfolio. If we isolate that, there may be long-term scalability we're overlooking."

I paused, expecting at least a follow-up. Nothing. Someone clicked a pen near the back of the room. A yawn slipped out from one of the Irish team members.

I pressed on. "Also, I ran a variance analysis to control for seasonal volatility. Once we normalize that and layer in wage growth sensitivity, the priorities could shift."

Still silence.

Then Raya, lounging effortlessly in her chair across from me, leaned forward and said, "That's great, Jess. I'd just like to add that some of those Galway sites are near major universities. I have a hunch that the manager pipeline is what's dragging down some of the numbers. If that turns out to be the case, I have some ideas for recruitment."

A few heads bobbed. Townsend's did too.

"Smart," he said.

Raya gave a confident little shrug. "Galway's got better food and cheaper rent. That's where I'd rather work."

Chuckles rippled through the room, killing me slowly inside. Even Townsend cracked a grin.

"Can you work with Jess to explore that angle?"

I smiled politely and looked down at my notebook, trying not to wince.

The meeting ended with the familiar shuffling of notebooks and water bottles. Townsend closed his laptop with a sharp click.

"Jessica, a quick word before you go?"

My stomach sank. I remained seated while the rest of the team filed out.

Raya offered a sympathetic look as she passed, though I couldn't tell if it was genuine or smug. Likely a bit of both.

Townsend stood, adjusting his cufflinks with the kind of focus that made me wonder if he was giving me a moment to compose myself. I sat up straighter and took a quiet breath.

"You're clearly prepared," he started, looking at me. "The research you've done in a short amount of time, and given the move abroad, is thorough. Very thorough."

"Thank you," I said, too quickly. My voice came out higher than I intended.

He smiled. "But here's the thing, Jessica. At this level, it's not just about being right, memorizing data. It's about thinking outside the box, considering the *qualitative* data and making people want to listen to you."

I nodded, throat tight. I wasn't sure where he was going yet, but I didn't like where we were starting.

"You'll notice the energy in the room changed when you were speaking," he continued. "Not because you were wrong, but because you were leading with data instead of insight. Oftentimes the shortest answers are the most impactful."

I forced a small smile. "Got it. Less textbook, more point of view."

"Exactly," he said, gathering his laptop and coffee. "You're here because the partners in your office think you have potential. Just . . . trust yourself more. Really put yourself out there. Like Raya."

Ah, shit.

I hoped my face didn't give too much away. "Thanks. I'll work on it."

His knuckles lightly tapped the table. "Good. Now go get yourself a decent lunch in town."

I laughed softly, grateful for the shift in conversation. "Sounds like a plan."

Walking out, I replayed every second of what I'd said in the meeting—cataloging my tone, my posture, the way I clutched my notebook. I dropped my things off at my desk and slunk into my chair.

After a few minutes of staring at a blank screen, as if summoned by Townsend himself, Orla and Simon appeared with an invite to lunch.

Warmth flooded my body at the invitation. Then guilt followed close behind.

"I'd love to join, but can I take a rain check? I have something I want to get done."

Neither of them made any attempt to hide their confusion at what I could possibly have to do already after only three hours on the assignment, but they spared me the explanation and frolicked along without me.

***

That first day, our team left the office at 6:30 p.m.—or as I had learned, "half six." There was barely enough time to swing by Dunnes Stores to pick up bedding and towels. The ones that came with the apartment looked and smelled like they'd been hanging around a few years too long. With crisp, white bedding and matching white towels in tow, I made it through the checkout just as security was locking up.

With a linen closet in my arms, I half ran to the Luas and made it on board just before the doors shut. Three stops later, a voice announced "Ranelagh" in English and then in Gaelic. The latter sounded like the English version, but with more throat action. I chuckled at the thought of how much spit must spray to make that pronunciation.

The amusement was short-lived. The handle on one of my bags ripped as I hauled them from the floor, so I shoved it under my arm. In the shuffle, my ChapStick fell out of my unzipped purse, but I was too focused on not missing my stop to care.

I stood in front of the door, waiting for it to open.

It didn't. Of course it didn't.

I shifted closer, thinking maybe it had a motion detector. Nothing. Panic set in as the Luas lurched forward.

I fucking hate this place.

"Awk, love, ye have to push the button," came a deep, Irish voice beside me.

Of course there was a button. Of course.

My eyes watered as a grey-bearded man held out my ChapStick.

"Erm . . . I'm gonna stick this in your wee bag here, so I am," he said gently, tucking it carefully into the shredded paper sack.

"Thank you," I murmured.

He must have seen the tears pooling. "Ye can get off at the next stop and catch one going back the other way. Or sure, ye could walk it just the same. It'd hardly be ten minutes for ye."

"Oh? Thanks for letting me know."

"It's no bother. Good luck to ye."

His "bother" sounded like "bodder." It was endearing and made my lip twitch despite the lump in my throat.

At the next stop, I disembarked. The display board revealed a seven minute wait. Considering the walk from the Ranelagh stop to my apartment would be about ten minutes anyway, I decided to go ahead and walk it.

That was when it started to rain. Not a mist, not a drizzle, but rain. More like standing fully clothed in the shower.

My leather loafers were done for.

A couple of blocks from home, with my hooded head hanging low, I slammed straight into a metal traffic sign. The bang echoed through my head the way it does in cartoons. Then came the cherry on top of my shitty Monday sundae: one of the soaked, eco-friendly paper shopping bags gave out, and my brand new white towels spilled across the sidewalk like I was waving the flag to surrender.

I dropped everything—my laptop bag, my purse, my dignity—and let the tears fall fast and free.

Mascara streaked down my cheeks. My hair clung to my face. Anyone passing might have assumed I'd just been dumped, mugged, or escaped an institution.

I wanted to go home. My *real* home. In Tampa. Where my friends and family were. Where things made sense. Where you didn't need a friggin' instruction manual to open a tram door.

I fumbled for my phone, wiped the screen with my undershirt and called Dad.

"Hi, sweetie!" he answered, voice chipper.

With only a sniffle for a reply, he asked, "Jess? Honey, are you all right?"

And that did it. The sob that escaped was guttural. "I can't do this. I wanna come home."

"Where the hell are you?" he barked. "Jessica Lynn, tell me right now where you are."

Remembering the time we'd watched *Taken* together, I briefly imagined him as Liam Neeson, and it snapped me upright.

"I'm . . . fine. Sort of. I'm sitting on the sidewalk not too far from my apartment. It started raining and my bags ripped, and all my shit fell on the ground, and everything is wet, and I think my laptop is ruined."

"All right, all right, take a big breath, sweetie."

I did it, sniffling and hiccupping through the inhale.

"Honey," he said, calmer now, "you're being too hard on yourself. It hasn't even been two weeks. It's going to take time."

"I don't belong here. Everything's a huge ordeal. I can't do anything without fucking something up."

"Hey, now! Watch your mouth, young lady."

I laugh-cried and managed a "Sorry."

"Jess, if anyone can move across the world and make it work, it's you."

"You have to say that, you're my Dad."

"I wouldn't say it to your brothers, that's for sure."

Another smile unleashed itself.

"Give it time, sweetie. It'll get better. But right now, get yourself home. Your current home. And don't hang up until you're inside."

"Okay." I sniffled more.

God, I was an awful, selfish daughter, making him worry like that.

Taking another deep breath, I stood and began collecting all my spilled belongings from the ground. I shoved a towel into my purse, another one into my laptop bag, and wrapped the last two around my neck.

Why in the world did I buy four towels anyway?

I held the bedsheets in one hand and phone in the other as I began walking to my apartment.

"You know what, sweetie? They say it takes six months to really adapt to a new place and start to feel settled."

"Who's *they*?"

"Some psychology experts, but mostly people who have moved abroad. I've been reading the blogs some of them make—they're called expats, did you know that?"

The thought of Dad, who takes five minutes to send a one word text, sitting at the computer reading blogs from people around the world dried my tears and warmed my heart.

"Make the most of it, Jess. Work hard, but don't forget to play some too."

I reached Charleston Road and the black cat I'd seen before darted across my path.

Of course a black cat would cross my path.

"I'm home," I told him. "Finally. My feet are soaked, and my shoes are ruined. So is my hair."

"Were you wearing the rain boots and the rain jacket your mom and me and Lindsay got for you?"

"Umm. No. I can't wear the boots at work, so it'd be a lot to carry."

"Did you have an umbrella?"

"Negative."

He sighed. "Jess, you're in Ireland. It's famous for raining a lot. You're always so prepared in every other sense, you gotta be prepared for the weather. Especially when you're walking everywhere."

"You're right. Thanks, Dad. I love you."

"Love you too, sweetie."

Three hours later, wrapped in new sheets that smelled like detergent instead of the tenants from the nineteenth century, I got a text from Dad. A photo of a micro pig tucked inside four tiny red rain boots.

I laughed loudly just as another text came in, an unexpected one.

Brad.

Brad: *Hey there. I heard you're in Ireland now?! Wow, that's really cool, Jess. Just wanted to say I hope you're settling in okay and wish you luck. Not that you need it.*

I read it a few times, surprised by how reassuring it felt. Not exciting, not complicated, just . . . sweet. We'd both moved on, and the only time I'd heard from him in the past two years were the "Happy Birthday" texts, but it was nice to know that he still cared enough to check in. I typed a quick response.

Me: *Thanks for checking in. I'm still finding my footing, but I made it.*

I set the phone face down on the nightstand and turned off the lamp.

I didn't necessarily feel better about the whole situation of being in Ireland, but I did feel like I'd survived a test and would come out a little bit stronger than the day before.

The next day, I'd be prepared for the rain and try again. There was no grand plan for wowing Townsend, but at least I knew one thing: how to push the button to exit the Luas.

8

THE NEXT DAY, AFTER my disastrous orientation, I considered bailing on lunch again. At 11:55 a.m., I even drafted an excuse about "catching up on onboarding materials." What I actually planned to do instead was rehearse my Helix talking points until they didn't sound, well . . . rehearsed.

As I read the message a few times, agonizing over the punctuation, Orla appeared at my desk, shimmying into her purple coat.

"Come on, Yankee. No excuses, we're getting lunch."

Simon stood behind her, perfecting his hair in the reflection of a monitor. "Trust me, love, she's not letting you wiggle out of it," he said. "Neither am I."

Hesitating a beat, my dad's advice reverberated in my head.

I hit the 'Ctrl' and 'L' keys.

"No wiggling here." I held my hands up in mock surrender.

Outside, the sky was its usual Dublin grey, but dry, which as far as I was concerned, counted as a win. I grabbed my trench coat and followed them out the door, hoping lunch wouldn't feel as overwhelming as everything else had.

We entered a cafeteria-style deli called KC Peaches which buzzed with clinking utensils and overlapping conversations. We slid trays along the display window, piling our plates with as many different salads and potato variations as we could fit. At the end of the line, a carvery station with ham and roast beef looked like something out of a holiday dinner instead of a casual workday lunch.

Orla snagged a table in the middle of the chaos and waved us over with the same level of enthusiasm she had when explaining how to make a cuppa tea.

I took mental notes on how they both ate. The fork remained upside down and in the left hand. Knife in the right. No switching hands, no flipping the fork over to how I'd used it my whole life.

Orla caught me staring. "Go on, give it a go, Yank. We won't judge."

"Too harshly," Simon finished the sentence.

A sly grin tugged at my mouth. Flipping the fork over and into my left hand, I speared a piece of ham and used the knife to load some mash on top of it and stuck a carrot onto the mash for good measure. It felt like trying to write my name with my left hand. I knew I could do it, but it was unnatural.

"It's much more efficient," Simon said. "No faffing about with switching hands every five seconds."

The bite felt too big, but I managed to land it without any casualties. It was a small, silly thing to anyone else, but it gave me a flicker of confidence. Like I was a little less of a visitor and more of a local.

Orla rattled off recommendations at machine gun speed as if we'd remember them. Simon might, given he'd been to Dublin several times for short work trips, but now he'd agreed to relocate for the duration of the Roadrunner project. Lucky for him, if he got homesick, London was a forty minute flight and less than a hundred euro away.

"If ye need proper shopping, don't bother with Grafton or Henry Street. Take the Luas to Dundrum, there's a massive shopping centre there with everything you could need."

I nodded, pretending I'd remember. Although, I did vaguely recall seeing Dundrum somewhere on the Luas map.

"Oh! And for the best scones, go to Bread 41. But ye gotta get there early because once they sell out for the day, that's it. And then for sausage rolls, it's without a doubt Brixton's in Ranelagh."

Her accent was thicker than anyone else's I'd met so far, which made it even harder to store the names she tossed out.

"Where are you staying, love?" Simon asked.

Staying? What an odd choice of word.

"Um, my apartment's in Ranelagh," I said, trying to mimic Orla's pronunciation. *Ron-uh-la* and not the way I'd said it to my parents and to the taxi driver which was *Ranel-ag-ah*.

Orla lit up. "Oooh, Ranelagh is quite posh now. Brilliant brunch spots, great pubs and . . . absolutely *crawling* with rugby players." Her decorated fingers quickly wiggled like spider legs in the air.

Simon adjusted in his seat. "Rugby players? As in the ones with rock-hard abs, tree trunks for legs, and dreadful haircuts?"

"Bingo," Orla said, pointing at him. "Ye can't swing a tote in D4 or D6 without hitting one."

Simon fanned himself with a napkin. "I know where I'll be exploring."

We all laughed, and for the first time since arriving in Dublin, I felt lighter. Taking our time to eat, Orla moved onto Irish sports, rattling off differences between hurling, rugby, regular football a.k.a. soccer to me, and Gaelic football. Again, I tried to keep up, but without my notebook it was going in one ear and out the other. When the conversation moved from the players to the technical aspects, Simon didn't even pretend to listen as he instead checked his phone between bites of roast beef.

After we cleared our plates, Orla returned to the table carrying three coffees, two slices of cake and three clean forks.

"You didn't have to—" I started.

"Shush." She plopped a slice of lemon-blueberry pound cake in front of me.

The first bite melted on my tongue.

"Right," Orla said, leaning onto her elbows, chin on fists. "Since ye two are technically outsiders, we need to discuss one more thing. Dating."

I inhaled a bite of cake, nearly choking. Simon, on the other hand, perked up like a meerkat.

"So. As a rule of thumb," Orla began, cutting into the rhubarb cobbler. "Irish men are absolute arseholes when it comes to dating. They'll text ye for weeks about everything under the sun but won't just ask ye out."

Simon groaned. "I'm too old for Peter Pans. Not that I want to grow up and settle down—quite the contrary, actually. But in order to have a cheeky shag, they can't stay in the text zone."

Orla bobbed her head in agreement. "My advice for dating here—lower your expectations."

My brief post-Brad stint on the dating apps had already taught me that late twenties dating is a jungle, regardless of country. Besides, I wasn't there to date. I was there to dazzle Townsend, lock in his backing for Associate Partner the following year and get out. Arsehole Irish guys be damned.

"I take it you're single?" I asked.

Orla laughed. "Sweetest god, no. My old man's back home in Galway. I figured I'd give Dublin a few years, make some money, and live in the big city. Sure, I'll go back eventually. Or not. We'll see how it goes."

"Oh," I said, trying not to appear startled. I'd known people to do long distance, but it was always tied to school or a job assignment. Not so voluntary and unorganized. "And he didn't want to come with you?"

Again, her reaction was as if I were the funniest person in the world. "Once you meet Gearóid, you'll understand why I'm laughing." She looked up, wiping underneath her eye. "He hates the city, hates public transport, hates traffic, hates crowds . . . hates people in general."

"A real charmer," Simon mumbled.

"Oh, he's a grump all right," Orla said, cheerfully. "But he's *my* grump. Plus, he works the family farm, so he'd never move. It's grand, really."

I swallowed my cake hard. A farmer. Maybe Lindsay's joke about meeting farmers wasn't as stereotypical as I'd thought.

"Wow. That's really cool," I said. "How'd you two meet?"

"At a pub on Stephen's Day during my final year of uni. Our families had known each other, but we'd never met until then."

"Final year of uni? So . . . four? Five years ago?" I asked.

"Seven."

Simon and I glanced at one another.

He spoke first. "Seven years, love, and you're slagging Dublin lads for dragging their feet?" He'd said exactly what I was thinking.

"I didn't say *Dublin* lads dragged their feet. I said *Irish* guys. Exhibit A: my own fella."

We dissolved into laughter for what felt like the hundredth time. Eventually, we made our way back to the office—ninety minutes after we'd left. I tried to slip in unnoticed, but no one from Roadrunner was around anyway.

As I hung my coat, it struck me that the lunch probably wasn't anything special for them. Just another Tuesday.

But for me, it felt like a sigh of relief. And I couldn't wait to tell Lindsay and my parents about it.

9

EACH DAY CROSSED OFF the calendar hanging in my kitchen felt like another step further away from home. Turning the page to reveal the adorable pug puppies modeling for the month of July, my heart stung seeing that the fourth landed on a Friday—so in addition to having no plans, I'd be working all day.

I'd finally cracked the code on doing laundry in the baffling all-in-one miniature unit. It didn't wash clothes well, more like sloshed them around gently without an agitator to really clean them. The drying was even worse. After two full hours, the clothes would be damp at best. On Sunday, which was my designated laundry day, items would hang from the clothes horse, the shower, and every doorway in the apartment. A fondness had developed for grocery shopping in small batches every two or three days, but I missed having a car, especially with the temperamental weather. The sporadic rain meant I never left home without an umbrella or my trench coat.

But it wasn't home. And it wasn't just my Acura I missed. I missed my parents, Lindsay, and other friends, but more than anything, I yearned for the small, everyday things—my favorite yogurt, my makeup and skincare brands, and decent water pressure.

The biggest downside was that I wasn't impressing Townsend as much as I needed to or had planned. After two full months, I'd barely gotten even one compliment. That is, if you count "Much better than your last presentation, Dunhour" as a compliment. He gave praise more freely to others on our team, especially to Raya. Being on the project and relocating for a year had to win me some brownie points, but if you only had those first two months to go off, I wasn't sure I'd be in the running to get his backing for Associate Partner in a year or two.

During a one-on-one feedback touchpoint, Townsend's comments boiled down to two painfully generic takeaways: improve my presentation skills, and work on networking and building professional relationships. Groundbreaking. Of course he wanted us to network and schmooze so we could sell more work.

Orla mentioned an annual charity 5K taking place the following weekend that our office always participates in. It'd essentially be a giant networking event that most Irish companies, regardless of size, participated in to benefit research programs for children's cancer. Each business had a tent set up and after the run, there was a DJ and raffles, and it'd be a good opportunity to meet other local businesses. At the very least I'd be showing some level of initiative to try and meet people outside of my new coworkers. Surely Raya would attend, and the last thing I needed was for her to get another leg up, so I internally rolled my eyes and signed up.

***

"We should probably call it a night. I've already had my two beers and if I have another, I won't be able to run tomorrow." In my mind, we were celebrating the Fourth of July a day late, but in Simon's, we were celebrating his birthday for the second weekend in a row.

"Oh piss off with your two drinks and home for midnight. It's my birthday week, Cinderella," he whined.

"Your birthday was two weeks ago . . . I'm over it. Plus, we have that networking race thingy tomorrow."

"Ah, bloody hell. Why'd I agree to that?"

"Because I asked you to, and you love me." I batted my eyelashes. "And you jump on any excuse to rub elbows with potential clients."

"True to both. But tomorrow is Sunday . . . it's my sacred day where I sleep off a hangover, ignore the piles of laundry and dirty dishes, watch *Buffy* reruns and order Zaytoon," he said matter-of-factly before taking a swig of his whiskey. "Now I have to . . . exercise? It's sacrilege."

"You can lay around in squalor after the race. I need a buddy to network with. The only other person I'll really know is Orla and she doesn't need to network for her role."

"God, I love it when you use me." His eyebrows waggled quickly. I shook my head.

"Hey, serious question?" I asked.

"Serious answer," he raised his finger and chin toward the bartender. "What's on your mind?"

"Townsend, um . . . well, he said I need to work on my executive presence." I curled slightly into myself. "I mean, I *know* that. I'm not oblivious. I've known for a while, and I try to work on it. Like, I've read all the stupid articles and blogs on LinkedIn about *'Taking Up Space'* and *'How to Talk Like a CEO'* and all that nonsense." I waved my hand casually through the air. "I practice my presentations at home, but I feel like it just makes me more self-conscious."

He looked at me with sympathetic eyes.

I rubbed my forehead. "I'm not getting better, at least not fast enough. I'm not . . . I'm not Raya, and I'll never be, but I need to at least like, move in that direction." I looked at him and finally said it. "Could you maybe, um . . . help me?"

The words barely left my mouth as he indicated agreement.

Hand on heart, he replied, "I'd be honored, Cinderella."

I smiled and mouthed, "Thank you."

He took a sip of his drink, eyes flicking toward the bar like he was deciding what his next words would be. "Besides," he said, "I've got skin in the game too."

I squinted at him.

"I've been an Associate Partner for four years now. The last two years have been a lot of 'Next year looks promising,' and 'You're right there,' and 'Just keep doing what you're doing, we all support you.'" He made air quotes around the last part. "I'm hoping this is finally my year to drop the Associate from my title."

"Aw, man, I'm sorry," I said.

He leaned closer. "Helping you find your voice will sharpen mine too. Not to mention I'll get mentor brownie points. Not that I wouldn't do it regardless."

"Hey, I get it. Mutual self-interest."

As I reached for my phone to check the time, I noticed a text banner from Lindsay: *Did you get my voice note? Jason wants to meet my mom!*

"My best friend from home," I explained casually, flipping my phone face down on the table. "She's got her own drama back in Florida."

"I love drama. Do tell," Simon pleaded.

"Lindsay, that's my friend, had a tough upbringing. Her dad left, Mom is crazy, etcetera, so she never wants kids. Like, it's a hard stop for her. But she met this guy and he's perfect, yada-yada-yada, but . . . has a four-year-old. Anyway, it sounds like it's getting serious, and he wants to meet her mom. She's freaking out."

"Ooh, I'm invested. Shall we stay for another round? You can call her and put her on speaker. Please, please, pretty please?" He pouted.

"No way! First of all, that's tacky. Second, I'm done and want to get some sleep before the run."

He rolled his eyes and blew out an exaggerated breath.

We argued over the tab, but he had his card ready and was able to tap it on the portable device quickly before he pulled my trench coat from the chair and helped me into it. It was only a fifteen minute walk back to my apartment, but Simon hailed a taxi and insisted I get in. With a small peck on each cheek, he opened my taxi door. "We'll start your boss bitchin' lessons next week."

I scrunched my face. "Is someone trying to make boss bitchin' happen?"

"Oh, I'm going to make you a boss bitch whether you like it or not." He rolled his eyes. "Safe home, Cinderella."

As the taxi pulled away, Simon, with hands in pockets, set off in the opposite direction of his apartment.

***

The Luas ride to Phoenix Park the next morning was quiet. As we glided along Henry Street, a few tourists were beginning to spill into and out of cafes. Phoenix Park was enormous; less a park and more like a small town. It took twenty minutes just to reach the race start, and I passed an actual zoo on the way.

My office group, minus Simon, was stretching in the grass while Orla entertained us with a story about the knobhead her younger sister was dating. He had shown up to a date in a grey tracksuit *and* forgot his wallet. I was midlaugh when someone ran right past me doing warm up sprints. Cutting across my peripherals, I turned to see the long body stretching.

He had long, wavy hair, ridiculous legs and what had to be the world's shortest running shorts. He had the confidence of a peacock—except instead of teal feathers, it was neon green nylon shorts daring anyone not to look.

This guy made an absolute performance out of stretching. Each move was precise and exaggerated. Every time he rose from a lunge, I'd see his eyes flick back toward our group.

No, not our group. Toward me.

Shit, he probably caught me staring.

I pulled my sunglasses from atop my head to make spying less obvious, but it didn't help because I swore he twitched one side of his mouth upward in a sly half smile.

Shit, what do I do back?

Nothing. I do nothing.

"Tell me," Simon's voice boomed behind me, "does one bloody park need to be so bloody big?"

I tore my gaze away from Tiny Shorts to see Simon with his own oversized sunglasses and an equally oversized coffee, greeting all the ladies in our group with a double cheek kiss.

Orla yelled at him for being late while I tried to coax out of him what he got up to after I left the pub.

"Whelan's had a band, so I went dancing, and now I'm paying for it." He began stretching like a ninety-year-old, barely turning his back but making a face as if he were doing a full split. "I got a hot dog from the stand outside of Whelan's. God, hot dogs are so fucking delicious," he blurted.

"Ew. How drunk were you?" I asked, turning my head just a tad to look at those slutty, little green shorts again. Tiny Shorts Guy looked my way, but I couldn't tell if he knew I was looking at him behind my glasses.

"No clue, but I went back for a second."

A gag face formed involuntarily. "Gross."

After a ten minute roll call of corporate team names, the race finally began. We ran past grazing deer, horseback riders, and serious cyclists who looked annoyed that joggers were cluttering their turf. Simon somehow stayed ahead of our group despite his whiskey and hot dog hangover, and I lost sight of Tiny Shorts Guy somewhere around the first kilometer.

After the race came the mingling portion, which was the whole reason I signed up. Simon, true to his word and to his image, was a phenomenal wingman. Or maybe I was his wingwoman? No. I was more like a networking barnacle. Before bringing me to the other company's tents, he introduced me to everyone he knew at our office outside of those I already knew from working on Roadrunner.

"Jess, this is Colin from IT, good guy to know," Simon said, gesturing to a tall guy with a buzz cut and windbreaker adorned with our company's boxy logo.

"Ah, I just tell people to restart their computers and half the time that works." We all chuckled. "So, you're one of the new consultants from the States, right?"

He was slightly awkward in his movements. I liked that about him.

"Guilty." My shoulders raised. "But now I'm living in Ranelagh." I quickly mumbled the name of my borough to disguise the pronunciation that was still far from perfect.

"Fair play. I'm on Rathmines Road, practically your neighbor, so I am."

It wasn't the first time I heard someone tack on "so I am" at the end of a sentence.

Thankful for the common ground and for someone I could maybe ride into the office with on a rainy day, I excitedly replied, "Oh yeah? Good to know. Maybe you can give me a ride sometime." I don't know why I chose that moment to give a wink when I'm not a winker, but I did. Colin's eyebrows shot into his hairline, and Simon made a choking sound.

Both their eyes darted around until Simon eventually chimed in, "Ah, she means a lift. Jess doesn't have a car and has had a few rain mishaps."

The redness in Colin's face slowly faded. He opened his mouth, closed it, and gave a mature answer. "Ah, well, yes. If you ever need a lift, I'd be happy to help out."

Simon clamped onto my elbow. "Right. Good seeing you Colin but we must venture."

As he dragged me away and toward the other tents he explained, "Just so you know, a *ride* means a shag."

"And a shag is . . . sex? Or kissing?"

"Kissing is a snog."

Shit.

"So I just asked Colin from IT . . . for sex?"

"You did. And don't forget the wink."

I smacked a hand over my face.

"Don't sweat it, he's friendly and if anything, you made his day."

I groaned, imagining how one or both of us will blush every time we see each other in the office.

"Relax," he said. "We cleared it up, now let's meet some local businesses."

Effortlessly, Simon introduced me to half of the tents. I was awestruck at how much he knew about so many people, especially considering he lived in London and not Dublin. The first few meetings went smoothly, but when he introduced me to Maeve Donnelly, the CEO of Strazmark, he added that she's been hiking in Georgia. I'd assumed he said it for me to jump on the Florida-Georgia connection, so I blurted out that I was from Florida and asked if she ate any peaches while in Georgia. Unfortunately, he meant Georgia the country, and I took a beat too long to register what was going on. Maeve politely confirmed she did not have any peaches while there.

Between the minor embarrassments and all the Sunday tasks I needed to do, I decided to call it a day early. Simon kissed me on the cheek and said we'd start the boss bitchin' lessons immediately the next day.

I'd only restarted my running playlist when Orla called out, "Hey Jess, wait up!" She was jogging to catch me. "I was gonna grab a bite. Wanna come?"

No, no, no. I wanted to get back to my apartment, shower, and get organized.

"Sure, sounds great," I fibbed. Since she was one of only two friends in Dublin, and I was hungry, I chose to be sociable.

"Great. Oh, my best friend's brother is here. He's going to come too, if that's all right?"

Ugh, why didn't I walk away faster?

"Of course." My lips stretched into a smile.

A few minutes later she emerged with . . . no.

Tiny Shorts Guy? The one with the staring problem.

"Jessica, this is Aidan."

His eyes were trying to decide if they were light or dark brown, almost the same color as his hair. Almost the same color as mine. Bumps formed on my arms, and it felt like I was on a rollercoaster. I paused before pulling out my headphones.

"I was wondering how long it'd take you to finally say hi," he said, with a deep voice and posh accent, as if us talking had been inevitable. Was he flirting or was it cultural? Or was he a jerk?

He held out his hand, but as I shook it, all I could look at were his shorts and imagining what was behind them. Trying to remember when my last date was, all I could recall was fog.

Grow up, Jessica. Stop looking at his bulge. Look at his face and introduce yourself like a normal person.

"What were you listening to?" he asked.

A tap of the screen revealed Brendan Urie smoking a cigarette on the cover of an old Panic! At the Disco album.

"Uh, currently "Far Too Young to Die." It's just a running playlist."

"How melodramatic." He tilted his head as his eyes slowly inspected me.

Presumptuous asshole. First he said he was wondering when *I* was going to come say hi when *he* was the one staring at me, and then he was sticking his nose up at my song?

"Excuse me?" I tried to keep my tone neutral. "Is it not up to your musical standards or something?"

"I meant the song title was melodramatic, not you. Although, after that reaction . . ."

A faint laugh escaped. I could feel every inch of him trying to get under my skin.

"And what do you run to? Beethoven?"

"I run without music. It clears the mind and allows you to take in your surroundings. You really ought to try it sometime."

Fucking prick.

"Thanks for the tip," I said flatly, before turning to Orla. "Shall we go eat?"

10

Ireland was having one of the warmest and driest summers in recent history, which meant I had no excuse for how out of place I still felt. The green patches around the entrance to Phoenix Park were littered with people drinking pints in the sunshine. Laughter and conversation harmonized with the clanking of trains pulling into and out of Heuston Station. We ordered sandwiches from a nearby deli and found a spot to eat them, using our canvas bags that came with the race merch for seating on the freshly cut grass.

In the short stretch of time since we'd met, I'd been analyzing everything about Aidan. The way he took up space reminded me of Townsend—almost cocky. Or was he coming off that way because of my own micro failings during the networking hour? Or maybe it was a cultural thing? Nonetheless, I couldn't take my eyes and ears off him, and it wasn't just because of the tiny shorts.

He and Orla were discussing the last time they'd been home, which was amusing considering Aidan's parents only lived about ten kilometers from his apartment, while Orla's trips back to Galway required a full weekend. She'd met Aidan through his sister, Emma, when they were at university together in Galway. Just like Lindsay and I. From what I could gather, Orla had taken trips to Dublin with Emma before moving here herself.

Aidan mentioned he hadn't been home in over a month, so was due a visit before his mum disowned him.

"She's bluffing, sure she is. A son can do no wrong in a mum's eyes," Orla countered as she handed out the sandwiches.

"Not Babs, you should know she's not the typical Irish mum. She wanted her only son out of the house after secondary school, and can you believe she won't iron clothes for me?"

When she asked Aidan who he was living with these days, I perked up.

"Still living with Killian, just renewed our lease."

"Is he the guy you met in Japan?" Orla asked nonchalantly.

"Yup. Two solo travelers brought together at the Mt. Fuji summit."

I knew travel was more commonplace in Europe than what I was used to, but a casual trip to Japan *alone* still caught me off guard. I didn't know anyone personally who had been to Japan, so I was fascinated to hear more.

Aidan told us the story of how their group climbed all day and night, so they were at the summit for sunrise. He and Killian hit it off and traveled together the rest of the trip. From monkeys stealing his phone at a park to getting lost in the complicated maze of the train system, the trip didn't sound relaxing. They tried squid sashimi, fish prostate, fermented soybeans. The one thing he didn't try? Pufferfish. It was number one on his bucket list, and they sought out one of the best chefs because apparently there is a risk of paralysis if not prepared properly. Killian went through with it, but Aidan bailed at the last minute. Can't say I blamed him—it's a lot to risk for dinner.

It struck me how casually he talked about traveling Japan, as if it were no big deal.

When their adventure came to an end and they returned to Dublin, they moved in together.

He'd also been to Cambodia the year before Japan. No mention of who he went with, but "they" went to see the temples where *Tomb Raider* was filmed. Beer was cheaper than water, three dollar massages every day, and enough wild stories to last a lifetime. Listening to him filled me with excitement, but made my life feel small. Not in a bad way, just . . . I don't know, predictable? Lindsay always says I'm predictable, but I've always seen it as a strength. Until I heard Aidan's casual stories about Japan, I hadn't ever thought about or cared how little of the world I'd actually seen.

About an hour later, Orla announced her departure. "Right so, I better get going. I need to run a few errands. It was lovely to see you, Aidan." They exchanged cheek kisses before she turned to me. "And I'll see you tomorrow. Thanks a mil for coming out."

Sitting there alone with Aidan felt awkward. Was he also wondering if we should leave? My hands smacked my knees in a way that could have been interpreted as getting ready to leave, or, if he was going to stay, just a nervous tick.

He shifted onto his side and propped himself on an elbow. The sunlight caught the stubble on his jaw. Based on composure and the way the fine lines around his eyes lingered after squinting, he had to be well into his thirties, but then again, there's a certain type of confidence that ages a person, and Aidan had it.

"What do you think his deal is?" He raised his chin toward a man in a plaid flat cap, sitting cross-legged on a bench. Overdressed for the weather, he scribbled in a notepad with the determination of someone trying to capture a moment, or a thought, before it passed.

"Huh?" I said, unsure what exactly he was asking.

"His name's Cormac. Loves crossword puzzles and calligraphy. Used to be a professor at Trinity, but he'll be ten years retired next spring. He's secretly writing a manifesto about the Irish government's lies and obsession with bureaucracy."

I shook my head, realizing the game. "Nah, I think Cormac is just lonely. His wife died three years ago, and his only son lives in America—trying to become a Hollywood movie star. That's not a manifesto. He's sketching that tree he and his late wife used to have picnics under."

His mouth pulled to the side and eyes widened. "Now I feel like a jerk for making him sound like a conspiracy theorist."

"You see a curmudgeon, I see heartbreak. Both are fair assumptions."

Thinking about "Cormac" or real people in the world like him that were struggling with much worse than being inconvenienced by a move abroad made *me* feel like a jerk for how I'd been processing the past few months. Picking a blade of grass, I became acutely aware that my resisting the move to Ireland was a first world problem.

With a sudden topic shift, Aidan said, "All right, tell me three things you love about Dublin."

Three things I love about Dublin? I'd been so focused on what I didn't like and how it wasn't home that I hadn't really thought about what I did like.

"Hmm, you see, love is a tricky word," I sighed, biding my time to think. It was less about things I loved and more about starting to accept certain things. "I do appreciate the character," I said. "Especially the buildings and houses with Georgian doors."

"Really?" He pulled his head back slightly.

"Yeah. And little things, like how most of the pubs have flower baskets hanging outside. That's pretty cool too." I hadn't spent enough time exploring the sites, but I really did notice the character of the city. "I don't know, Tampa has some cool areas, don't get me wrong. But it's mostly cookie-cutter neighborhoods and huge apartment complexes."

"Ah, yeah, well, America is still new. Hasn't had time to develop that kind of character." Still on his elbow, he edged closer like he didn't want to miss a single syllable. "Okay, what else you got?"

"Oh, the pressure! Let's see . . ." I gazed up, tapping my finger on my chin.

"You clearly *don't* love rocket," he said, eyeing the pile of arugula I picked off my sandwich. "What do you think of the food here?"

"I actually *do* love the food. Everything's fresh; even with these sandwiches, the bread was baked in house. And although I really only dine out with my coworkers for lunch, it seems so much more relaxed. They don't rush you out to turn the table quicker. It's like you have to chase them down for the check in order to leave."

"I take it that's not how it happens in America?"

A quiet scoff escapes before I can answer. "Usually when they clear the plates, they also drop the check."

Again, he looked intrigued. These differences were not that exciting, certainly not like the cultural differences he'd experienced on *his* travels, but nonetheless, he treated my observations like they were equally fascinating. Like I was truly being seen.

"And I love how every drink here comes in glass—even the mixers are served in those tiny glass bottles. I never see soda fountains or those spray guns." And they charge you for that little soda, but I left that part out, so I didn't sound like a cheapo. "And you guys love to use saucers for tea and coffee, it's all very fancy," I said with hands in my lap and shoulders back, mocking a demure pose.

"There were a lot of *loves* in there. Maybe you like Dublin more than you think?"

"It's more complicated than that, or I mean, tricky. Ooh, I have another one."

He leaned in. "Hit me."

"The grocery stores. At first, I hated them, but now I'm starting to . . ." I scrunched my face, realizing what I was about to say. "Love them. At home, there's a whole aisle for peanut butter. Another for pasta. Here, it's like, crunchy or smooth peanut butter? Spaghetti or rigatoni? Bam, you're done." My hands were animating for dramatic effect.

"I've heard that Americans do love their options. That's cool that you're starting to appreciate the simplicity." He looked to the clouds, eyes nearly closed due to the sun. Only the left side of his mouth lifted. Crooked, but sexy.

"So you've been to the U.S., I take it?"

"Actually, no." He seemed surprised by his own answer. "I've been to about thirty countries, but never North America. I'd like to go, but I wouldn't do that one alone." His focus moved to something off in the distance. Did that rule come from a lesson learned the hard way or just a preference, I wondered.

"Thirty countries? That's amazing!"

"You are *so* American," he laughed.

"Whatever. I'm practically Irish now."

"Ah, sure, look, it's like, so awesome and amazing." I fought the urge to shove his shoulder but couldn't stop the smile pulling hard at my cheeks.

We gushed about our favorite movies, discussed our mutual fear of clowns, and shared stories from our "uni" days. I told him about Lindsay and how we lived together throughout college and how she's like a sister to me. He told more travel stories while hours passed and clouds rolled in, bringing with them a drop in the temperature.

"It's getting late. I should go," I said, brushing the grass off my legs. I didn't want to leave, but on top of being cold and needing to pee, time was running out to prep for work the next day.

He agreed, and we walked together to the park entrance where he said he'd be heading in the opposite direction.

"Right, so. It was great chatting with ye. I'm sure I'll see ya around sometime."

I took note of how he cycled through "ye", "ya", and "you" much more than Orla did, but couldn't get a sense of how he felt or what we should do for the goodbye.

Should we hug? Shake hands? Do the double cheek peck thing?

My mind raced. Would he go in for an actual kiss?

No, no, no. I wasn't getting first kiss vibes from him. Or was I? No.

It'd been so long since I'd been in a legitimate flirty situation. I had no clue how to read signs or how to tell if there were any signs to read. Eventually, I convinced myself that a handshake would be the safest option.

But my brain short-circuited and instead sent signals to my body to perform the worst possible option.

With one hand on my hip and the other enthusiastically waving like Forrest Gump, I said, "Welp, have a nice night." And then I saluted him.

His head fell as he laughed. "You are *so* American."

What I was, was so embarrassed. I shrugged as if that were a sexy response and scurried away.

During the commute home in the Luas, I combed through everything I'd learned about Aidan, mentally filing it away. I ran through his superlatives like a checklist . . . well-traveled, spontaneous, undeniably sexy.

With a dumb grin and butterflies in my stomach, the reality finally hit—we didn't exchange numbers.

But did he want my number? Or was the whole afternoon just him being polite?

I didn't want politeness, I wanted more. I wanted to see him again. And again and again and again. But at the same time, I wouldn't be the one to reach out; the ball was in his court, and I'd wait patiently for his serve.

But what if it didn't come? No, there was something there. I was sure of it.

Still, the grin faded. Then returned and faded again.

He could easily get my number from Orla.

The smile returned.

11

It was Tuesday—a full week and two days since I'd met Aidan—and I hadn't heard a peep. Sitting at the wooden desk in our modern, open concept office, I kept a close eye on Orla, waiting for her to head to the break room. My plan was to follow her in and casually tease some information about Aidan out of her. Her bright saffron-colored, wide-leg trousers and matching sleeveless vest made her impossible to miss when she finally emerged.

I diligently made my Irish cuppa tea the way she'd taught me on my first day almost three months prior—boiling water, Barry's brand, stir counterclockwise, milk then sugar. No microwaves. Orla recapped her weekend back home in Galway. She'd gone for her boyfriend Gearóid's birthday and organized a long romantic weekend getaway at a spa and castle.

I willed myself to listen and engage instead of searching for a moment to snake my way in and ask about Aidan, but the right moment never presented itself. Eventually, Orla dashed out, saying she was late for a meeting. I was left alone with just my tea and theories about why he'd ghosted me.

It was obvious—he had a girlfriend. Or at least, that's what my brain decided as a means to protect my feelings.

As I wiped the tea that had splashed onto the counter during my twenty-seven vigorous stirs, two loud snaps near my ear made me jump.

Simon shouted, "Hurry up and get your cute little fanny into the James Joyce room, Cinderella."

"Umm, HR . . . did you hear that?" I looked around for a camera. "Workplace harassment."

"Yeah, yeah, yeah. Come on, we have work to do," he said, knocking back a shot of espresso.

"I love how serious you're taking this whole helping me out thing. The two lessons last week were so helpful, but I gave the client presentation yesterday. It went well. I think Townsend may have even smiled. You don't need to keep this up."

"Oh no. This wasn't a one week gig. You're a really shite speaker."

My mouth fell open. "Ouch."

"It's true," he said, unapologetic. "But I'm in this until you're promoted—not flattered."

As we walked toward the James Joyce room, Raya was deep in conversation with Townsend. He looked to be laughing, which was something I hadn't managed to get out of him.

My phone buzzed and like I'd done with every buzz since I met Aidan, my stomach assumed it was him.

But it was Lindsay.

Lindsay: *Any word from that guy yet?*
Me: *Negative.*
Lindsay: *Then he has a girlfriend. On with the next.*
Lindsay: *Did I tell you I met Cody this past weekend?*

Lindsay: *Cute kid, but I definitely broke out in hives trying to talk to him.*

Lindsay: *I really don't have the mom gene!*

Me: *Why are you up so early?*

Lindsay: *Reformation Pilates at 5:15*

I'll occasionally rise at the crack of dawn to get to work before everyone else, but never to workout. Lindsay had done so religiously since college.

Snapping back to the present, I turned to Simon. "I feel bad. You're about to make full-fledged Partner this year and you're like, babysitting my confidence crisis."

"Don't get it twisted—you getting promoted to Associate Partner helps my numbers too. And don't like, say like."

I huffed a laugh. "Okay, but I'm not up for promotion this year. You are."

"Doesn't make me any less invested." He winked and nudged my arm, directing me to the conference room he reserved.

When Simon wasn't slamming whiskey and hotdogs or being brutally honest, the man radiated pure professional "It" factor. Conversation came effortlessly to him no matter who he was speaking to. He could sell sand to a beach and make it feel like a deal. And he wasn't just a charming salesman—his technical knowledge ran deep, which made it obvious why the firm had pulled him onto Roadrunner in the first place.

In the couple of months we'd worked together, he'd closed one piece of work for the London office and another for Dublin. They'd be fools not to name him a Partner.

He still called our lessons boss bitchin' 101, which I refused to say—not because of the language, but because of the cheese.

Lesson one was all about body language. He'd brought in a mirror to show me the difference between how I normally stood versus how I *thought* I stood. Being tall, I never tried to appear taller, but when he recorded me, I looked like the hunchback of Notre Dame.

Lesson two was all about taking up space. He drilled into me opportunities to physically fill space and still look natural. Feet always shoulder width apart or wider. Owning my seat. There was even a whole methodology for when to smile, when to pause, and when to ask questions to appear both likable and authoritative. It felt a tad manipulative, but I loved knowing the secrets, even if I wasn't comfortable using them yet.

As we settled into the small conference room, I asked, "What's the topic today, boss?"

A mischievous look spread across his small, handsome face. "Thinking on your toes."

Oh no. No.

A montage of my stiff presentations in front of Townsend, asking Colin from IT for sex, asking a local CEO if she had peaches in Georgia—the country—and my goofy wave to Aidan all flashed through my brain.

"Great," I muttered.

"I'm going to rapid fire topics," he said, alternating pulling a trigger with his finger guns, "and you simply talk about it until I fire off a new one."

"I really regret this."

"Oh, if I had a euro for every time I've said that, or had it said to me . . ."

Before we started, I flipped my phone. The email notification sent my heart plunging to my stomach.

Aidan McGovern 9:36 A.M.

Subject: Awesome American

Simon told a story about a guy he took to a silent disco, but I couldn't focus on his muffled words.

"Okay, shall we begin?" he asked.

"Hold on, I need to respond to this client email quickly."

I feverishly opened it and immediately deflated.

From: Aidan.McGovern@ESKlaw.com
To: J.Dunhour@mcafeeconsulting.com
Subject: Awesome American
Time: 9:36 a.m.

http://www.mediawire.com/10-things-americans-say-and-what-they-really-mean
Please see #1.
Aidan

That was it? No, 'I can't stop thinking about you, wanna grab a pint?'

Annoyed, I clicked the link anyway. Taking its sweet time to load, the heading finally popped into view: *Ten Things Americans Say . . . and What They Really Mean.* I laughed out loud while reading through the list.

"Everything okay?" Simon asked.

"Yep," I said quickly, surely sounding like a liar.

Number one was about how when an American shop assistant says, "Have a nice day," what they actually mean is, "I don't care what kind of day you have, but please tell my manager I was friendly so I can make a commission."

My favorite was number nine—how an American saying they need to use the restroom doesn't mean they're looking for a room to have a quiet lie down in. Just the loo.

He must have gotten my work email from Orla, but surely she'd have given him my phone number too? Regardless, did he have to wait a week and two days to reach out? And then *this* is what he sent? What an odd bird.

Okay, I can play this game.

I searched for an Irish equivalent and found something on IrishMai l.ie. Following his lead, I replied with nothing but the link.

The article was about Irish mothers believing their sons could do no wrong and that no woman would ever be good enough. There was even a quote from "Paddy, age 32" saying his mum gets worried when he doesn't go home to Edenderry at the weekends to be fed and have his laundry done.

Below the link, I typed, "Stereotypes come from somewhere."

Satisfied with my response, I turned my attention back to Simon, happy to have the distraction. I even put my phone on silent and placed it face down so I wouldn't fixate on his reply.

Simon snapped his fingers and stood at attention, like a game show host. "All right, Cinderella. Enough faffing around with emails. The rules are simple. I bark out a topic, and you've got thirty seconds to convince me it's fantastic. Ready?"

"No," I deadpanned.

"Perfect. Topic one. Squirrels. Go."

My mind went blank. Squirrels? What the f—

"Uh, they . . . umm, they . . . they have fluffy tails, which are . . . very nice and fluffy. Okay, this is so cringe. I can't do this."

Simon groaned dramatically. "What's cringe is your lack of effort. Deep breath, try again."

A deep breath. "Fine." I swallowed. "Um, squirrels are so fantastic because they . . . um, they . . . are entrepreneurial."

His head jerked back.

"That's right," I pressed on. "They have to gather all their things . . . their, um, their nuts to eat and sticks for shelter. They're scrappy. And strong. Oh, so very strong."

I looked at Simon as if to say, "I'm all out."

"You didn't use the full thirty seconds, but since you're roadkill, we can move on. Next topic. Reality TV. Go."

I winced. "I don't watch reality TV."

"Irrelevant. You can always find an angle. Think, Cinderella."

I inhaled loudly, blew out a raspberry, closed my eyes and let nonsense spill. "Reality TV is great because . . . it allows you to . . . study? Human psychology, and, um, social hierarchies and sometimes even, um, mating rituals of the young and the beautiful. And, uh, you can learn all of this from the comfort of your own couch."

Simon nodded slowly, reluctantly accepting the attempt.

"Also, without reality TV, we never would've gotten the Kardashians and then where would Simon be without their lip plumpers and contour kits?"

He gasped, grabbing his chest. "Personal attack? I love the sass. All right, topic three. Hot dogs. Go."

I made a quick gag face and thought for a few seconds.

"Hotdogs are great because . . . um, they bring people together?" My face was surely unconvincing. It was difficult to praise a stick of mystery meat.

"Whether it's a baseball game or a backyard BBQ, they are synonymous with sunshine and good times. Are they disgusting? Yes. But for less than a dollar a dog, you can feel the . . . nostalgia of simpler times. Or you know . . . some of us choose to pay twenty euro for two from a rolling stand outside the pub on a rainy night."

Simon's mouth fell. "Personal attack again?"

"Last one," he said. "Rain. Go."

"Rain? Really?"

"Yes, sell me on why rain is fabulous. Tick, tock." He tapped his wrist.

I pushed out another big breath and mentally made a list. "Well, rain practically sells itself," I said with a smile. "It's not *just* water, it's part of the water cycle. Some people complain about the rain, but they forget that without it, Ireland wouldn't be so green . . . and so beautiful." Dublin wasn't very green, but I'd seen enough images online and in the Ireland book my mom gave me to know the countryside was notorious for its greenery.

"By golly, that *almost* sounded like you believed it. Not bad, Cinderella."

I couldn't wait any longer to see if Aidan had responded, but Simon wanted to debrief the exercise and give pointers. For almost fifteen minutes, I tried to focus on what he was saying, but the urge to tap into my email kept pushing harder and harder until I caved. I insisted I needed to confirm if a client had sent something. Quickly tapping at the screen revealed his message.

From: Aidan.McGovern@ESKlaw.com
To: J.Dunhour@mcafeeconsulting.com
Subject: Re: Re: Awesome American
Time: 10:45 a.m.

Well played, Miss America, well played. But I told you, my mum is not the standard Irish mum. She doesn't do my laundry and actually wants me to get married. She'd much prefer to talk to you than me. It's true, she's a different species . . . almost American if you ask me.

So what does an American living in Dublin do at the weekend? Any plans?

Aidan

She'd much prefer to talk to you than me?

Okay, so not only was he single, but he was eager for me to meet his mom.

Jessica McGovern.

No, absolutely not. Way too soon. But still . . . it had a nice ring to it.

Was he asking about my weekend plans to be polite, or was he going to ask me out? I drafted a response immediately but waited a couple of hours to send so I didn't appear too available.

From: J.Dunhour@mcafeeconsulting.com
To: Aidan.McGovern@ESKlaw.com
Subject: Re: Re: Re: Awesome American
Time: 1:07 p.m.

Your mom sounds awesome! [smiley emoji]
I'm going to a concert at the Olympia with a friend tomorrow. What does a Dubliner do on the weekend in Dublin?
Jess

In the middle of a Project Roadrunner team meeting, I failed to hide the giddy from my face.

From: Aidan.McGovern@ESKlaw.com
To: J.Dunhour@mcafeeconsulting.com
Subject: Re: Re: Re: Re: Awesome American
Time: 3:41 p.m.

And I was afraid you were going to say you go to Temple Bar! The Olympia Theatre is brilliant, enjoy the tunes. This weekend my housemate, Killian, and I are heading to Kerry for some golf. Maybe a bit of hiking if the weather holds out.
Ok, I'm signing off, have an AWESOME weekend!
Awesome Aidan

Of course he would sign off like that. Of course.

I left the focus room with the rest of the team.

"You're gonna tell me what's bloody gotten into you, right this instant," Simon demanded.

"Huh?"

"Eh, eh, eh, eh, eh, eh, don't even go there. I saw "the look" not once, not twice, but thrice." He shoved three fingers in my face.

"The look?"

"I can spot "the look" from a mile away. Did Cinderella find Prince Charming and not tell me about it?"

"Not Prince Charming." I rolled my eyes. "And I *did* tell you about him."

Confused, he made a face while processing. "The guy from the race? He finally got around to asking you out?"

"Well, we haven't exchanged numbers. And he didn't exactly ask me out yet, just . . . reached out. Through email."

"I don't like him," Simon blurted.

"You take first impressions to the extreme."

"First impressions are almost always correct," he said flatly. "And my first impression is—he waited a week and a half to make a move and when he finally did, it was indirect at best."

He gathered his laptop and phone before wagging a finger at me. "In fact, first impressions will be the topic of our next lesson."

12

The witty emails with Aidan continued for over a week, progressively growing deeper. On the ninth day, he finally asked for my phone number—said it was to send photos from a trip he took to Colombia a few years prior. They picked and roasted coffee beans, went parasailing, and even did the Pablo Escobar tour. Similar to other trips, I never asked who "they" were in case he went with an ex-girlfriend. I liked seeing his photos, but loved that they were an excuse to move our communication from work email to texting.

Texting meant communication during weekends and late nights. It meant that our flirtation had fewer boundaries, but what it didn't mean was that we were any closer to a date. Orla had warned Simon and I that first day of work that Irish guys are notorious for dragging their feet in the relationship front. I always thought she was exaggerating, but as I was experiencing it firsthand, I started to think maybe she was right.

A game had emerged where we'd send each other songs that matched our conversations. When I told him Orla said he "had a hold on me," he returned a link to Smokey Robinson's "You've Really Got a Hold on Me." The song stayed in my head for days along with the thought that we were more than we were.

But I didn't tell him *all* of Orla's comments, like the one where she casually dropped that he "loves the chase." I wanted to dismiss it, but the more time passed with no actual invitation to go on a date, the more it stuck.

But after weeks of being pen pals, my patience was wearing thin. I pulled away. Stopped sending the morning memes, let his messages sit unread a little longer, responses became a little shorter. Even though I hadn't dated much outside of my one serious relationship with Brad, I knew exactly how the game worked.

Simon and I met up with Orla and her boyfriend Gearóid at a pub before a concert at Iveagh Gardens. I promised myself I would just have fun and not stress about Aidan or work or anything else.

The four of us sat around a tiny pedestal table littered with our fresh round of pints and plenty of emptied ones too. Gearóid gave a lesson on Gaelic slang. Orla teased him while Simon flirted with a tattooed biker group at the next table over. It was all in good fun until I checked my phone. Still, no message.

Simon noticed. Of course he did.

"Whatever is the matter, my love?" he asked, one hand on my shoulder and the other clutching what had to be his fourth pint.

"Nothing." I shoved my phone back in my bag and smiled.

"Bullshit," he slurred. "Don't you bullshit a bullshitter."

"It's just . . . Aidan. We kind of fizzled before we ever started."

"Ugh. That guy again?" Simon rolled his eyes. "Didn't know that whole *thing* was still going on."

"I don't know what to call it. We were texting every day. Just Friday morning, he sent the song "Friday I'm In Love." I replied with a smiley face, and that was the last message."

Simon looked genuinely confused. I hadn't mentioned Aidan to him since his reaction in the office when I first told him that Aidan had emailed me. He didn't like that he waited so long to follow up and then didn't ask me out straight away.

"So why don't you ask him out?" Simon asked.

"I don't do that."

He tilted his head. "Come on. You're a modern woman."

"Yes, and he's a modern man. Who clearly doesn't want to ask me out."

"Look, I already told you I don't like him. Who takes eight bloody days after meeting someone to send one cheeky email? Seriously . . . an email? Really? He's either bored or he's a player." He shook his head.

I didn't answer; he was right.

"But . . . if you want to go out with him . . . make a move. What do you have to lose?"

As we walked along the sun-soaked sidewalk, past small crowds congregating outside pubs and taking advantage of the weather, Orla suggested we smuggle in a bottle of Jameson. My heart raced and palms sweated at the thought of bootlegging liquor into a concert in a foreign country especially because the only two people I could maybe call to bail me out of jail were the culprits. No, I needed to look out for myself and stay away from trouble, plus I'd already had two pints of Smithwick's, so I needed to wait a while before considering one more. I waited outside the off-license while the three of them stocked up.

They returned, giggling like teenagers instead of the late twenties to early thirties that they were. Each took turns passing the bottle, taking swigs like it was a bottle of water. Beads of sweat formed at my brow as the security guards looked over our tickets, the sweet and distinct smell of whiskey pouring from their breath as they spoke. The taller of the two guards looked inside Orla's bag as the shorter one half-heartedly looked in mine. As he waved me through, Orla's guard winked at her before saying, "Enjoy the show."

Once we entered the venue grounds, I stood in line to purchase my overpriced but entirely legal plastic pint of beer while they were getting three sheets to the wind on a plaid blanket that Orla brought.

She danced barefoot in the grass holding her makeshift mixed drink in one hand and twirling a stranger around with the other. Orla's new dance partner placed a flower in her wild dark curls and she reciprocated by pouring some of her whiskey concoction into her new friend's mouth.

Gearóid sat on the blanket listening to music while Simon was completely sprawled out on his back, tapping his head behind a pair of Union Jack sunglasses. I sat next to him, occasionally checking that he was still awake and alive. Each time Orla tried to get me to dance with her and her new friends that were ever-growing in number and toxicity, I politely smiled and shook my head, remaining seated. Peering down to an empty cup, I debated switching to water or joining in on the whiskey with them. Between Orla swaying with every person there, Gearóid with a tattooed smile, and Simon feeling every beat as he stared at the sky, I felt out of place. Too rigid, too sober. Maybe a whiskey and Coke wouldn't hurt?

Being around Orla and Simon was infectious. Wanting to loosen up like them, like the night in college when Lindsay dragged me out to a hurricane party, and I met Brad. I decided to go for it.

I grabbed a Coke from a nearby vendor truck and as I took a sip to make space in the bottle, I froze.

The label taunted me. "Share a Coke with Aidan."

Goosebumps formed on my arms. Of all the names Coke printed for that campaign, I got *that* one? In *that* moment?

Thinking of who I was that night I wore the Rolling Stones shirt while Brad held my legs during my first keg stand, I wanted to be her again, if only for a moment. I snapped a picture and muttered "Fuck it" before sending it to Aidan. Almost instantly, he replied.

Aidan: *Haha! Well played!*
Aidan: *I trust there isn't just Coke in there.*
Aidan: *I see you're at Iveagh Gardens.*

Wait, was he there too? Panic rose.

Aidan: *My flatmate's there. I wanted to go but had to come home for my little sister's birthday.*

Oh thank god.

Me: *Yep, I'm here. It's so AWESOME!*

Satisfied, I left it there and went back to mixing my crime drink and enjoying the music, finally loose enough to stop overthinking.

The next morning, I stared at my ringing phone.

Aidan McGovern.

13

Damn, Simon was right about giving him a nudge.

I cleared my throat and practiced my best, "Well, hello there," to make sure my voice wouldn't have any weird cracks when I answered. Ugh, it sounded sarcastic. I tried again, "Hey, you." Oh my god, no. Too friend zone-y.

Come on, make up your mind before he hangs up or worse . . . hears your lame voicemail.

"Heeyy."

Good one. A slutty sounding "Hey" was the best I could come up with?

He laughed. "How ya doing today? You in bits after the concert?"

"Ah, I had a headache this morning, but nothing a coffee and some Panadol couldn't sort out." I was proud of the smooth delivery and effortless use of "sort out", a common Irishism.

"Good stuff. So what are the plans for this bank holiday Monday?"

I had planned to do what I'd typically do on a Sunday, just a day later: go food shopping, meal prep, laundry, iron, plan my outfits for the week, and get ahead of some work. I couldn't tell him that because it'd sound like I was too busy being lame to meet. But on the other hand, I didn't want him to think I had no plans.

Ugh. Think, Jessica.

"No major plans, just running a few errands," I said in my best attempt to sound nonchalant. Meanwhile, I couldn't stop pacing back and forth and sweating from every pore on my body.

"Well, if you're not too busy running errands, I wanted to see if you fancied meeting in town tonight. Posh pizza and craft beers?"

Oh my god, oh my god. Oh. My. God. It was happening! Thankfully he couldn't see me jumping and mouthing silent screams.

"Hmmm, that depends. Will you be wearing those short shorts?"

"If that's what it takes."

"Sold. When and where?" I needed to hang up so I could properly scream, report to Mom and Lindsay and start getting ready.

"Skinflint at eight? Do you know where it is?"

"No, but I'll find it."

"Are you sure? The door's a bit hidden down an alley. I can meet you at Trinity and we can walk over together?"

"I have maps on my phone, I'll be fine."

"Is that, like, American confidence, aye?" he teased.

If only he knew Simon was giving me lessons on how to appear more confident. "That's right. Okay, see you at eight. I'll be looking for the shorts."

"I better run along and shave my legs," he said. I could sense his smile through the phone. "See you soon. Looking forward to it, Jessica."

God, he sounded sexy.

I immediately texted Mom and Lindsay so they could wake up to the news. They wouldn't believe that after a month and a half of being pen pals, I was finally going on a date with Aidan McGovern.

***

Where is this friggin' place?

Google Maps showed it on Crane Lane, which I had turned onto after passing it twice. I scanned both sides of the alley for a Skinflint sign but came up short. At the end of the lane, I turned and tried again. Still nothing. My phone was already in my hand to call the restaurant when Aidan's text lit the screen.

Aidan: *It's on the right when you turn from Dame Street. Blackout windows, no sign, looks abandoned. See you soon.*

Ah-ha. Immediately, it became clear which door it was. Interesting choice to have it be so hard to find. No way that could be good for business.

Inside, six or seven tables filled the dark and cozy space. Aidan emerged with a huge grin, and I could feel my face getting warm. Thank god for the dim lighting of the Edison bulbs hanging above each table by a wire pendant. He wrapped his arms around my shoulders and pulled me in. The mix of laundry detergent and musky cologne was subtle enough that you had to be in his embrace to smell it.

"You look well," he said, pulling away. "Come sit, I ordered you an IPA."

Ugh, my least favorite type of beer. "Perfect." I placed my trench coat over an empty stool. It was too warm for it, but I knew the temperature would drop at night. The tabletop was made of a distressed wooden door panel. Exposed industrial pipes complimented the eclectic décor.

"So I have to admit . . . it was quite entertaining watching you walk back and forth out there, talking to yourself." He flashed a mischievous smile as he poured us water from the repurposed Martini & Rossi bottle. The label had been stripped, but after all of the martinis Lindsay had made us over the years, I could recognize the bottle anywhere.

"What? No, I was singing," I said unconvincingly.

"It's okay. I've been on dates with crazier," he said with a sly wink. "Right so, I think Tess and Maria look absolutely scrumptious."

I nearly choked on my swig of nasty beer.

"Oh yeah? Wanna tell me about them?"

"Well, Tess is thick and meaty with pulled pork and braised fennel, whereas Maria is more delicate with potato, truffle oil and mushroom." He pointed to the menu. "What do ye reckon?"

I kept a straight face and scanned the menu quickly.

"Hmm . . . I don't know. Olivia is lookin' mighty fine. Harissa, hen's egg, serrano ham and mozzarella—she sounds both complicated and delicious," I said, pretending to know what harissa was. Our server approached, donning tight leather pants and a blurry tattoo on his thin neck.

Aidan ordered the Maria and the Olivia, commenting that he likes complicated things.

He asked if I was a foodie, which although a fair and simple question, still felt odd. I had a few foodie inclinations like drizzling overpriced olive oil on top of overpriced gelato and sprinkling it with overpriced Himalayan rock salt, but I wasn't adventurous with trying new foods the way he was in Japan. I was even dreading the unusual pizzas he ordered but told myself not to show it.

"I appreciate good food, but a foodie? Nah, not me."

"My sister's taking classes at the Ballymaloe Cookery School. It's grand because she'll go to Mum and Dad's and try new recipes because they buy all the ingredients *and* clean up. I just eat. She's a really good cook."

"That's awesome." I internally reprimanded myself for the overused phrase and took another gulp of piss water to calm my nerves. "And this is Emma? Orla's friend?"

"Nope, Kate. Kate is the baby, twenty-five. She's shy, keeps to herself, reads a lot. Emma is the opposite. If she thinks it, she says it. And I have an older sister, Fiona. She's in Australia. Recently married, settling down."

"A wee Irish family of only four children. Which one are you closest to?"

"Fiona because we're so close in age. I'm only eleven months younger so we shared all the same stuff . . . toys, sports, friends."

"Ah, so that explains the short shorts—they're Fiona's. Got it."

"You laugh but wait till you see the box of baby photos. I was always in something pink or flowery."

Assuming that box is at his parents' house, my heart skipped as I read into it. *Wait till you see the box of baby photos.* Singing it in my head to the tune of "Here Comes the Bride," I schooled my face to not give away how psychotic my thoughts were.

He switched the conversation back to me, asking about my family, upbringing, and earliest childhood memories in a loaded and direct manner. I felt guilty; sharing about my family and how we grew up relatively happy and normal, whatever "normal" even means. Many of my friends had divorced parents and Lindsay's upbringing was the polar opposite to mine. I sometimes felt boring for not having any family drama to relate to, but Aidan was in the same boat. He spoke highly of his family, and his parents were still together.

I reminisced about building indoor forts with my brothers during hurricanes which blessed us almost every year in the late summer to early fall. We'd pull out every single cushion, pillow, blanket and sheet; never knowing that our parents were panicking over whether the boards on the windows would hold and at what point we'd all need to move into their bathroom. I recounted our family vacations camping in Silver Springs. How we'd rent a pontoon boat, and how once, we came back from a hike to see a snake coiled on top of our cooler. My mom stopped coming after that.

Aidan's camping experiences were more elevated. He and some buddies went on a safari in Botswana and camped in the middle of a river delta, where they'd fall asleep to lions roaring and wake to elephants and hippos heading to a watering hole. My snake on the cooler story felt lame in comparison to his adventures in Africa until he added that he'd never seen a snake in real life especially because there were none in Ireland.

"Saint Patrick drove them all out," he said, with a telling wink.

The conversation pretzeled all over. Before I knew it, I was telling a story about how I used to cry in elementary school whenever other kids broke the rules and didn't get reprimanded. I'm still annoyed with Ms. Alberta for always allowing Carley McIntire to blurt out the answers when other kids, including me, had their hands raised. Why even ask anyone to raise their hands? Just let the chaos ensue.

Middle school and high school brought on their own challenges. I was hyper focused on my grades and far less invested in sports or a social life. It wasn't until junior year, after my brother Robby encouraged me, that I tried out for the volleyball team—and made it. I was late to the game but proud all the same.

Kid Aidan, on the other hand, only cried when recess was over. As a teen, he seemed a lot like he does as an adult—an all-around, stand-up guy. He did well in school, played football (i.e. soccer), and had a lot of friends. Of course he did.

He looked different from the day of the race. Not just because he wore brown, slim fit jeans and a chalky blue button dress shirt instead of barely-there running attire or the fact his stubble was now almost a full-on beard. It was the way people look different the more you get to know them. He'd become the most attractive man I'd ever seen. And he was with me at a hole-in-the-wall pizza joint, talking about everything and nothing. I didn't think I'd ever see him more beautiful than I did at that moment.

An hour later, our skinny server in skinny pants cleared our plates and brought a second round, switching to a chocolate coffee stout per Aidan's request. Anything was better than the IPA.

"So, how did you make friends here? From what you've said, it seems like you go out pretty often." I noticed a long scar on the outside of his forearm, near his elbow.

Conscious to not let my gaze linger, I scoffed at the notion that I was some sort of Dublin socialite. "I only have a couple of friends here, and I met them through work." Not wanting to exclude him from the short list of people I knew, I added, "Well, except for you, obviously."

His jaw clenched as he shifted in his seat. "Jessica, I'm sorry if I gave off the wrong impression, but I want to be very clear now . . . I don't want to be your friend."

His eyes held mine, daring me to understand exactly what he meant. I pressed my lips together, trying to fight a smile I absolutely did not want him to see. It was pointless. "I know it's a bank holiday and we've got work tomorrow, but I don't want the night to end. Do you like cocktails?" he said, lifting one cheek.

I had an 8:30 a.m. with Townsend the next morning, and I'd planned on waking super early to prepare for it, but I didn't care. It was future me's problem.

"I do," I said.

"All right, Missus, we're going somewhere pretty touristy."

Missus? Was it an Irish thing or was he already giving me a nickname? It was suspicious that he first used it immediately after declaring he didn't want to be just friends.

"But it has a nice roof top bar, so you can see Dublin from a different perspective," he continued.

God, I loved his accent. "Sounds perfect."

He exited the restaurant first, holding the door and offering his hand. As we stepped onto the uneven cobblestone, he squeezed mine twice in quick succession.

"The stones can be quite tricky." He winked.

Live music spilled from every pub doorway, clashing with the chatter that filled the streets of Temple Bar. It was the signature hustle and bustle of Dublin, a violin here, a banjo there. I didn't know if those were the actual instruments being played or not, but it felt like every instrument was in use to serenade us.

As we took our drinks—his looking like something you'd order on a girls' trip to the Bahamas—we settled into a spot against the railing of the roof. I leaned my back against the metal bar and tipped my head back toward the stars, feeling the bittersweetness of my Moscow Mule travel down my throat.

"What do you think is going on at two o'clock?" he asked.

To my right was a pretty woman sitting at a table by herself, sipping a cocktail through a tiny black straw and scrolling through her phone. Before I could register what he meant, he was answering his own question.

"It's Mia. Twenty-five years old, works in marketing but is trying to make content creation a full-time gig. She's waiting on a guy that's ten years older, so she ordered mezcal thinking it makes her appear more mature, more interesting."

I tilted my head. "Are we looking at the same person? Or are you projecting?"

He grinned. "All right then, Missus. What's your take?"

"Mia looks twenty-five but is actually early thirties. She's meeting her best friend for a long overdue catch-up and arrived early to savor the time alone and this weather. She's sipping a spicy margarita—with regular ole' boring tequila—that reminds her of a trip she took to Mexico after graduation when life seemed easier."

"First of all, there's nothing boring about tequila. Second, I don't buy it. I think I know Mia better than you. Hell, I bet I know what you're thinking."

"Oh yeah? And what is that?"

"You're overthinking."

True. I nodded silently.

"And you're wondering how you ended up here, tonight . . . with this charismatic, devilishly handsome man."

A laugh escapes. His hand brushed against my cheek, slowly, seductively. He gently twirled a lock of hair framing my face. A slow heat gathered low in my stomach.

"And most of all, you're thinking how you're so . . ." He leaned in closely, his nose scraping my ear and his husky breath scattering down my neck. "So . . ." Something ever-so-gently grazed my collarbone; could have been lips, a nose, a finger. I wanted any and all of it, right there in front of Mia.

"So . . . thirsty." He snatched the empty glass out of my hand and beelined to the bar as I remained against the rail with my jaw dropped and legs crossed.

What was happening? How did we go from awkward occasional pen pals to him turning me on in public. And another drink? I was already in complete violation of my two drink rule *and* my mom's words of "Nothing good ever happens after midnight."

But fuck it. I'd stay out as long as Aidan wanted. I'd worry about the consequences with Townsend in the morning because there was something about Aidan that I wanted to—no, *had* to—know more about. It'd never felt like this before, not with Brad, and certainly not with any of my dalliances after him.

As he returned with our next round, Mia embraced a woman her age and complimented her on her dress. "It's from Penney's!" her friend said as she shoved her hands downward and exclaimed, "And look, it has pockets!"

With a defeated look on his face, Aidan handed me my cocktail and said, "She must be meeting Mr. Midlife Crisis tomorrow." I bit the tiny black straw, grinning stupidly like the Cheshire cat.

At 12:30 a.m., the bartender unenthusiastically declared "last call" over the clatter of bottles being shoved into a crate. Had we really closed another place down? Who was I? I was seriously tipsy, that's who I was.

With his arm around my waist, we strolled through Temple Bar again as he fed me tidbits of Irish history. The black streetlamps, styled to look like the traditional gaslights, glowed against the pub windows and brick walls. I wanted to slow time down so I could take it all in, every small detail of the city I'd missed until that moment.

Eventually, we were walking along the River Liffey, and the city's iconic white bridge was coming into focus. From researching Dublin before the move, the gentle arch had been etched into my brain. Aidan began telling me about the history of the Ha'penny Bridge. Back in the early 1800s, small ferry boats would take people across the Liffey. As the city grew, they couldn't keep up so they built the iron bridge in 1816. I couldn't believe he knew the exact year. I didn't know the exact year that anything in Tampa was built or even when Florida became a state, nothing like that. I should probably learn more about my state's history.

"Ireland had its own currency back then and the fee to cross the bridge was a half of a penny . . . or, a ha'penny."

I nodded in appreciation for the historical fact, imagining a little man sitting at a little table at the foot of the bridge, wearing whatever little men wore in the nineteenth century and collecting a halfpenny coin in one of those metal lunchbox looking things. I could envision the women in beautiful dresses cinched at the waist, holding a sun umbrella in one hand and a gentleman's arm with the other, gliding across the bridge after tossing their "ha'penny" to the little man.

Aidan continued that the bridge had been there for over two hundred years with only a small refurbishment in 2001. Ascending the steps was literally going to be like stepping through history.

"So they named it after the fee?" I asked.

"Well, it's actually called the Liffey Bridge, but the Ha'penny nickname stuck around for centuries."

"Impressive. The bridge for keeping its name for so long and you for knowing all of this. You're like a walking Wikipedia page."

He gave a sly smirk as if to say, "I know," or "Tell me more."

"I take it you haven't heard the superstitions of the bridge, huh?" he said.

I shook my head. He held my hand as we ascended the steps, smiling like he was about to share a big secret. The wind intensified with each step until we reached the center of the curve. He took in the quiet view of the city.

"Legend says that anyone who crosses and doesn't pay the toll will be haunted by the ghost with the lantern. He paces the bridge at night."

"So he haunts the bridge at night and the freeloaders during the day?"

"I hadn't thought about it, but yeah."

"I just hope he knows that it's free to cross now, otherwise he'll be one very busy ghost." He cracked a smile and squeezed my hand twice, just like before. "What's the other superstition?"

"Well . . . the other one, I actually happen to believe in. So no jokes, okay?"

"Okay." I squeezed his hand back, twice in agreement.

"It's that couples who have their first kiss in the middle of the bridge, underneath this arch right . . ." He looked up, ensuring we were centered under the arch. "Here."

He used both hands to push my windblown hair back and left them on the sides of my face. "They will fall madly in love . . . and stay in love forever."

A millisecond later, our mouths were pressed hard against each other before slowly opening for our tongues to collide. Sweetness lingered from the cocktails. I let myself feel all of it; the wind atop the idyllic bridge, the rough prickle from his overgrown stubble, his hands tugging at my hair as he pushed backward until my back hit the iron rail. There was no overthinking what to do with my hands or my mouth; I gave my body permission to take over.

It was only when we pulled away for a moment, foreheads pressed, that I thought about what he had said.

They will fall madly in love and stay in love forever.

Was that his way of saying he was falling in love with me, or was it a cheesy line he'd used before?

Just before the pause felt uncomfortable, like one of us would have to say something, he kissed me again. Harder and faster than before. A tingle between my legs traveled up to the back of my neck. My heart raced, and the city faded until all I could see were the brightly colored doors of Dublin mixing behind my closed eyes. Among all of the doors, the red one washed all the others out.

I had to remind myself to breathe.

14

THE THREE WEEKS AFTER our first date were both vibrant and a blur. We'd meet several nights a week for dinner, drinks, gigs, and one night, he dragged us to pub trivia. He, of course, shone while I was of limited help, especially as most of the topics were outside my forte: Irish pop culture, European politics and soccer—or football. The nights we didn't meet for a date, we usually met over our lunch break. Most things got better: the weather, the food, my perspective on being away. I tried to keep Lindsay updated with voice notes and texts, but we hadn't actually spoken on the phone in over a month. I saw myself getting wrapped up with Aidan too quickly but there was no chance of slowing down. Lindsay understood the honeymoon phase as she was still in it herself with Jason. Still, I wanted to share with her what was going on. I'd tell myself that I'd call her "next weekend" or send a long, thoughtful text update "tomorrow," but those tomorrows came and went without anything more than a one liner and an emoji.

The thing I loved most about getting to know Aidan was how much I learned from him. Despite being a nearly straight-A student my whole life and excelling at work—at least pre-Ireland—I realized how narrow my definition of smart had been. I didn't feel smart when I talked to

Aidan, didn't feel well rounded. But I felt like I could be. And it wasn't just all his travels and big adventures and pub trivia knowledge; he really *knew* things. Knew about people and what makes them tick, knew how to read and motivate them the way Simon did.

I'd learned the history of Ireland from him; from the Celtic invasion to the potato famine and their fight for independence, including The Troubles in Northern Ireland. I hadn't known about any of it. Thanks to Aidan, I vicariously lived through the Irish economic boom in the early 2000s. His dad opened a beer distribution business during that time and was able to move the family into a bigger home; the one his parents still live in and plan to stay in forever. When the 2007 global financial crisis hit, his business collapsed, and although his dad eventually recovered, Aidan admitted it was partially why he chose to pursue law.

While walking past Trinity after having lunch in City Centre, we noticed some pranksters had dumped soap into a fountain about a block down from the university, causing it to erupt with bubbles. It swallowed the statues and spilled onto the pavement surrounding it. Aidan couldn't resist covering my face with suds, and when I retaliated, we ended up in a foam war just long enough to soak our work outfits. The fight ended in a soapy kiss just in time for the Viking Splash Tour bus to roll past, prompting a chorus of delighted "oohs" and "ah's" with several of them growling at us in their horned Viking hats.

Every time we were together, another core memory was being formed. I don't know if I'd fallen in love with him those first few weeks, but I know for certain that's when I fell in love with Dublin.

I spilled out of the Luas after smacking the button. Out of breath from running down Grafton Street, I passed the statue that looked naked without all of the soap. After only a few weeks, he'd already imprinted himself on so many places in town. Everywhere I turned, there was another street we roamed, a corner we kissed in, a pub we drank in.

Running to meet Simon and Orla for brunch, I was annoyed I'd be arriving at 11 a.m. on the dot, possibly a minute late. Catching my breath at the hostess stand in vain, I waited fifteen minutes before Simon arrived and another ten before Orla decided to bless us with her presence. How could two grown, successful people manage to be late to everything? Sure, I wanted to catch up with my only two friends in Dublin, but I also wanted to tell them that I was likely going to be sleeping over at Aidan's later that night. I needed someone in the same time zone to analyze it with.

After reading the menu in silence and placing our orders, Simon, giddy like a teenager, gushed about Merrick, whom he'd met on a dating app. He was half Portuguese, half British and raised in Leeds, so they had the UK connection. Merrick was an entrepreneur of some tech start-up thing that he was trying to expand into Dublin. Simon didn't know all the details of Merrick's career aspirations, but he sure did know about his abs and pecs, showing us at least twenty shirtless pictures and raving about his height of six-one.

Orla's eyes rolled. "Ah, sure, anyone's tall next to ye."

"Rude," he shot back. "I'm almost five-eight."

"Yeah," she scoffed, "maybe in platforms."

"He's cute. When are you guys meeting up?" I asked, handing him the phone back.

Simon grinned. "Next weekend. He's gone this week, but we've been texting constantly."

"Just don't get stuck in pen pal land like I did. Remember how quick you were to write Aidan off?" I teased, trying to veer the conversation to Aidan so I could gush about him and our likely sleepover that night.

"Fine, I *might* have been wrong about Aidan now that he and I have talked about music. He's a synth lover after my own heart."

"That's Aidan for ye. He sure knows how to lay on the charm." Orla's eyebrows raised and her head shook. It was subtle, so subtle I might have missed it if I hadn't been analyzing any and everything relating to Aidan.

What did she know that I didn't? I'd considered asking her about Aidan's dating past, but I never could bring myself to. Partly because it might get back to him and partly because I wasn't sure if I wanted to know.

"He reminds me a lot of myself in that regard—full of charm." Simon winked. "Speaking of, Cinderella, your dry run on the phase four presentation for the client next week? Spot on. You were confident and charming in all the right ways. Townsend was impressed, I could tell."

Orla snorted. "Impressed in the silent, judgmental way or impressed-impressed?"

"The silent kind," Simon said definitively. "But coming from him, that's something."

Her elbows pressed down on the table as she leaned in. "The real way to know you nailed it is that Raya was scowling in the corner," Orla said.

I scoffed. "Can you believe she corrected me on that slide about inventory costs for the regional cash flow models? My numbers were right, but I didn't want to sound petty correcting her."

"You should have," Simon said. "She's absolutely circling."

"I must be improving," I said, with a sly smile.

Simon and I did our not-so-secret, secret handshake, careful not to knock over our peach Bellini's.

Orla looked on, amused. "You two are adorable. Can I join in on the love fest and secret meetings ye have in the James Joyce room?" It still took me a second to process her thick, country accent.

"You can join, but only if you tell us when you and Gearóid are getting engaged," Simon coaxed.

"Funny, we were just talking about the opposite—maybe taking a year of travel, like a late gap year," Orla said.

"You didn't answer the question," Simon said, to which I shot him daggers.

"Do you want to marry him?" I asked.

"I do." She laughed. "Pun intended."

"So you propose," he said, as if it were the most obvious and natural response.

Orla and I teamed up to protest why that was not going to happen. Sure, we wanted to be strong, modern-day women, but we also wanted to be swept off our feet when it came to a marriage proposal. And considering I wouldn't even ask Aidan on a date when he was dragging his feet, there was no way I could plausibly encourage her to propose.

Eventually Simon conceded, most likely to shut us up.

Feeling my phone vibrate in my purse shot electricity through my body at the thought of it being Aidan.

Aidan: *Since your unfamiliarity with the classics is appalling, we'll be seeing Casablanca tonight.*

He could have sent a happy face emoji, and I'd probably blush, but that? He wants to introduce me to classic films because he's a cinephile and knows I haven't seen many. The high ten from Brad after completing my first ever keg stand flashed in my mind. It was right before he asked about the Rolling Stones t-shirt and declared he'd turn me into a fan. To have Aidan showing that same level of enthusiasm toward me about movies and travel and culture was like being covered with a weighted blanket—warm and secure.

Me: *That's fine, but since your unfamiliarity with rom-coms is appalling, I'll be picking the movie next time.*

Aidan: *[wide-eyes emoji]*

Aidan: *I'm all set for dinner at my place afterward. Be kind about my cooking.*

Me: *Sounds like a recipe for a sleepover [winky-face emoji]*

Aidan: *There will be a lot of wine so I can't drive you home. And you're not taking the red line at night.*

Aidan: *But I'll call you a taxi if you want.*

I bit my lip. I wanted to stay the night, I just didn't know if I wanted to sleep together yet. If I was ready to give up that special time in a new relationship where it's all good, all tension, all butterflies. But also, I really, really wanted to.

Me: *[link to "How D'ya Like Your Eggs in the Morning?"]*

Aidan: *Well played.*

Aidan: *I'll pick you up at 4. Can't wait.*

Aidan: *P.S. Over easy.*

As our food arrived, and I shoved the phone back into my bag, Orla chided, "There's only one person that could have been."

"What's Prince Charming up to?" Simon added.

"He's visiting his parents, but I'll see him tonight . . . it's actually going to be our first sleepover." I covered my face with both hands before slowly peeking out.

"Shut up!" Simon said in disbelief. "Isn't there like a three date rule? Surely you hit that mark in the first week?"

"We just . . . I don't know? We always meet in town and just haven't gone back to each other's place. To be honest, I'm not sure I'm ready."

"Shut it, love. Flies will get in," Orla said, tapping Simon's chin.

"You're really taking the Cinderella thing to a whole new level."

"It's not the . . . act itself," I said, lowering my voice. "I'm not ready for how it might change our relationship. I just want to hold onto this a little longer."

Orla chimed in, "How are ye legs?" Before I could register the question, she'd snuck a hand under my loose fitting jeans and rubbed my calf.

"What the hell, Orla?" I lashed back.

"Right. These legs will keep ye safe tonight."

"Huh?" I said.

"You could seriously knit a sweater from those legs, so don't shave tonight."

"You really think he's going to be scared off by some leg hair?" Simon asked, making a stank face.

"*He* won't care, but our Cinderelly will be self-conscious. Hell, even I'd be with those things."

"Okay, okay, I get the point." I gulped my Bellini. "I don't shave, so I don't make a bad decision in the heat of the moment?"

"Exactly."

"You bitches are crazy," Simon said, shoveling the perfect bite onto the back of his fork with his knife.

Sure, it was silly . . . childish even, but I couldn't deny it made sense. I knew well enough that the first time I slept with Aidan, I wasn't showing up with cactus legs. And they were definitely more like cacti than a sweater.

My decision was made. No shaving. And with that, I ordered another Bellini.

15

THAT EVENING, AIDAN HONKED the horn of a sleek black Audi A5 outside my apartment at 4 p.m. sharp. I didn't even know what car he drove until then because we always met in town and used public transport.

During the drive, he asked about my parents. I told him Dad was sick, so Mom was tending to him with her famous chicken soup recipe. He in turn, told me that during his visit earlier, his mom was *dying* to meet me.

Turning right to face him felt as strange as being on the wrong side of the road. "What did you say to make her want to meet me so badly?" I asked, more interested in the fact he'd already told her about us than how he described me.

"It's more that she thinks I spend too much time with Killian. Like, I'll end up alone."

His attention alternated between the road and me. "Oh, and she loves that you're American." He changed his voice to imitate either his mother or an overly enthusiastic aerobics instructor and carried on, "I know most people are insincere when they say, 'Have a nice day,' but I think Americans actually want you to have a nice day. God bless them for that." He bobbed his head and shimmied his shoulders to exaggerate the impression. I laughed hysterically as he continued, "Bring Jessica over so I can get out the photo albums, and I'll make my famous raspberry buns." He switched back to his regular voice and explained the raspberry buns were purchased off the shelf from Tesco. He felt a part of his childhood had been a lie when he caught her transferring them from the box to a pan. She warms them in the oven and sprinkles powdered sugar on top before calling them her own.

"Does that mean I'll get to see those baby photos of you in pink floral hand-me-downs?"

His left hand squeezed my right on top of the console. "Does that mean you'll come?" he asked. "To meet the family?"

"Wait, the family? You mean the sisters too? Oh, the pressure!" I paused to look at him. "Yes. I'd love to."

At a junction, he leaned over to kiss me.

***

I found *Casablanca* to be boring and couldn't wait to leave the hipster movie theater, not at all because I was eager to see his place and eat whatever he'd cook for me.

The apartment was modern and tidy. Killian was in Munich visiting a friend, so we conveniently had the place to ourselves. He put on a record and as "Try Me" began to play, he poured us wine and got to work in the kitchen.

"I love James Brown," I said.

"How do you know music, but live under a rock when it comes to film?"

I thought about it. "Strict parents, I guess. Movies and TV were only allowed on weekends after all homework was done, and they'd often screen it first."

He paused midchop of the zucchini, or courgettes in Ireland, and raised an eyebrow.

"But music was always on. My parents played their old records. Mom loves jazz and older country like Loretta Lynn, Patsy Cline, Johnny Cash. Dad's more into rock 'n' roll. And I had a friend in college that played in a garage band."

I don't know why I described Brad that way. Surely, *first love* or *boyfriend of almost five years* would have been more accurate but calling him a *friend* wasn't entirely a lie either.

"Please don't ever drag me to a country gig," Aidan said. "I'm a music snob and country will make my ears bleed."

It was a tad dramatic, especially considering how many music genres influence one another, but it wasn't a hill I felt like dying on, so I didn't push back.

His sister, Kate, who was in culinary school, had sent him the recipe. It was called "Marry Me Chicken" which he said she chose purely to be funny. I couldn't remember the last time someone cooked for me. It turned out delicious, albeit slightly overcooked.

After dinner, we snuggled on the sofa with our wine, legs tangled beneath a throw blanket.

"So, Missus, are you religious?" He said it so casually that it took my brain a minute to catch up. When it did, I nearly choked on my wine.

"Wow. Jumping right in."

He shrugged. "Well, it's important."

Was it? It had never been important to me what someone's religion was, but it occurred that it might be a deal breaker for him.

"Well . . . I'm the only one in my family who's not baptized. Guess my parents gave up or were too busy after my two older brothers." I let out a nervous laugh before turning more serious. "I remember being super interested in religion as a kid. I read Bible stories all the time and begged my parents to take us to church. But we only went on Easter and Christmas. Even that fizzled out over the years."

He listened quietly, absentmindedly rubbing my foot with his free hand.

"But now?" I continued, "I don't think the world and space and time is just science. I just can't believe that we're just balls of matter spinning through the universe without meaning. It'd be too sad. So I believe there is something bigger . . . I'm still figuring out what that is."

He seemed to agree. "I get that. And same here, but don't tell Babs I'm not a true believer."

"Your mom? Why, were you raised Irish Catholic?"

"Yeah. Same story, really. It fizzled in our house too. By the time I was in secondary school, we didn't even go for holidays."

"What's Christmas like for you?" I asked, veering to a lighter topic. "You're one of those families that starts celebrating a week early, aren't you?"

He made a face that said "absolutely" and he was proud. "Yep. Assuming I'm home for Christmas and not off traveling. My aunt, uncle, and cousins who live just outside of Dublin come over, sometimes family on my Dad's side from Wexford. Christmas Eve is spent in town . . . at the pubs and watching the Christmas busk.

"The Christmas busk?"

"Yeah, it's where Grafton Street fills with musicians. Some famous ones have been there unannounced over the years—Bono, Hozier. It's mental."

"Wow, that's really cool." Ugh, did that sound sarcastic?

"Then by Christmas Day, Babs has already been cooking for a week so the roast goose and stuffing are extra dry by the time we eat." He grinned, relishing in the chance to mock his mother's cooking again. "And on Stephen's Day, we lounge around and watch *Father Ted*."

I let out a warm sigh. "It sounds . . . magical. And a bit chaotic."

"What about you? What's an American Christmas like?"

"Quieter than yours. My family's smaller but we're really close and have never missed a major holiday together," I said, filling with excitement to see them again for Christmas that year. "We open stocking stuffers the night before. My dad always gets those scratch off lottery tickets and then we play board games. They're super competitive, but not me. Christmas Day is turkey and spiral ham with all the fixings, served at five o'clock on the dot. It's all very predictable—the jokes, the movies, the gifts—but that's what makes it feel like home."

"I'd expect nothing less from you," he said with a joking wink. "You still talk to them a lot while you're here?"

"Almost daily; the family group chat is super active. And I call my parents on Sundays. They lived near me in Tampa, so I'd go over most weekends. My mom supported my move here, but I think she's still in shock that I actually did it. And so am I."

"I know it was a big deal for you. You're brave," he said, as if it were a fact. He lifted his glass. "To Dublin."

"To Dublin."

Just as the silence started to feel too long, the record skipped.

He blew on the vinyl to troubleshoot before swapping it with a new one. As he poured us more wine, I wandered around the living room, admiring his art and collectibles. Several framed paintings that looked one of a kind decorated his white walls; knick-knacks were thoughtfully arranged on open shelving that looked like the popular Ikea one.

Most of the décor I owned, which was boxed up in Tampa, came from Crate & Barrel or Williams Sonoma. Pieces I loved because they were neutral and timeless, not because they held any meaning. Looking around Aidan's apartment, I realized that distinction mattered to him, and I wished it mattered to me too.

"This one's from a lads' trip to Rome a few years ago," he said, pointing to a vintage travel print, the only framed piece that wasn't an original painting. A man on a turquoise moped zipped through a European street with a high-heeled babe on the backseat. The colosseum dominated in the background. "Four lads exploring one of the most romantic cities," he said, a laugh buried within the words.

"I can't believe they're not wearing helmets," I said, eyes still locked on the couple in Rome.

He laughed. "Of course that'd be your takeaway."

I moseyed onto the next piece which was a scene of downtown Tokyo.

"I try to get a piece of art, or simply something to decorate the apartment, from every city I visit."

"That's way better than magnets or shot glasses," I joked. "Man, you've really been everywhere. And you don't just do touristy stuff in capital cities . . . you really experience the culture. I wish I were more like that."

"Hey, you're here, aren't you? I'll show you Irish culture."

"You already have. I've seen more of Dublin in a few weeks than I saw in a few months, thanks to you."

"Yeah but that's just Dublin. We'll get outside the city too. There are some places I want to show you." He paused a beat, visibly choosing his words. "Starting with my family home." His face winced. "Maybe next weekend?"

A wry smile slowly crept in. "Okay, but . . ."

It was my turn to hesitate.

"Can I ask something? You know what—never mind."

"Oh come on, you can't do that," he said, nudging my shoulder.

I took a sip of wine for courage and looked him in the eyes. "Why?"

"Why what?" he asked.

"Why do you want to show me Ireland? Why introduce me to your family?" I bit my lip and looked away before returning to his smoldering gaze. "Why do you like me?"

He sighed, and I immediately wanted to take it back, realizing how pathetic it sounded.

"I don't mean it in a self-deprecating way, I know I'm great," I said quickly, trying to recover. "But you've traveled the world . . . you collect cool art . . . your life is *here*."

A deep but concealed breath left me. "None of that is true for me."

The base of his wine glass clinked as he placed it on the glass coffee table. Just as gently, he rubbed the tops of my arms. "First of all, I think it's cool that you haven't seen much of the world. But you're curious. I see a future traveler in you and it's exciting." His tone was soft and assuring. "I love seeing Dublin through your eyes. It's easy to miss the beauty of what's right in front of you."

He said it to me like he was choosing me.

"Like these freckles just around your nose, they're beautiful."

Otis Redding's "These Arms of Mine" started playing.

"May I have this dance, Missus?"

I set my wine next to his and he pulled me in close. Our swaying fell into sync, or at least it felt that way after a bottle of wine.

He didn't acknowledge the part about his life being in Dublin and mine not.

Let it go.

I wasn't ready to decide which truth mattered more—that this felt real, or that it couldn't last. A part of me thought it'd be weird to have that talk before sleeping together. Another part of me thought it'd be weird to sleep together before having that talk.

Was I thinking too much? God, it was so loud inside my own head.

Focus on the present.

He mouthed the lyrics as his nose brushed against mine. After a few lines, we kissed. Slowly, his mouth worked its way down my neck. Goosebumps rippled across my skin as my legs trembled. I could feel my body waking up to every place his mouth touched. My head tipped back; a shaky breath escaped me as he dropped to his knees, gathering my skirt in his hands. I threaded my fingers through his thick hair, gently scratching his scalp with my unpolished nails, pulling a moan from him that rippled through me.

He rose, lifting my skirt with him as his hands grazed the outside of my legs.

"Ouch!" He half laughed, dropping the fabric and looking at his palms. "Those should come with a warning."

Fuck! Orla. Seriously, fuck you, Orla.

I covered my face with my hands. "Sorry."

"Come here, Godzilla," he said, pulling my waist to him and lifting me. My legs instinctively wrapped around him as he walked us to his room.

Sensing some sort of micro hesitation, he pulled back. "Is something wrong?"

"Nothing's wrong. I want to, I really do. It's just . . . after all the wine and . . . these legs."

A small smile immediately appeared. "You don't have to explain. And for the record, I love the legs," he assured, rubbing my thighs as my ankles interlocked behind him.

He kissed me once more and set me down.

"I have a spare toothbrush in the drawer and there are towels under the sink. I'll sleep on the sofa."

My chest flickered. I didn't want to throw cold water on the night.

"I'll get you some clothes you can sleep in," he said, heading into his room.

Think Jessie, think. Do not make this awkward. Act confident for once.

I grabbed his arm, just below the scar.

"No. I want you to sleep in your own bed."

Confusion filled his face as his lips parted slightly.

"With me," I added softly.

"Are you sure?"

I nodded—excited to wrap around him again and also thinking that nothing good happens after midnight.

He scooped me up, and his mouth found mine again. Hard. Passionate.

And we crossed the threshold into his bedroom.

16

I WOKE THE NEXT morning tangled in Aidan's sheets. The sunlight spilling across unfamiliar walls accentuated my headache and cotton mouth—and the fact that he wasn't beside me. I lay still, staring at the ceiling, reliving the night and fixating on what it all meant.

Pots and pans clattered from the kitchen, jolting me back to the present. I pulled on his t-shirt and followed the noise.

"Morning, Missus." He handed me a glass of water and two Panadol. "Get back in bed. I'll bring coffee. Milk, sugar and cinnamon, right?"

"How do you even know that?" I tried to think of the times we actually had coffee together. Maybe once? I didn't remember adding cinnamon in front of him.

"I pay attention."

He worked on a full Irish breakfast as I perched myself on a stool at the kitchen bar instead of tucked back into bed.

"Your phone was beeping like mad. I hope you don't mind—I put it on silent."

I scrolled through the notifications: a few work emails, messages from the family group chat and some from Lindsay. I shrieked when I opened her message.

"What is it?" Aidan asked, turning from the hissing pan.

"My best friend, Lindsay. She booked her flight to come visit!"

"Deadly. Soon?"

"Yeah, the end of October . . . for my birthday." He paused midflip of the rashers. He didn't know my birthday. And I didn't know his. "And she's bringing her boyfriend, Jason."

"They must be serious, aye?"

I confirmed, though I wasn't entirely sure. With the distance, most of our updates had been text messages or the occasional voice note. Oftentimes we'd respond a day late because the time zone difference meant receiving them at inconvenient times.

Coffee sloshed around in my mug as I turned it slowly. I needed to give my hands something to do as I rehearsed the next sentence.

"I know it's two months away, but . . . if you're around then, maybe you could meet them? We could . . . ya know, grab dinner or drinks?" I traced my finger around the handle of the mug. "No pressure."

He turned the knob on the stove until it clicked, then slung a tea towel over his shoulder like a chef.

"If I'm around?" Deep lines formed between his brows. "I'll be around. And I'll meet your friends . . . on one condition."

I gave a look, urging him to go on.

"*We* take a trip together for your birthday. A real trip, outside of Ireland." He plated the crowded meal as I processed his condition. "I want to be your first real passport stamp."

He wanted to go away? A trip? On a plane? To somewhere romantic in Europe? With me?

This was big.

How much time would I need off work? I hadn't taken any while in Ireland, though others on the team had. Surely it'd be fine? What would Townsend think if I took vacation?

Stop thinking about work, you loser. The memos and spreadsheets can wait.

He wanted to whisk me away for my birthday—to eat pasta, drink wine, look at expensive art, and make love every night. Was I excited about going to a new country? Not really. I'd rather do a road trip within Ireland, but I was excited to go anywhere with Aidan.

I concealed my concern and elation with a smug smile. "I accept this condition." I sipped my coffee, trying not to take in the thick layer of cinnamon in one go. "Where did you have in mind? I'd love to go to Spain. I heard Barcelona has incredible architecture. Plus the tapas, the flamenco dancers. Maybe after a few cervezas, I could test out my Spanish. Did I tell you my grandma was Cuban? She taught me some when I was a kid, plus we had to study it in high school."

I knew about the architecture from when Brad would talk about it during college and after. He came alive when he'd talk about Gaudí, the mastermind behind the designs. Although I'd never really wanted to go, Barcelona had lived in my imagination through Brad, especially when he was trying to convince me to go, right before we broke up.

"Whoa, whoa, whoa," Aidan laughed, interrupting my stream of consciousness. "Can we say American tourist much?" He set my plate in front of me. It looked gorgeous, like Ireland on a plate, but yet the smell of the blood sausage or *pudding* made my stomach churn.

"Leave it with me," he said. "I'll plan something incredible. A trip you'll remember forever."

A cautious smile tugged at my lips before returning to a state of bliss.

***

The next day, the Project Roadrunner team, minus Simon, gathered in the conference room for our weekly status meeting.

Townsend tapped his pen against the table and peered over his glasses. "Raya, you're up on restructuring."

Raya leaned forward with a big, mischievous smile. "Certainly. The overall restructuring plan is slightly behind schedule, so we're proposing to re-prioritize the roadmap. We'd like to push back any non-critical initiatives and instead focus on a dependency matrix. It will help us map system interlocks across the regions and flag any bottlenecks early."

Her voice was crisp and confident, but I had no idea what she was talking about. It sounded like buzzwords designed to impress Townsend because there hadn't been a strategy shift, and I'd never heard of a dependencies matrix. It sounded made up.

She continued, "I discussed this with the client last week and management has approved the plan. They're eager to see the new models for each region. Jessica is working on them."

Wait—what?

What the actual fuck did she say?

My stomach plummeted as everyone turned to look at me.

I was certain it hadn't come up in any of the planning syncs or status meetings, and it definitely hadn't been discussed with me. My assignment had been clear: work with local management to build region-specific forecasting models to identify underperforming divisions. From that, I help management decide what to buy and what to sell. What Raya was describing was something I was unfamiliar with.

Townsend looked up from his notes. "Jessica, where are we on those models?"

I straightened and cleared my throat nervously. "Uh, well, I—I've been focused on scenario-building based on three-to-five year financial projections. The dependencies matrix isn't something my team has formally been looped into."

Raya smiled—pleasant and professional to the others in the room, but I knew it was a piece in her game of chess. And Raya was moving first.

"From my experience," she said, "having both financial and operational modeling really strengthens leadership's decision making. If you're spread too thin, Jessica, I'm happy to help reallocate your workload. Seriously, anything I can do to help."

What a snake.

She'd glossed right over the fact that I'd never been involved in this decision, making it seem like I'd failed to deliver.

Before I could speak, Townsend chimed in. "Jessica, I'd really like you to be the one to work on those. Let's see some drafts next week, please."

"Yes, sir," I said, nodding once.

My insides buzzed as my fingernails dug into my palms, wishing it were Raya's throat.

I'd spent the last three weeks laser-focused on the agreed assignment. I'd been neck-deep in spreadsheets for all the regions, working with local management on product mix and headcount efficiency to project their bottom lines at various scenarios. This matrix Raya had mentioned was never flagged. Not once.

My eyes burned into Raya. She didn't look.

I scribbled in my notebook: Dependencies matrix? WTF? Simon? I underlined the *WTF* twice and circled *Simon* as the pen tore through the page.

Townsend moved on to the next agenda item as I forced myself to appear calm and engaged. This wasn't just about getting back at Raya.

It was about proving to Townsend that I could lead and that I belonged on the Partner track, even if I was still a couple of years out.

I needed a win.

But now, thanks to her, I'd be scrambling to deliver something I didn't understand.

This wasn't about winning anymore.

It was about making sure Raya didn't.

***

I found Simon in his office, sleeves rolled up, tie loose, with three empty espresso cups on his desk. He barely noticed as I hovered in the doorway.

"Are those all from today?" I asked, not sure which was worse—three shots before lunch today or yesterday's mess still sitting there.

He gave me a look. "None of your business. How can I help you?"

I shut the door behind me and sat in the chair opposite him.

He slid a package of digestives in my direction. Whose idea was it to name tea biscuits digestives? "Debrief me," he said.

I bit into a crumbly biscuit and filled him in, starting with the dependencies matrix bombshell and ending with the tight-lipped "Will do" I'd given Townsend.

Simon let out a high pitched *reeer*—the sound a cat would make if you tried to bathe it. "Classic Raya. All strategy jargon and delegation, no substance."

"She made it look like I didn't do my assignment. But it was an assignment she invented in the meeting." I exhaled sharply. "And the way everyone just nodded along like she was Mother bloody Teresa of cross-functional alignment. I swear, I could feel my credibility slowly dying in real time."

"First of all, I'm rubbing off on you a little too much," he interrupted. "Second, you didn't lose credibility . . . just didn't grab it."

I frowned.

"You're too careful, Cinderella," he went on, checking each of the espresso cups for remains. "You *wait* for your moment to be handed to you. But in the boardroom, you have to *make* your moment."

"How?" I snapped too aggressively. "I didn't even know what a dependency matrix was. How can I make a moment when I don't know what I'm making?"

"Instead of freezing over what you *don't* know, flip it to what you *do* know. It'll buy you time and keep credibility."

He snatched a dry erase marker and drew a horizontal line on the glass wall. "This represents clarity," he said. "Vagueness on the left. Specificity on the right." Then he drew a vertical one, creating four quadrants. "And *this* is confidence."

With the mannerisms of a professor, he continued, "Right, so, this chart is every meeting you'll ever sit through in a nutshell." He drew a circle in the top left. "This is where Raya lives," he said, tapping the marker against the glass. "High confidence, low clarity. Throws around big words, sometimes big ideas, but rarely actionable. People just *feel* like she knows what she's doing."

Then he drew a circle in the bottom right quadrant. "You like to hang out here. Overly specific, but low on confidence. Polar opposites." I rolled my eyes in agreement.

The graph burned into my brain.

Next he drew an arrow from Raya's circle to the top right. "Your job is to move her here. You don't fight her points, you ask for definition. Force her to get specific and she'll expose her bluff."

"Show me, master," I said, gesturing toward him.

He switched to a serious voice. "That's interesting, Raya. Can you clarify exactly how the dependency matrix maps to our scope and why we need it? I want to make sure we are fully aligned."

"Oh, that's good."

"It's neutral. It shows you're thinking of the big picture—how does this bring us closer to the deliverable—and it makes her explain. If she's bullshitting, she'll trip. If she's not, you just learned something without looking weak."

Using my thigh as a table, I scribbled notes.

"And what about how she sprung it on me? She made it sound like I was already working on it. How do I flip that without looking like a tattletale?"

Simon sighed, as if it were obvious. "You say, 'Happy to explore it, but as I'm sure you can appreciate, we've been focused on the original scope—financial modeling and ROI projections. Local management is actively involved. If you're telling me there's now appetite to expand the scope, I'll adjust resources and focus accordingly.'"

I tapped my pen against my chin. "Remind them of the original scope, management's involvement, and show willingness to adapt if needed. Got it."

"Exactly." He pointed his marker at me. "You've got the hard skills, Cinderella. Now you need presence. Tactic."

I exhaled. "I also need to figure out what this damn matrix is and how to build one."

Simon grinned. "Lucky for you, I know a guy."

He scurried behind his desk and typed rapidly. "Tadeusz Mitkowski. Polish guy in our London office. He's an absolute machine—built half of the interlock framework for a big aerospace client last year. Not that this dependency matrix will be anything like that."

"And you think he'd be willing to help me? Like, today?"

"He owes me. I saved him from a data protection nightmare when he cc'd a client on the wrong distribution list. A *very* wrong one. I'll schedule a call."

"Simon, I could kiss you!"

"It better be with tongue," he said, wagging his. I swatted his shoulder.

"Don't let Raya get in your head. You're not here to play defense."

"You're right. I'm here to win."

17

AFTER A WEEK OF working with Tadeusz and pulling all-nighters to get the dependency matrix in a good spot, Aidan picked me up from the office on Friday. I had to will my eyes open because we were meeting his family. In a way, it felt like a bigger deal than sleeping together. Sex only involved the two of us and had a fairly predictable outcome whereas meeting his family had way too many variables. Meeting the parents is always a big relationship milestone, but adding in two sisters, and the fact that I was in Dublin on borrowed time made the whole experience feel heavier. I climbed into his Audi, greeted by a prickly kiss from the stubble emerging on his face. The top three buttons of his powder blue shirt were undone and the sleeves pushed up. A folded striped tie was shoved in the center console. "Is this an okay 'meet the parents' outfit?" I made the *voila* hand motion, presenting my trusted uniform of high-waisted trousers, a white button-up with matching tan loafers, and belt.

"You look great; but don't worry about that stuff. They're going to love you."

Love.

I smiled.

"Also," he said, tapping a thumb on the steering wheel, "I pulled the trigger and booked our flights. Want to know where we are going?"

He had been waiting for me to give the all clear on getting the time off at work. I had only told him that morning that I got it approved.

"Oh? So it's happening? Ah, yeah I wanna know where we're going. I don't like surprises."

I don't think I'd ever seen him look that happy.

"Morocco," he said with excitement.

Huh?

My face reacted before I could fake enthusiasm. I searched deep into my mind for something, anything I might know about Morocco, but similar to the country of Georgia, I had nothing. Jeesh, I really needed to study up on my knowledge of other countries.

"It's been on my bucket list forever. I was torn between there and Turkey, but since Turkey is in Europe and Asia and I've been all over both continents, I figured Morocco would be better. I've only been to Africa once before."

What other places were on his bucket list that he'd considered for our trip?

"But with Morocco . . . the colors, the smells, everything about it is meant to be unreal. I can't wait to see it." He grabbed my hand and squeezed it twice. "With you."

Warmed by his enthusiasm, I imagined Morocco as an exotic, romantic Arabic destination based on his short description.

"Me too." I placed my hand on his and returned the double squeeze. "Thanks for organizing this."

He knew way more about travel than I did, so although it wasn't romantic Barcelona or Paris or Rome, I told myself to trust the process and be happy about the trip he was planning.

As we turned onto the street of his family home, he gave a final word of advice. "Oh, I do apologize ahead of time for the actual dinner. Hide it in your napkin, push it onto my plate, give it to the dog—whatever you need to do, but don't eat it. We can go to a chipper on the way back."

"Oh, stop!" I smacked his arm. "It's my first 'Irish mum made meal' and I refuse to believe that she can be that bad of a cook."

He peeled his concentration off the road and looked at me.

"And they don't have a dog!" I said.

We parked outside a narrow, three-story brick home connected on one side to another home that was its mirror image. As we scaled five steps, the bright red quintessential door of Dublin stopped me in my tracks. It was larger than a front door needed to be, although, perhaps the deep red color and surrounding glass windows made it appear bigger than it actually was. If I could have any front door in the world, it'd be that one—not some small, tacky turquoise door.

"What do you have there?" Aidan looked at the Tupperware I pulled out of my bag.

"Just a little something I made. It's rude to go to someone's home for dinner and not bring something."

"You are so American." With his hand on the small of my back, he opened the door, nudging me in first.

"Maaa! We're here." Loud banging came from the kitchen as we looked at each other, trying not to laugh.

"Oooh," she shrieked as she emerged from a hallway, taking off bright yellow rubber cleaning gloves. She raised her arms and made a beeline to me. "It's so good to have you, dear. Come, come make yourself comfortable. Aidan, take her jacket," she said, in between the kisses planted on my cheeks. "You two must be absolutely *wrecked* from the drive? And coming straight from work? Oof."

The house was about five miles from the city. Although with rush hour traffic, it took about forty-five minutes, it certainly was not going to *wreck* anyone.

"It's so nice to meet you, Mrs. McGovern. Thank you for having me over. Aidan mentioned you always serve sweets after dinner, so I made my mom's favorite. It's called gooey butter coffee cake."

"Oh, bless your heart. You are *actually* the sweetest thing. We'll have it tonight," she said, taking the Tupperware from me. "Aidan—a girl who can bake, aye?" She winked at him. "But please, call me Barbara, dear."

"Or Babs. She likes it when people call her Babs—don't you, Babsy?" Aidan teased, squeezing her shoulders. She rolled her eyes and gave him a light smack to the arm.

"It's super easy to make; there are only a few ingredients. I wrote a recipe card and taped it to the lid." I hoped it didn't come off as "I heard you're a terrible cook and thought you might need a foolproof recipe."

"Ah, you're very good. Come; let's get you a cuppa tea, dear."

"That'd be great. Can I help with anything?" I asked, wishing she had offered whiskey instead.

"Ah, no, pet. It's gammon. It basically cooks itself. You just sit right here and tell me *all* about yourself." She set my Tupperware next to a package of Tesco raspberry jam filled rolls—her "famous" raspberry buns. "Aidan, you're getting too skinny. There isn't a pick on ya." Babs pinched his waist. Skinny wasn't a word I'd use to describe Aidan's tall, slightly muscular, but mostly average build.

"Hiya." Emma said loudly, joining us in the kitchen. "So Aidan is finally bringing one of his girls home, so he is?" Pieces from her messy bun fell into her overly made-up eyes as she filled two glasses with white wine. "You're much prettier than he let on, and your teeth—my god, they're so white." Even though her directness caught me off guard, I immediately liked her when I realized the other glass was for me. It was clear how she and Orla were such close friends.

"Ah, you're very kind, but I only cleaned up for tonight."

"Don't be daft. Now Aidan, he's a slob. I still can't get over seeing him in an ironed shirt; it's actually so unnatural," she joked.

Kate walked in and quietly introduced herself. She was even more shy than Aidan had described. Her light freckles complimented her small face and strawberry blonde hair. When Aidan's dad joined, we moved to the table to eat. The conversation naturally skewed toward me, which was difficult to manage as I struggled to cut, chew, and respond in a timely manner.

At one point, Emma spoke in Gaelic. Aidan's dad laughed and responded, also in Gaelic. Having no clue what they were saying, I smiled awkwardly and cut small pieces of the overcooked ham, hoping to chew it easier.

"Have you picked up any Irish since you've been over here, Jessica?" Babs asked.

"Not much, but I know *sláinte* means cheers." I raised my glass and everyone lifted theirs to cheers.

"Perfect pronunciation, Jessica, well done," Babs said warmly.

"Except it doesn't actually mean cheers . . ." Aidan said, amused. "It means health. As in, to your health. Good try though."

I should have stopped there but my awkwardness was determined to shine. "We have a sign in the office of 'hello' in every different language. I know the Irish one is die-a-doo-it."

Emma choked on her wine while Aidan stopped midbite.

"Well, that's a new one!" Aidan's dad joked.

"Oh bless you, pet," Babs said.

Why couldn't I just leave it at sláinte? The heat had risen with nowhere for it to escape.

"It does look that way, but it's actually 'jee-uh ditch'. The alphabet is really tricky. You're very good for remembering the word though," Kate said sweetly.

"Okay, I'm officially retiring from Gaelic. I won't butcher it anymore."

The table chuckled politely, while Aidan looked on at me while shaking his head.

After dinner, we gathered in the sitting room with mugs of tea and polished off the whole gooey butter cake. It was entertaining to watch them interact. Aidan and Emma took after Babs; extroverts who spoke with their hands and facial expressions. Kate was their father's child. He was quiet and mild-mannered; happy to sit back and let Babs shine. The way everyone spoke over one another without irritation, the way they were so comfortable around each other reminded me of Sunday dinners at home.

Sitting next to Kate, we talked about her culinary school in Cork and the trendy new restaurant called Hawthorne & Rye where she started working in Dublin's City Centre.

"It's French technique with locally sourced Irish ingredients," she explained before going into a passionate rant about Jerusalem artichokes and beetroot. "You guys should come by one night. You can be my guinea pigs on a new dessert I'm trying."

As I was accepting Kate's invite, Babs reappeared with a photo album in hand. She quickly opened it and began flipping through the crackly pages.

"Here it is!" She smacked her hand on the plastic sleeve.

Aidan groaned, begging her to put it away.

It was an eight-year-old Aidan standing on a coffee table in a full magician's costume. In front of him, a group of kids sat cross-legged on the carpet, fixated on him.

"This was at *my* birthday party," Emma said with an eye roll. "Aidan was putting on one of his 'Great McGoverni' magic shows. He'd practice and plan for hours, go through lines in the mirror, then act like it was all improvised brilliance."

"You loved it," Aidan shot back, grinning.

"Yes, I just loved how you had to be the center of attention—even at my party," she said, dripping in sarcasm.

Babs chimed in. "When little Jack O'Sullivan said he wasn't impressed, you cried. It was the worst thing someone could say to you. Probably still is."

Everyone laughed, but once she said it, I couldn't unhear it. He did light up when he had someone's full attention and laid on the charm when I was interested in his travels.

I tucked the thought away, smiling at the next photo of little Aidan covered in mud, holding a frog.

***

On the drive back, Aidan wanted to stop and show me Bull Island, not far from his parents' neighborhood.

We turned onto a narrow access road that led to a rickety wooden bridge, just wide enough for one car to pass at a time. Aidan yielded, allowing the oncoming car to cross before proceeding.

After parking we strolled along the worn island path in silence, holding hands. The wind grew sharper, bringing a light drizzle with it, but neither of us acknowledged. I'd long stopped worrying about what the mist was doing to my hair.

Aidan pointed to a statue at the end of the run. "That's the Star of the Sea. It was built to honor Dublin port workers." He paused, seeming to reflect. "Funny how she's facing toward land instead of the sea."

He gestured to a flickering light in the distance. "And that over there, that's Dún Laoghaire," he said. "We'll go there one weekend. It's not too far from your place, so we can cycle."

"You have a lot of plans for us."

"You have no idea, Missus."

Turning toward me, he sandwiched me between himself and the railing. His damp shirt clung to his chest. I wrapped my arms around his neck and tousled his hair more than the wind already had.

"It's going to be a pretty packed couple of months," he said.

"Oh? Is that right?"

"Yeah. I have a few things on my list to show you. Now I gotta squeeze in Dún Laoghaire before the weather turns to shit. Then Morocco for your birthday . . . "

"And Lindsay and Jason will visit," I added.

"Ah, yes, the best friend visit." His tone was a shade too light, but I shook it off.

My waist tightened under his grip. "And before we know it . . . it'll be Christmas."

I shook my head, in disbelief of how fast the months had flown.

"And since my family loves you," he continued, "I wanted to ask if you'd stay here in Dublin and spend it with us. With me."

Oh.

Giddiness surged through me—then stalled. I had planned on going home to Florida for Christmas and already booked the flight. I couldn't miss Christmas with them. On the other hand, I couldn't miss Christmas with him.

Before I could answer, Aidan was already launching into the details: ice skating in City Centre, the Christmas busks, a road trip to Kilkenny, maybe a quick pop over to London for New Year's. It was sweet, but something about the way he skipped to the list of activities made it feel like he was booking an itinerary rather than asking me to share a special time with him. Then again, this was Aidan. Mr. Full of Life. Enthusiasm for trips and events was his default setting.

"Are you sure?" My face asked it more than my mouth did.

He set his hands on my shoulders. "I'm positive. I want you here with me for Christmas and New Year's. For as long as I can have you."

Oh shit, was he about to say he loved me?

The first time Brad told me he loved me, I was so caught off guard I said thank you without reciprocating.

"What I'm trying to say is . . . " He hesitated, then stepped even closer so our chests were pressed to each other's. "Don't go back to America. At least not yet." He cupped my face gently, forcing my eyes to his. It reminded me of our first kiss on the Ha'penny Bridge, but now it was layered with something heavier. "You could keep doing your job here, right? Stay with me. Please?"

The tiredness from earlier had disappeared. Life pulsed through my veins.

I *did* want to stay, to see where this was going. But if Aidan weren't in the picture, I'd be ready to go home. I still wanted to lay down roots near my family, make Associate Partner and then Partner. I wanted marriage and kids—near my own parents, the way I'd always pictured.

But I felt like I was approaching a fork in the road where half the life I wanted was in Tampa, but the other half might be in Dublin. I didn't want to wake up ten years later and wonder if I'd made a wrong turn. My mom always said I needed to trust my gut. Now was my chance.

"Okay." I nodded firmly, despite the racing in my chest. "I'll stay here for Christmas." A long exhale. "And I'll talk to my boss . . . maybe try to extend my visa another year?"

"Really?" His voice cracked.

"Really."

He squeezed my hands tightly and kissed me for a long time on the rickety bridge. I let myself feel it fully. The rush of choosing something unplanned was something I'd never felt.

"But you better not let me down with this agenda of yours," I added.

Holding both my hands, he brought my left hand to his chest and said, "Cross my heart."

I smiled at the endearing, childish gesture before he covered my mouth again with his. It was how I imagined taking drugs would feel like. I knew the high was destined to fade but wanted it anyway.

If things kept going well, I'd continue pushing the fork in the road a little further down. I didn't know what would happen when the visa expired—whether Aidan would ever move to the U.S., or whether I could truly stay in Ireland, away from my family and the career I'd worked so hard for.

As the night shower turned into a proper downpour, we hurried back to the car, my trench coat over our heads as we ran. It did nothing to keep us dry—but everything to burn the word *stay* into my mind.

That was worth changing the plan for.

18

A FEW DAYS LATER, the conference room had already filled by the time I arrived. Spending the night at Aidan's had become a regular occurrence even during the workweek, but on this particular day, he pulled me back into bed after I got up and had coffee, causing me to get ready at warped speed. He insisted on driving me but I'm confident that driving anywhere in Dublin takes longer than public transport or simply walking.

Although technically on time, to me, I was late *again*, but knowing the reason was him, I didn't mind.

I took a seat halfway down the table, across from Simon. It was always hit or miss whether he'd show up to the weekly touchpoints or if he was out with clients. He mouthed a silent "You got this."

Raya, in her usual spot near Townsend, connected her laptop to the projector. She saw me but showed no emotion.

Townsend kicked us off without pleasantries. "Let's start with the restructuring update. Raya, you flagged some items last week. Where are we now?"

Her smile was cool, the way someone in the top left quadrant of Simon's graph would be. "As mentioned, we're prioritizing a dependencies matrix to preempt integration risks. Jessica was going to explore this with regional data. I imagine it's still in progress?"

My fingers interlocked, ready to be confident and specific. "Actually, I completed it over the weekend."

Several heads turned. Even Townsend paused.

"It outlines cross-functional system interlocks for all five regions, highlights key bottlenecks, and models four levels of operational risk if delays occur. I leveraged the experience of a colleague in the London office who built a similar structure for an aerospace client last year. He reviewed it with me on Friday and validated the logic. Management approved the input assumptions, but I still ran sensitivities to see which ones to focus on."

Raya blinked. "Well, that was . . . fast."

"I wanted it to be ready before the steering committee review this Thursday," I said. "I'll circulate the latest version this afternoon. I also added a visual heat map for an executive overview."

Townsend adjusted his glasses to the middle of his nose. "You just . . . added a heat map?"

"Yes. It's linked to the forecasting models so it will automatically update if assumptions change."

Simon gave a small, proud shake of his head.

Townsend looked between us. "Impressive. I'll review it right away."

Raya cleared her throat and flashed a fake smile. "Sounds great. We'll want to ensure it's consistent with the broader transformation themes."

I recalled Simon's example.

"That's a good point, Raya. Can you clarify exactly how the dependency matrix will map to those broader, uh, transformational themes, was it? I just want to make sure we're fully aligned."

She looked like furniture. Immobile.

"I, ah, ah—" she sputtered.

"It's okay, I just didn't want to steal your thunder. I've actually already done it," I said, flipping my notebook shut. "I included key terminology and assumptions aligned to Phase Six messaging, so it should tie in neatly with rollout communications. If that's what you meant?"

There was a small silence. Then she nodded once, definitive.

"Excellent," Townsend said. "Let's keep going."

As the meeting wrapped, and I collected my laptop and notebook, Raya approached.

"Good job with the update, impressive you finished the models so quickly," she said as if she hadn't thrown me under the bus.

Once all my things were gathered, I responded, keeping my voice neutral. "It's amazing what getting backed into a corner will do." Even though I had on flats and she had on heels, I looked slightly down at her. "Don't *ever* again attach my name to something without looping me in. Now if you'll excuse me, I have to go impress Townsend some more with my dependency matrix that you so cleverly volunteered me for." Her smile twitched and then faded. As she searched for a reply, I headed straight for Townsend's office. His door was open, so I tapped the glass twice as I let myself in.

He did a double take, glancing up from his keyboard. "Jessica," he motioned to the leather chair opposite him. "That was excellent."

Finally. Finally, a compliment. I tried not to beam.

"You had command of the room." He leaned back in his chair and Simon's voice subconsciously reminded me to mimic his body language. According to Simon, we are all a little narcissistic and like to see our actions reflected back to us. "You were clear, measured, no fluff. And that matrix work with finance and getting the client onboard in such a short amount of time? Now that's leadership."

"Thank you, sir."

He raised his eyebrows slightly, a twitch of a smile in one corner of his mouth. "You know, you're not bad at this, Dunhour."

More praise? What was happening? I didn't hide my grin that time.

"I'm serious. Keep up the momentum, and when we're back in the States, you'll be well-positioned for the next step."

When we're back in the States.

The phrase took me out of my bubble.

All I could think about was Aidan and the rickety bridge and his hand over his heart. Dún Laoghaire, Morocco, Christmas, New Year's all on the horizon. That long kiss in the rain where I could feel that he loved me, even if he hadn't said it.

I cleared my throat. It was now or never. "Actually, I wanted to talk to you about that. About my return timeline."

He raised a brow again. "You're not wanting to leave early, are you?"

"No. The opposite actually. I'd like to request an extension. I know the project is scheduled to wrap before the end of the year, but I think I could continue to add value. Especially with the restructuring. I've already spoken with several of the local managers, and they seem receptive to having someone stay to help with transition planning."

Townsend didn't speak right away. He stood and walked to the window, the low profile of the city blurred in the dreary greyness behind him. Hands in his pockets, he rocked slightly on his heels. Standing up to match his body language didn't feel appropriate so I didn't mimic him. Plus, there weren't pockets in that pencil skirt, so I didn't know what I'd do with my hands if I stood.

"You're asking to extend your visa and stay after the project is finished?"

"Yes. I've loved working on Roadrunner, and I think there's still more I can contribute. I'm not looking for a vacation or anything," I added quickly.

He turned back to face me. "It's not just about your performance, Jessica. The Irish government did our client a favor with getting the visas processed so quickly. It's not usually that easy so I don't know what it'd be like to extend. The client would have to approve, I'd have to approve, your office in Tampa would have to approve, and they're already planning your client portfolio for Q1. We can't keep you abroad for sentiment, I need a real business case."

"I understand, and I'll work on it. I just wanted to start the discussion."

He studied me. I suddenly felt vulnerable and weak sitting while he was standing. Per usual, Simon had a point. Just as I slapped my knees and stood, he said, "I'll bring it up with Kent from your home office. Can't promise anything, but I'll try to make it work. Just six months though."

"Thank you," I said, my voice sincere. "That means a lot."

He sauntered back to his desk and added, almost offhandedly, "Do you remember that assignment I was telling you guys about? The one I took in California twenty some odd years ago?"

"Yes. You said it launched your career and changed the trajectory of your life."

He nodded once and smiled. "That's because I met Mrs. Townsend while on that assignment."

19

Walking into the stadium felt like entering a freshly kicked anthill. I followed Simon and Orla, weaving past groups chugging plastic pints of beer before heading into the stands. The low autumn sun had just set behind the curved walls of the stadium, making it immediately feel colder.

Simon stopped to take a selfie with the field behind him. "I need to document my first rugby game."

"Except that it's not rugby, it's Gaelic football," Orla said, slipping past him.

It was a rare chance to see a match at Croke Park during the off-season, but thanks to it being some kind of fundraiser Simon scored tickets from a client that couldn't make it. The second he mentioned Galway was playing, Orla claimed a seat and dragged me along too, insisting I needed a "proper Irish sporting experience."

What I needed was to do something outside of work and outside of Aidan—something fun without consequences attached to every decision.

"Rugby, Gaelic football . . . same thing right?" he replied.

"I'd expect something like that from Ms. America here, not you. Surely you follow rugby in England?"

Simon scrunched his face. "Only to check out the uniforms and their commitment to leg day."

Orla rolled her eyes. "Rugby looks like American football without the protective gear. Gaelic football is a hybrid of soccer." She made air quotes around "soccer" while looking at me and continued, "And rugby with some basketball vibes because you can dribble the ball, catch it, punch it."

We both half-heartedly nodded, not at all understanding.

"Honestly, have you two learned anything about Ireland since moving here?"

"I've learned that there really can be four seasons in a day. Oh, and how to do a dependency matrix," I said.

She laughed as we settled into our seats. A group of rowdy dudes behind us wore their Dublin county scarves and began a chant that picked up momentum. "Let's go, Dublin, let's go!"

Orla turned around to the guys and screamed, "Ah, shut up, ye knob-heads! Galway is gonna kill 'em like they always do."

They flirted back in response to which Orla hissed, "Ah, piss off."

Turning to Simon and I, she warned, "If ye clap for Dublin, I will disown ya."

"Listen, love, I live in Dublin, and I hate the song "Galway Girl," so I know exactly what to do." He joined in with the bros behind us, chanting "Let's go, Dublin, let's go!" smirking at Orla. I snorted into my coffee that had turned cold thanks to the early October weather.

During a lull in the action, I pulled out my phone to check the time and saw a voice note from Lindsay. I popped in one earbud.

"Jessie! Hey, just checking in. I feel like we keep missing each other with this stupid time zone difference. I can't wait till we're in the same city again. Any who, are you getting excited for the trip to Morocco coming up? I can't even imagine all the cool stuff you're gonna see there. Say hi to Aidan, I can't wait to meet him. I know I'll love him too! See you in a couple of weeks!"

I smiled, but as the message ended, a knot tugged at my chest. It was like listening to a message from someone I used to know and not my best friend. I didn't really know how things were going with Jason, and more importantly, if she had gotten used to dating someone with a kid. How often did she see him? What did he call her? How did she feel about being a stepmom? And similarly, Lindsay didn't know much about Aidan, beyond the couple of flirty texts I'd screenshot when we first started dating plus a few distracted calls over the summer.

A roar rushed through the stadium; it'd be too loud to respond with a voice note. My thumb hovered over the reply button, debating what I wanted to say. When I finally settled on the message, I sent it with a selfie. She responded almost instantly.

Me: *Heard your message, I miss you so much and can't wait to see you guys! I'm at a Gaelic football match, no clue what's going on. Call you later xo.*

Lindsay: *OMG the shorts are so short!*

Lindsay: *And the legs are so THICK [heart eyes emoji]*

As the game went on, Orla all but gave up on answering the ridiculous questions Simon and I kept asking. I joined in with a half-hearted cheer whenever she did, and Simon continued to chide her by only cheering for

Dublin. When the big screen panned to a couple making out, the whole stadium whistled and cheered.

"Gearóid would rather die a slow, treacherous death than have our faces snogging on the big screen." Orla kept her eyes on the field as if not to miss anything even though the players were on some kind of break.

"Oh, I'd happily let Merrick molest me in public. The bigger the crowd, the better. I'd just hope the camera caught my good side." Simon presented the right side of his face to us.

"Sure, look, ye know he's shy in front of people. But behind closed doors . . ." She waggled her eyebrows faster than humanly possible.

We all laughed, and Simon interjected, "I've said it before, and this tidbit confirms I should say it again . . . you need to ask that bloke to marry you because he's taking way too long."

Orla playfully jabbed Simon's shoulder but didn't respond. Instead she looked intently down at the field, willing for action. I turned to Simon. "Hey, so what's going on with you and Merrick? I've been so caught up in my own little bubble lately."

"Yes, you have, bitch," Simon said, dryly. "His mum and sister were in Dublin for a visit last weekend, and I met them."

My mouth hung open.

"Excuse me? I've seen you in the office this past week, and you're like the biggest oversharer . . . how am I just now hearing about this?"

"You've been busy meeting your own future in-laws." He gave a look that said "mmm-hmm."

"I know I've been a shit friend lately, I'm sorry. But I really do want to hear about you guys. Last I heard, you'd written him off when it turned out he exaggerated his height on the dating app. And now you're meeting the family. Talk about doing a one eighty on your first impression." I nudged him playfully.

"Ugh, I still can't believe he isn't tall."

"He's taller than you. I mean, most people—including children—are, but still."

"I've told you, I'm practically five-eight," he protested. Knowing I'm almost a head above him even in flats, I let his delusion linger in silence.

He proceeded to tell me how things were moving fast with Merrick. Said it felt easy, unlike previous relationships and hookups where they could never get on the same page. With Merrick, there was no, and I quote, "dicking around." He wanted things to keep moving forward and was confident Merrick did too. It wasn't even weird or stressful when Simon asked him to come home with him for Christmas. Merrick agreed as long as they could go to his home in Portugal for New Year's and stay in an all-inclusive resort. I couldn't help but think of the similarities between their relationship and mine and Aidan's. I looked out at the packed stadium, glad I decided to come to Ireland. Lindsay, and even Raya unknowingly, had nudged me to take the leap and Project Road-runner made it all happen. I wasn't just happy, I was in love. And not just with Aidan, but with Dublin and with who I was becoming there.

Still, I missed home.

Thanks to a play I hadn't watched, the ref made a call against Galway, so I joined Orla in booing while Simon cheered stupidly.

In the end, Dublin won 2-10 to Galway's 1-12, and Simon rubbed it in Orla's face all night. I enjoyed watching them bicker throughout my two beers after the match, but I couldn't wait to go to Aidan's place for the night.

20

We'd only managed to see each other once that following week as both of us were tying up loose ends before Morocco.

Aidan's fingers tracing my bare back woke me from a deep sleep.

"Good morning," I mumbled, eyes shut.

"Morning. Did you sleep well?"

"Mmm-hmm." My smile was slowly waking too.

"I was thinking . . . there's somewhere I want us to go today."

My hand managed to prop my head up. "But I thought you were meeting Killian and the lads in town for a match? I was going to run errands and pack." The early morning flight was in two days and despite my detailed packing list, the laundry still needed to be done.

"I'm not fussed about the match. Let's go on a road trip." He twirled a piece of my hair around his finger.

"So the guys bailed, huh?" I teased.

He started tickling me. "Hilarious, you are." Resisting only encouraged more tickling.

After a quick Weetabix breakfast, which I kept in the apartment just for him, we got dressed. I prayed my jeans still fit as I sucked in just a wee bit to secure the button through its hole. The oversized cream sweater covered the slight love handles that had developed since dating Aidan and all the additional calories that entailed.

The drive on the highway, or as I was growing accustomed to, the motorway, was easy and uninterrupted. The clouds increasingly gathered the further we drove out from the city. I assumed we were going to Dún Laoghaire since he'd mentioned it before, but he didn't confirm where he was taking me. The version of me from earlier in the year would have had anxiety going on a road trip and not knowing the destination, but somehow I was okay with it.

After thirty minutes or so, Aidan pointed toward the hills in the distance.

"That one's called the Great Sugar Loaf because, well . . . apparently it looks like a big mound of sugar."

I squinted at it. "Yeah, I'm not seeing it."

"And since we're such creative people, can you guess what the smaller one next to it is called?"

"Uh, the Great Baking Soda?"

He laughed. "What? No! It's the *Little* Sugar Loaf, obviously."

"Baking soda's better. So, is that where we're going? To the, uh, Sugar Loaves?"

"Not quite. We're headed to Bray. I thought it'd be good to get some fresh air and scenery."

"Will I see sheep like in the movies?"

"I don't think so. It's a seaside town, but you never know."

I thought about it all the time, but man, I liked his accent. I liked the way his hands gripped the steering wheel. I liked the way he still made me nervous. Maybe time was playing tricks on me, but I didn't remember feeling butterflies with Brad in the beginning. Not in a bad way—not like

I wasn't drawn to him or smitten by his smile—it was just . . . different. With Brad, I felt safe. Steady. I always knew we were a sure thing.

At least until I started working at McAfee.

Once my career took off, and I was required to put in much longer hours than he did at his architecture firm, that's when the doubt crept in. I'd started to wonder if he'd be willing to share me with my career. Could he keep up with the hustle I wanted to put in during our twenties to ensure we'd be set in our thirties? A flutter in my stomach did eventually form, but it wasn't butterflies; it was more like a beehive of ambition and doubt.

Why was I thinking about Brad? Stop it.

The rolling hills and grey stone cottages could have been straight out of the coffee table book my mom gave me after I told her I was moving to Ireland. She'd smiled through glassy eyes, both proud and sad. I could almost hear her narrating the drive and pointing out every observation the way she did to avoid silence. I wondered what she was doing, what my dad was doing right then. Probably something ordinary like having coffee and fighting over the remote which somehow made me wish I were there.

More and more road signs sprouted as the green countryside dissolved, and the town unfolded. Our parking spot on a narrow unpaved road behind an O'Neill's pub came with ocean views, free of charge. When was the last time I'd been to the beach? Even though it was only a thirty minute drive from my apartment in Tampa, between working all week and cramming everything else into the weekends, the thought of going to the beach always felt like a chore as an adult.

College graduation weekend. That was the last time I'd been to the beach.

With Brad.

Oh my god. Stop, stop, stop thinking about Brad!

"My aunt and uncle live just down there, in that wee village," Aidan said, pointing down the hill. "We used to come here a lot when I was a kid. They've got three lads around my age, slightly younger. We'd sneak beers up to the cliff. Tasted like piss, but no one wanted to be the one to say it, so we'd push through a few cans each."

I pictured it vividly. That's kind of how I felt about most beers but drink them anyway because it feels weird to "go out for beers" and be the one person drinking wine or soda.

He held my hand and led me up a rocky path, steadying me where the terrain became loose and covered with pebbles. The blue-grey ocean stretched to the horizon, the sun straining to break through the clouds. Behind us lay the town. To our left, a sleepy village curled along the coast. To the right, sprawling fields stretched wide, dotted with grazing sheep. It was a panoramic postcard that came to life, and I was mentally printing it to keep forever.

We sat on a grassy patch and leaned against a boulder that had been smoothed by time. As a teen, Aidan, in his own words, had been popular but hot-tempered and always getting into fights. It was new information from how he described his adolescence during our first date and I'd only ever seen him getting along with everyone so it was surprising. He also mentioned he didn't keep in contact with any of his school friends, preferring the ones he met later through his roommate, Killian. Teenage Aidan was also athletic, trying every sport under the sun and—surprise—being good at them all. But he could never commit to just one, so there wasn't a single sport he could call *his*. I was the opposite. My closest friends were the same ones I had since high school and college with the exception of Simon and Orla. I loved volleyball, and although I wasn't very good, I stuck with it once I started in high school.

"And what about law? I know you said you wanted a more secure path than your dad's after he lost his business with the crash, but how'd you actually get on that route?"

"I had good grades in uni but didn't know what I wanted to do so I took a gap year after graduating. It's pretty common here but I hadn't planned on taking one. Just felt like the right thing at the time. Some of the trips I've told you about were during my gap year."

I knew he'd gone traveling for a year but didn't realize it was partly because he didn't know what to do with his life.

"So you ran out of money and decided that law pays well?"

He huffed out a laugh. "Pretty much." His gaze remained fixed on the ocean. "I asked them for money, so I could stay another couple of months. Babs said absolutely not, that if I wasn't back in two days, she'd throw all my things onto the garden. I didn't believe her but two days later, she sent a picture of my stripped bed and several bin bags scattered out back. Said they were expecting rain soon." He let out an annoyed breath. "So I bought a return flight."

My eyes widened, impressed with her clear communication. "Wow, you weren't kidding. Babs really isn't a typical Irish mum. Not a typical mum, period."

There was a small shake of his head. "Things were different after that. The pressure was high to get a job and get out. A neighbor was a solicitor, and they were looking to take on an apprentice so—"

"You took it," I finished.

He fidgeted with his clasped hands. "I took it."

"Do you . . . regret it?"

The pause answered my question more than words could have.

"No," he shook his head, looking past me. "The pay, the benefits, the networking would all be hard to beat." His hands were still wrestling with each other when he looked at me. "Plus, it funds my travel."

There was more that he wanted to say, but the words didn't quite break, and I didn't push. As much as Aidan shares—all of his stories, his travels, his charisma—he's never been that deep, that raw, with me. And I could relate since I also had a secure career path I was proud of, even with its faults.

"I'm starving, let's go to O'Neill's. They have the best fish and chips," he said, already standing, holding his hand out. And with that, the conversation was over.

***

Aidan and I were the only ones with menus. The rest of the pub leaned into pints and chatter. The two elderly men nursing Guinness at the bar looked like they'd been there all day.

After our fish and chips, we hit the road back to Dublin. Just a few minutes into the drive, we began slowing to a stop on the shoulder.

"All right . . . your turn." He clicked the release of his seat belt.

"Oh no, no, no." I shook my head and scissored my hands vigorously. "I tried once to drive a friend's stick shift, and it was a disaster. So no, thank you."

It was another half-truth where I classified Brad in the friend zone. He drove an older but cared for manual transmission Volkswagen Jetta in college and had tried multiple times to teach me. I could never get the hang of releasing the clutch while simultaneously pushing the accelerator. He was always patient, but the last attempt ended with me stalled in the middle of a four-lane intersection. Sheer panic consumed me, so

Brad sprinted around the car to switch seats while every car in a three block radius blared its horn. He drove us to the nearest parking lot where he held me tightly and apologized for putting me in that situation.

"I'm an excellent teacher," Aidan said, stepping out to walk around to my side.

I clutched my seatbelt as he stood at my door. "Did you know that only like five percent of Americans can drive stick? That's counting the ones who *say* they can but really can't. And I haven't driven at all in like six months, I probably forgot how to drive all together. Plus, the wheel's on the wrong side, and you all drive on the wrong side of the road."

He leaned against the open door, arms crossed, face bored.

"And I don't want to ruin your transmission," I added, out of breath.

He paused. "I taught an ex who'd never driven a day in her life. She picked it up in ten minutes."

Ouch.

He hadn't brought up exes before, and anytime I mentioned Brad, it was under the friend guise. The thought of him being patient with another woman who didn't have a full-blown panic attack at the idea of a clutch was enough to make me unclick my seatbelt.

"Fine," I said.

I stomped around and climbed into the driver's seat, adjusting the mirrors with trembling hands. "So . . . is first gear still top left, or is it reversed too?"

"Still top left. But make sure you push the clutch all the way in before you shift. And when you're ready, ease off the clutch slowly while gently pressing the accelerator. You'll feel it catch. Don't overthink it."

Don't overthink it? I hate when someone other than me says that to me.

My next breath was silent but deep. Pressing down on the accelerator, my face scrunched tighter and tighter, waiting for something to happen.

Please, please just work for me.

I released the clutch as slowly as I could and the engine sputtered. Instinctively, I applied more acceleration but in doing so, totally released the clutch. His bachelor mobile jolted like some broken down junker before dying completely.

I also died, covering my face in embarrassment.

"Jesus, Jessica, open your eyes!" Aidan shouted, slamming the center console with his palm.

A tingle crept in from behind my eyes.

What the hell just happened?

I never wanted to drive the car, but he insisted. I debated on how best to respond. Stay quiet and avoid confrontation like my mom? Something short and punchy like Townsend would? Flip the moment and stand up for myself like Simon taught me to do with Raya? I went with Simon's approach. But before I could find the right words, Aidan had opened the door and began marching around to my side.

"You were right, I shouldn't have pushed it," he said stiffly, holding my door open wide. "Come on." His head signaled, "get out."

In a panic, wanting to defuse the situation, I changed my approach. "No, wait." I grabbed his hand. "Let me try again, I won't freak out this time."

What was I doing? Why did I say that? I would absolutely freak out again.

His mouth twisted as he rubbed a hand on the back of his neck, deciding my fate. The door closed and he returned to the passenger side.

The Coral's "Dreaming of You" played from the shared playlist we'd compiled over the past couple of months. It was mostly music that'd come out more than ten years ago, because Aidan didn't like most contemporary music. With the exception of a few indie bands, he felt most modern music was overproduced and lacked texture, whatever that meant.

I gripped the wheel tightly and muttered a prayer before putting the car in first gear. As the car revved, I released the clutch more than the time before. There were a few small jerks, so I pushed it back in and released the acceleration. Back at square one, but this time because I chose it, not because I lost control.

Breathe.

And again.

I was unsure whether I had actually mastered the sweet spot between acceleration and clutch or if it was pure luck. But I didn't care because after a vibration from the engine, it caught, and I was driving. I didn't know exactly how I did it or what to do next, but for a few exhilarating moments, I was proud.

"I'm doing it!" I squealed. "Look, I'm actually—"

"See? It's really not that hard," he cut in.

Maybe I was coming across like an overexcited toddler, so I toned it down, at least until we went around a bend where . . . sheep with blue markings on their fur were crossing the road.

"Sheep, sheep!" I squealed.

"So stop the car!"

"I don't know how!" It didn't sound like my voice and even in the moment, I knew I sounded like a moron for not knowing how to stop the car, but I wasn't sure if I needed to change gears first or press the clutch or could I simply brake like in a normal car?

Shit. I was about to be a sheep murderer *and* break my boyfriend's car in one fell swoop.

"Clutch in!" he yelled.

I pushed hard with my left foot.

"It's in."

"Now brake." He shifted for me as we came to a stop, just as the last little lamb cleared without a care in the world.

We sat for a while as the song faded leaving only the sound of the sheep's baa-ing outside.

"That felt like something out of a movie," I said, with labored breath. "Actually, it did happen in *Three Men and a Little Lady*. Have you seen it?"

His eyes burned through, as if trying to understand why I was so stupid. "No. But just to clarify—you hadn't seen *Casablanca* before we went, haven't seen *American History X*, or *The Godfather*, but you *have* seen *Three Men and a Little Lady*?" A scoff grated on my nerves.

"Yeah." There was an "and so what?" tone packed into the simple word. "I told you, I'm not really into movies. But I used to watch that one with my grandma when I was a kid." I looked out at the shepherd, wishing that I could trade places with him. "There's a scene with sheep on the road in Ireland, and it made me think of her. Sorry. Wrong time to have brought it up."

No acknowledgement. "Right, so." A loud breath. "I'll take the wheel now."

We switched back to our original seating arrangement as I wondered if he was upset with me or just annoyed about the driving lesson because there was an undeniable shift from the first half of the day, almost like someone had turned the volume down.

Or was there? I really was overthinking everything.

As we drove off, he switched off our playlist to turn on the radio. Meanwhile, I combed through the day searching for clues. He was sweet in the morning, supposedly canceled with his friends to take me to Bray, seemed fine on the drive. Maybe a little distant when talking about his career path but nothing crazy. At lunch, I told him the itinerary I had planned for Lindsay and Jason's visit right after we returned to Dublin from Morocco. He didn't have much to add, so I felt like I had planned a good trip with the right balance of culture, fun, and relaxation.

It hit me like how I'd imagine a cold plunge would. We hadn't kissed all day. Hadn't even held hands. But we did have a silly tickle fight in bed. He hadn't called me Missus all day. Actually, all week.

What did it mean? Was our relationship simply normalizing after a honeymoon phase, and I was making something out of nothing? Or was it something more? Should I mention it or would that make it worse?

I commented on the scenery a few times, and he'd reply back politely with nods and smiles. Maybe it wasn't fair to expect him to be charming and interesting and perfect all the time, the way I saw him the first month or so. I sure wasn't.

As we turned onto my street, the black cat that often lurked around was weaving in and out of the thin iron rails of my neighbor's front stoop. Parked outside of my apartment, Aidan placed his left hand on my right leg and rubbed just above my knee. "Thanks for a lovely day, Missus. I'll see you at the airport Monday morning."

Missus. There it is.

"Any chance you'll send me the itinerary?" Besides knowing we were going to Morocco, I didn't know what we were doing there, where we were staying, how much it would all cost, and who was paying for what. It drove me slightly insane, but I wanted to be the cool girlfriend and at least pretend to be spontaneous.

"Not a chance," he said, leaning in to kiss me.

Missus *and* a kiss? I had definitely been overthinking—making a bigger deal out of an off moment.

When I opened the car door, he grabbed my wrist and pulled me in for another kiss. It was hard at first, then sweet. He gently stroked my face and twirled my hair around his finger. His classic maneuver.

Everything was fine between us, and I *had been* overthinking the day's events. I needed to focus on our romantic weeklong trip to Morocco.

21

THE NEXT MORNING, I woke up with the driving lesson weighing heavy on my mind. And my heart. It occurred to me that he was always taking charge, and perhaps it was tiresome. He planned all our dates, planned the trip to Morocco, often drove me around, and tried to teach me to drive stick. Maybe that's why he snapped?

As a way to show my appreciation, I searched the internet for concerts that were coming up in the next couple of months. I quickly settled on The Paper Keys, a Scottish indie group he'd sent me a few links to. They were playing at The Academy a few weeks after we returned from Morocco. I secured the tickets, made reservations for before the show at the restaurant his sister worked at, and added it to my calendar.

After packing, I FaceTimed Lindsay to go over their trip to Ireland, which would be the weekend after we returned from Morocco. We covered everything she could borrow from me, particularly warm outerwear to save suitcase space. I reminded her to bring comfortable shoes, which caused her to groan about how her feet were still recovering from trying to break in a pair of too-small Louboutin's.

I ran through their itinerary again. They'd arrive on a Friday morning, the day before my birthday, which I'd mostly written off to jet lag, but

Aidan would meet us for drinks or an early dinner. On Saturday, we'd go out in town for my birthday, and Sunday, Aidan would drive us to Howth. Monday, they'd rent a car and head west to the Ring of Kerry for five nights. Similar to Aidan and I, it was their first real trip together, save for a couple of weekend getaways in Florida.

Jason was determined to check golfing in Ireland off his bucket list and wondered if Aidan would join him—giving us ladies half a day to ourselves. I lied and said I wasn't sure if Aidan golfed. He had his own clubs and went with Killian every couple of months or so, but I was worried he'd feel cornered into going with him.

Before we hung up, I cautiously asked about Jason's son, Cody. She pinched the bridge of her nose. "He's good. Cute. Well-behaved," she said. "I just don't know how to be around him yet. Like, what does he expect from me?"

Lindsay doesn't do dinosaurs, monster trucks or kid appropriate small talk. As expected for someone who never had a model for any of it growing up. Since the day I met her, she's insisted she doesn't have the mom gene. I was starting to think she actually believes it.

I couldn't quite picture how it would work long-term between her and Jason—not because of him, but because of what loving a child demanded. Still, it felt like crossing a line to say that out loud. Lindsay, being almost thirty, wasn't going to build her life around my observations.

When the call ended, the familiar ache settled in—the kind I'd felt before when realizing how much life can happen when you're not around. I couldn't shake the reality that I knew almost nothing about Jason. Or Cody. Or what a normal day for her even looked like anymore. And she didn't know Aidan. We'd always sworn we'd never grow apart, but that's the kind of promise friends make when they share a zip code.

Once the laundry was done, my out-of-office was set, and my suitcase zipped, I microwaved my last prepped meal and collapsed on the couch as the opening credits of *Mad Men* rolled. I was halfway through an episode when my phone rang.

Unknown number.

"Good evening, Jessica. Crawford here. Sorry to bother you on a Sunday evening. Do you have a minute?"

"Uh, Mr. Townsend? Is everything all right?"

"Yes, everything is fine. I saw your out-of-office and remembered you'd be away this week, so I wanted to catch you before you left."

"If this is about Phase Nine, I've got it under control. The client's all set, I'll be checking email, and Simon's running point on any emergencies, should they arise."

"It's not that. We just received a request for proposal from Pioneer. It's big, Jessica. We're talking up to eight-figure billings a year for the next five years if we land it."

"Holy shit—uh, sorry. That's incredible." I sat up straighter.

He chuckled. "Don't apologize."

"I know ATB & Co. has been eyeing them for years," I said.

"We were eyeing them too, just didn't think they'd submit an RFP to us, given ATB's dominance. If we win this, we'll be the largest consulting firm in the world."

We were currently fourth—up from seventh two years ago. This one assignment would push us to number one overnight? Unreal.

"So does this mean you'll be splitting time between Dublin and the U.S.?"

"I'll be handing Roadrunner over to Patrick Cunningham this week. He'll see it through while I pop in occasionally for relationship continuity."

Patrick was a local partner, so it made sense to keep things on the Irish side as we wound down Roadrunner.

"Do you need me for the transition?" I asked, unsure why else he'd call—unless maybe to say goodbye personally? It'd be sweet but definitely could've waited until a workday.

"No, you've earned the time off. I'm calling because I want you on the proposal team."

I went still.

"I know you wanted to stay longer in Ireland, but Jessica, this is a once in a career opportunity. And if you join, we'll put you forward as one of two Associate Partners on the account."

Associate Partner? No, that couldn't be right. A twenty-eight year old Associate Partner would certainly be the youngest ever in our office, probably in the whole firm.

I shut my eyes and shook my head as if that'd help me to process. "Mr. Townsend, that's . . . incredible. And making Partner is definitely my endgame, so . . . thank you. Truly."

"So you're in?"

"Um, what's the timing? And when would you need an answer?"

"ASAP. National kicks off tomorrow. We'll need the full team on-site in Atlanta early next month. It'll be a rough few months, but Pioneer will make their decision by December first. Don't plan on having much of a Christmas break. If we win, we'll be busy."

Next month? That gave me . . . two, maybe three *weeks* to leave Ireland?

"Okay. Wow. That's so soon. I need some time to process this."

"Of course. Though, I want to be clear—the promotion is contingent on the proposal. This is your business case. Otherwise, it'll likely be another two or three years before your name comes up again."

I automatically nodded, even though he couldn't see me. "Understood."

His tone softened. "Jessica, if you do this, we could look into transferring an Irish national over to the U.S. There are ways to make it work."

I hesitated, chewing the inside of my cheek. "And if I don't join the proposal team, is the visa extension we discussed still on the table?"

"It is. I've discussed with Patrick, but if it's approved, you'd be staying as an Irish employee working on Irish clients since Roadrunner will be wrapping up soon. And just so we're clear, that won't really translate back home."

"I understand. Let me sleep on it for a few days, and I'll give you my answer this week."

"Uh . . . okay? Uh, yes. Yes, of course," he recovered. "Have a wonderful trip, Jessica. He's a lucky guy."

When we hung up, I stared at the wall.

I'd never felt more seen or energized professionally. It was the ultimate career high: Townsend handpicking me for a proposal that could launch the firm into consulting-world dominance. And yet, the knot in my stomach told a different story.

Aidan had asked me to stay. And God, I wanted to. But I knew, deep down, if I left in a few weeks, it would be the end of us. It'd be another relationship sacrificed at the altar of my career.

Just like with Brad. And the house with the turquoise door we'd almost bought.

I couldn't make that mistake again. I knew all too well how that kind of regret worked. It didn't hit all at once, but chipped away slowly, day by day and week by week until eventually realizing what I'd thrown away. Brad had been worth fighting for. We could have grown together and figured out our budding careers together. He would have supported my long hours and ambitious career timeline. He told me he would, I just didn't believe it at the time. I was too focused on the next rung on the ladder, and he became an obstacle instead of a spotter ready to catch me if I fell.

Then, seven months after we broke up—seven months after we viewed the house with the turquoise door—I reached out. I told myself it was just to talk, just to check in.

But it was too late.

He was already seeing someone else.

The door had shut. And for the first time, I understood what it meant to lose something quietly, because I didn't speak up in time.

I couldn't make that mistake again.

I'd wait a few days in the Moroccan sun before giving Townsend my answer.

<h1 style="text-align:center">22</h1>

The intercom cycled through Arabic, French and English in a jarring loop as we strolled through the Marrakech airport. Robes and head coverings were scattered throughout the crowd, but there was far more typical western attire than I was expecting.

Stepping through the automatic doors into the outside, the low sun had cast a copper haze over everything, and yet, the heat was still suffocating. A man wearing a faded Real Madrid jersey tried to usher us toward a taxi that wasn't actually a taxi.

Aidan respectfully waved him off like a pro. "Welcome to Morocco, Missus."

"I feel like I walked into the deep end of a very hot and humid swimming pool." I slid my sunglasses on, grateful for the cover. Boxy Mercedes sedans lined the curb, each in varying shades of tan and cream. A family of five wedged themselves into one, with the smallest child held on the mother's lap in the front seat. The driver struggled to close the trunk with their two large suitcases, so the lid bounced loosely as they pulled away.

"Is that normal?" I whispered.

Aidan grinned. "Perfectly normal. Not exactly the same safety regulations here."

He wasn't kidding. In our taxi a few minutes later, a family of four buzzed past on a single scooter. The father drove, followed by a toddler tucked between him and the mother with a baby tied to her back. No one wore a helmet. My knees squeezed my hands between them tightly as I forced myself to breathe deep.

"You good?" Aidan asked, rubbing my knee in the back of the taxi.

"Yeah. Just, um . . . adjusting."

I couldn't tell where the rural part near the airport ended and the city began. The outer neighborhoods were a blend of weathered apartment buildings, laundry swaying on balconies, and rows of olive trees with the occasional goat tied to a few of them. The billboards and road signs in Arabic were a busy backdrop to the men in long, tan gowns weaving through traffic as if collisions weren't possible.

"This is wild," I mouthed quietly to Aidan, my eyes glued on a pair of women in jeans and jewel-colored head coverings across the street.

"Mad, right?" Aidan's voice was full of energy. "I love the chaos here. You'll get used to it."

There was no way I ever would.

Our driver assured us that the riad was tucked behind a series of terracotta walls and narrow alleys where cars couldn't fit. We reluctantly followed a lanky teenage boy in a polo shirt and flip flops who offered to carry our bags in a wheelbarrow as the 1980s Mercedes sputtered away. While dodging stray cats and potholes, I tried not to lose sight of Aidan's brown hair in the crowd.

"Are you sure we're headed in the right direction?" I asked, unsure if I was asking Polo Shirt or Aidan.

"It's all part of the charm," Aidan said, clearly in his element.

Great. If being lost was the charming part, I was afraid of what came next. When the boy finally stopped in front of a massive wooden door and gestured that we'd arrived, relief flooded me so fast I had to catch myself on my knees. Aidan dished out a tip and a fist bump—meanwhile, I was quietly thankful we arrived with our luggage and passports intact.

The riad door had to be at least ten feet tall. More exquisite than its size was its shape—like an old fashioned keyhole. The wood had been carved with intricate floral patterns and embedded with iron detailing. It was the opposite of the doors of Dublin, which although candy-colored, were simple.

Inside the riad was stunning. It was exactly what I was hoping for when researching Morocco. We entered a serene courtyard just through the lobby filled with potted lemon trees, mosaic tile work, and a multi-layered fountain bubbling in the center. The citrus scent reminded me of the orange groves in Florida.

After a while, a woman in a white robe offered us mint tea while the boy disappeared up a narrow stairwell with our luggage.

"Now this is more my speed," I said, dropping onto a rich plum colored sofa.

"Don't get too comfortable," Aidan said, pulling me back to my feet. "We've only got an hour before sunset. Let's head out and get a feel for the place before it gets dark."

I blinked slowly. "Now?"

"Yep. No better way to shake off the flight. We'll walk through the souks, grab some food. Come on, let's live a little."

I hesitated. Processed. My head felt discombobulated. Between the early morning start, the plane ride, the heat, the sights, the language . . . the call from the day before weighing on my mind. I needed a minute to decompress.

"Maybe I'll stay here for a bit, and we can meet in an hour?" I smiled, trying to sound casual. "I want to unpack and take a shower. You go ahead and explore, I'll catch up."

"No way you're going to try to find your way to the square at night on your own. I'll meet you back here in an hour and a half," he said, gazing at his watch. "Be here in the lobby at six." A gentle kiss landed on my forehead which felt both sweet and unnerving.

"Don't you want to see the room? I bet it's romantic." I gave him *the* look.

"Eh, I'll see it tonight when we're back. Right now I want to explore Marrakech!"

As the courtyard door clicked shut behind him, I sunk into the velvety cushions and closed my eyes, pretending to relax. The trickle of the fountain echoed up the high ceilings.

We were on the trip I'd been so excited for and thought would feel magical. Instead I felt like I was already falling behind—my lack of travel experience already at the forefront.

I took one last inhale of the lemon tree and ran after him.

***

After fifteen minutes of tradesmen trying to lure us into their shops with "just a look, my friends," we finally reached the entrance to the main square. Smoke from open grills drifted across the medina, mingling with cumin, coriander and something I couldn't quite place—almost metallic.

Outside the main gate, Aidan bought macarons from a woman with a baby secured to her back with a shawl. Just like the one I'd seen on the moped. He didn't object when she overcharged us, and after he handed her the money, she added two more of the tiny French cookies to the bag and said, "Thank you," to which he replied "Shokran" with a small bow of his head.

We each popped a macaron into our mouths as we entered through the gates. The noises were individually familiar but together, they warped into something surreal. Drums. Shouting. A snake charmer's flute. Mopeds buzzing. Like drifting through a loud, hazy dream.

"I feel like I'm in a movie," I said, tightening my grip on Aidan's hand.

He grinned. "Mad, isn't it? Come on, let's see how lost we can get."

The getting lost thing again?

Before I could respond, he was already tugging me deeper into the square—past carts piled with dried figs and dates, past men holding monkeys on leashes, past women waving laminated henna menus.

At a lantern stall, I slowed, mesmerized by the kaleidoscope of colored glass casting patterns across the pavement.

"This is . . . wow," I said, mostly to myself. When I turned, Aidan was already halfway down an alley.

"Let's head into the medina," he called over his shoulder.

One last glance at the lanterns, and I hurried after him, nearly tripping over a black cat darting across my path.

Inside the medina, everything narrowed. Some alleyways were barely wide enough for two people. Leather bags and rugs brushed our shoulders. Merchants shouted prices and greetings in multiple languages.

Aidan moved as if he'd been there before. I jogged in short bursts just to keep up; my sandals and the uneven pavement didn't make it easy. Spice and meat smells thickened in the air, pushing me to the brink of sensory overload.

"Can we slow down a little?" I asked.

He stopped at an orange stall and turned, half smiling. "Someone a little out of shape?" he said lightly. "Too much time at the office maybe?"

I couldn't overthink it in the midst of all the commotion.

"I just want to take it in," I said, stepping beside him. "Together."

He studied me for a second, then reached for my hand. "All right, together. Cross my heart." There was the familiar double squeeze.

As we moved on, his grip stayed firm, but I could tell he was itching to take off again. His gaze kept drifting toward narrower lanes, the ones that looked darker and less touristy.

A rooftop café caught my eye. I tugged his arm. "What about there? We could watch the square from above. Maybe get a drink?"

He glanced up. "It'll be packed. And remember, most places don't serve alcohol. Let's keep going—there's probably somewhere more authentic for mint tea if we go a little further."

"Sure," I said.

The alleys began to blur together. We passed a butcher's stall where meat hung from rusty hooks and flies buzzed over dark puddles on the ground. The metallic smell from earlier, explained.

Both captivated and uncomfortable, I watched a man reach into a cage, grab a chicken, snap its neck like a twig, place it on the block, and chop its head off in one casual yet intentional motion. The smell of raw flesh and spice clung to my throat.

It was too much. I frantically scanned for the most acceptable place to throw up. An alleyway? My crossbody bag?

And Aidan wasn't beside me.

I spun around, but there were too many people, too many corners, too many lights. My pulse spiked.

"Aidan?"

I turned in a slow circle. The crowd moved frantically around me. My stomach twisted as I reached for my phone. I remembered he had his roaming turned off.

"Aidan!" I increased the volume.

Breathe. Stay put. He'll come back. He has to.

Or would it take ten minutes before he even noticed?

"Aidan?" My voice cracked and my stomach dropped lower.

What was I doing? Why was I there? Why were *we* there?

This was a bad idea.

The spinning worsened.

His words echoed. *Let's see how lost we can get.*

"Aidan!" I yelled, and heads turned.

Walk, breathe. Breathe, walk.

Tears pooled as I screamed his name one last time.

Then, two alleyways down, I spotted him. Bartering over a rug.

The smile on his face was as carefree as his wave.

I wiped my palms on my linen pants and crossed over to him.

"Found a souvenir to add to my art collection." He held a red, orange and gold patterned rug. "What do you think?"

And just like my mom when she was holding something back, my lips curled while my gaze dropped to the floor.

"Nice. It's really very nice."

23

Three days later, at 5:52 a.m., we were jolted awake by the first call to prayer blaring from a nearby mosque. Aidan scooted over, wrapped his arms around me and mumbled a sleepy rendition of the prayer while I giggled. It went on for about five very long minutes.

Although the first half of the trip in Marrakech had been amazing, it was clear this wasn't going to be the relaxing, romantic trip I envisioned unless I spoke up. We were traveling to Rabat for the second half of the adventure, and I was determined to slow down the pace.

"One down, one to go," he said, kissing behind my ear. He meant it because there was a call to prayer just before sunrise, and it was followed by another one about twenty minutes later.

I rolled onto him, kissing his neck and squeezing with my thighs. His hands traced designs on my back as warm breath tickled my ear.

"You know, the mosque wasn't the only thing that woke me," he said, gently pushing my hair back. I assumed he meant it in a flirtatious way so kept kissing. "You were farting in your sleep," he added.

Shit.

Those god-damned Moroccan spices.

I jolted onto my elbow. "What? No? Are you sure?"

He laughed.

My jaw dropped. "You're making it up, aren't you?" I smacked him around playfully.

"Be careful, you don't wanna upset your stomach," he teased.

"You jerk!" I grabbed a pillow and started hitting him.

"You're cute when you're mortified," he said lightly.

I couldn't tell if he was joking or not but being mortified over a fart was a bit extreme even for me.

Nonetheless, he grabbed a pillow, and we playfully fought until the next call to prayer called us back under the covers.

***

Later that afternoon, after checking into the riad in Rabat, we strolled to get a lay of the town and stopped at a cozy café for mint tea. The inside looked like it was stuck in the 1960s with a box TV hanging in the corner with antennae at the top. A few men huddled around watching it, one reading a newspaper and smoking a cigar.

Outside, at a chipped blue table, we watched a little sparrow hop from chair to chair. The silver teapot between us reminded me of something out of *Aladdin* as I sipped the delicious, albeit too sweet drink. Sweat gathered at the back of my neck making the hot tea outside feel slightly absurd, but it was what the locals did and Aidan was determined to do Morocco properly.

"I want to open my own law firm one day," he said casually.

"That's awesome. Have you looked into office space?" I stirred my tea, bruising the mint leaves.

"Not yet." He shook his head. "There are a couple spaces I saw for let just north of my apartment, closer to Phibsborough, but haven't inquired."

"I've worked on a few business plans. I have some great templates and planning tools. I could help if you want?"

A closed lip smile crept without a response. "What about you? What are your goals?"

To buy a house, make Associate Partner, get married or at least be engaged by age thirty. To settle down, have two point two kids, and be successful. The same as everyone else I know. Duh.

"Well, the main reason I came on this assignment to Ireland was to fast-track a promotion. I want to make Associate Partner in the next couple of years, but it's really competitive." I wasn't ready to tell him that I in fact had the position in the bag, but it would mean leaving Ireland to get it. I hated keeping something so big from him, but on the other hand, it felt like too much pressure to put on the relationship only three months in.

Or should I bring it up?

He sipped his clear glass of mint tea, his attention drifting just enough to notice.

"Yeah, but, are you passionate about your career? Or are you following this track because it's the one you're already on?"

I didn't know what to say. My job was never just a paycheck to me, but if I was honest with myself, was I truly passionate about due diligence, finding synergies—and thanks to Raya—dependency matrices? Probably not. But there was plenty that I did like and was good at. I love analyzing data and running models to see how tweaks to inputs change the bottom line. Plus, most people aren't passionate about their jobs, are they? Feels like something you tell little kids like, "Do something you love, and you'll never work a day in your life." Then you grow up and realize the stuff most people love to do doesn't pay all that great, so you look into something more steady.

Realizing I let the awkward silence drag too long, I responded honestly.

"I guess I haven't thought about it before. I like my job and even more so that it led me here." My hand gestured to the street and all around.

"I know you like your job and you're good at it, but what makes you tick? Hobbies? Travel? Sports? Any wild plans for the future?" he pushed.

One of my greatest fears was coming true.

He thinks I'm boring.

Lindsay always jokes about my predictability. Simon calls me Cinderella because I'm always home by midnight, even my parents often tell me to have fun and "live a little." I'd been so focused on work that I forgot what I even like to do when I'm not working.

Shit. I really was a passionless, workaholic, uncultured, boring person.

Hovering outside my body, I watched the spiral into an early midlife crisis on the streets of Morocco. No way I was going to bring up the promotion. It wasn't the time.

"Maybe I'm not passionate about my career, but I think it will afford me a life where I can follow passions in the future."

He didn't appear enlightened. The sinking feeling in my stomach doubled down.

"So . . . is law your passion? Law and travel?" I asked, trying not to sound as defensive as I felt.

"God, no, law is *not* my passion. I do love meeting so many new people in the community, building connections, solving problems, and being needed in my own little corner of the world. But my passion?" He sipped mint tea from the tiny metal cup. "Yes, it's travel. I want to visit another twenty countries before I turn forty. Maybe even live somewhere else and I don't know . . . volunteer, start a blog, get a job doing something completely different. An adventure I'll be proud of when I'm eighty years old."

He had his own checklist. That part was very cool. But—twenty more countries in the next seven years? That would mean roughly three big trips a year. I could never swing that with my job, or my budget given how much I set aside for savings. Also, I didn't want to. Moving to Ireland and visiting Morocco in the same year was enough excitement to last me a decade. I was thankful for both experiences, but I missed my structured life in Tampa whereas Aidan clearly craved variety. Were we really so different?

"What if we moved here? For six months . . . we could teach English, really immerse ourselves in the culture," he said, pouring another cup of tea.

"You're kidding."

"I'm not. How cool would that be?"

Cool for someone else, but not for me. Plus, it'd mean pausing life again as the rest of my friends charged ahead.

"It does sound pretty cool, but let's get through this trip first and then talk," I joked.

"Afraid it would derail your exciting corporate job?" He laughed.

The corners of my mouth barely flinched as I focused on my tea, willing for a change in topic. Finally, it did as he presented the itinerary for the next two days. My interest was piqued only when he mentioned a traditional hammam spa experience. But even a spa day couldn't ease the chaos in my head and pinch in my heart after that conversation.

With only a layer of soggy mint leaves in the pot of tea, Aidan went to the restroom while I conjured up a Wi-Fi password to check my messages.

Shit. There was an email from Townsend.

From: C.Townsend@mcafeeconsulting.com
To: J.Dunhour@mcafeeconsulting.com
Subject: Checking in
Time: 9:16 a.m.

Hi, Jessica. Just checking in to see if you've had a chance to think more about the Pioneer proposal? I told National you'd get back to us by Monday. Enjoy the rest of your trip. Call if you need me. Crawford.

It was as if I'd eaten a bucket of knots during teatime. With shaky hands, I quickly swiped out of the email app just in case Aidan could read it from the toilet. There were also two texts from Simon.

Simon: *Greetings from dreary Dublin. Is Moroccan Cinderella enjoying lots of nuts? Get your mind out of the gutter!*

Simon: *Something fishy is going on here. Townsend is transitioning Roadrunner to some local dweeb and going back to the U.S. He'll be gone next week. I'll keep you posted.*

He attached a picture of him and Merrick sipping hot toddies at a bar. Despite still being on edge, my heart smiled to see Simon happy with his not-tall-enough match.

Back to Townsend's email.

Aidan called from the counter of the café, asking if we should get pastries with the next pot of mint tea.

Shoving the phone into my purse, I called, "Absolutely, yes" and blotted the sweat from my face with the bottom of my shirt.

We still had a few days left of the trip. I'd formally give my decision back in Dublin.

24

For our last full day in Morocco, Aidan had booked a hammam experience. Knowing I'd likely never be back, I set two goals for the day: soak it all in and avoid the pit in my stomach where questions about our relationship had started to gather.

On the walk there, shop owners pulled out every stop to lure us inside. "My friends, my friends. Come, come . . . beautiful carpet and beautiful jewelry for the lady, one of a kind," they called, waving us inside as we politely acknowledged and kept walking.

The soft murmur of prayer came first, then the group rounded the corner toward us. Aidan stepped in front of me. For a split second, I thought he was about to steal a kiss or steer us into a shop, but his body language shifted—firmer, protective.

I leaned slightly to see past his shoulder. Four men carried a wooden board at shoulder-height, draped in linen.

A body. A woman's body. The shape was unmistakable beneath the cloth.

I gasped. There was no hearse, no ornate casket, no line of mourners. Just a handful of people shuffling behind in quiet prayer. The ceremony was so simple and so private, yet completely exposed. It felt wrong for me, a tourist on the way to a spa, to share the same winding street as that woman's final procession. But there we were.

Aidan's arms wrapped around me, letting me feel.

Neither of us spoke because what could we possibly say?

At the hammam, we changed into robes and slippers—me still in my underwear, him still in his boxer briefs. A petite woman in a jeweled headscarf and rubber slippers led us up three flights of stone stairs to a room that looked more like a jail cell than a spa. The floor was drenched and two large stone slabs—treatment beds—sat in the center.

The two women used charades to instruct us to lie face-up. They then disappeared for what felt like an eternity but was probably less than ten minutes.

I anticipated a blissful concoction of warm spa mud infused with exotic oils and healing herbs.

Instead, they grabbed hoses and blasted us with icy water like we were livestock. I shrieked, wiping under my eyes and instantly regretting the mascara.

So that explained the soaked floor.

The women bickered in Arabic while coating us in a gritty black scrub that smelled like cinnamon and coffee. My masseuse worked methodically, covering every inch of my body including behind the ears, between the toes, and deep into the scalp.

Some areas tickled, making me squirm as the stone slipped beneath me.

Then came the *really* deep scrub. I didn't see the tool she used, but it had to be either a Brillo pad or a horse brush because holy hell, it hurt.

Whatever tan I'd achieved during the trip disappeared along with several layers of skin.

We flipped to our stomachs to repeat the fun.

When the scrubbing session was over, they coated us with a different mixture and left the room.

A few minutes passed. I turned my raw, muddy, mascara-smeared face toward Aidan. He was already watching me.

"They kept staring at you the whole time," he said, his eyes and teeth the only visible parts of his mud-covered face. "I wanted to tell my lady, 'Hey, I know she's beautiful but look at me! Rub me! Over here, hello!'"

"Good. I want them to ignore you. You're mine." My cheek pressed against the wet stone. "How long do you think they'll leave us here?"

"According to my research . . . about twenty minutes. What do ye reckon I come over for a snuggle?"

"No way! We'll get in trouble if we get caught!" I whisper-yelled.

"Ah, we're leaving tomorrow anyway." He was already sliding off his block.

"Oh my god, oh my god," I recited, eyes closed.

The stone bed definitely wasn't made for two people. He climbed up with the grace of a baby deer on ice. I rolled onto my side and grabbed him before he fell off.

Our mud covered bodies were like those jelly toys where the harder you grip, the faster they slip. We laughed quietly, trying not to echo.

Eventually we found our sweet spot and froze, careful not to set off another slip-a-thon.

"This is very tricky," I whispered, our foreheads firmly touching, noses brushing. His hand moved from my shoulder to my face, his thumb circling my cheek, then tracing my lips. Like he was memorizing me.

"Tricky, huh?" he said, quietly. "Someone once told me *love* was a tricky word."

"Sounds wise, that person." The mud cracked as I smiled.

"Mm-hmm." He kissed me, slow and wet. "These lips . . . are tricky."

"This body . . . is tricky." His hand slid across my stomach, hip and eventually gripped my thigh, pulling it over his.

"This . . . is tricky," he murmured, brushing a clump of matted hair from my face. "But I want to be tricky with you. I'm so in tricky with you."

He kissed me again, harder. Then soft again.

"Thank you for coming here with me," he whispered. "Thank you for . . . thank you."

The words landed strangely. It was *our* trip so "thank you for coming" felt like he was glad I could tag along. Maybe he meant for agreeing to Morocco over somewhere romantic. Somewhere without chicken beheadings and street funerals.

"You're welcome." I smiled anyway.

"Right, I better get back to my block before we spend our last night in a Moroccan jail."

"Ah, the U.S. Embassy would be on me like white on rice. *You*, on the other hand, would be waiting a while. All the Irish are on holiday this time of year."

He agreed and slid back across the floor just before the women returned.

***

Later, on the walk back to the riad, we wandered the maze of streets feeling more at ease now—no longer checking the map, just letting the city guide us. We held hands, Aidan giving his double squeezes every now and then. I'd always return them.

We passed a small souvenir stand tucked between two alleyways. Aidan paused and pointed to a t-shirt hanging on display. "Look there, even in Marrakech, Che is with us," he said, chin darting toward the face printed on the cotton.

I followed his gaze and recognized the image. The black and red face on the poster frequented college walls and vintage t-shirts. My eyes squinted, trying to recall who it was.

"Jesus, don't tell me you don't know who Che Guevara is, either?"

The "either" stung. Another notch on the belt of things I'd gotten wrong. I huffed out a smile. "I know that he's really, really ridiculously good looking," I said, hoping the *Zoolander* reference would lighten the moment.

But he didn't laugh. "Are you serious?"

"I was kidding."

"Were you though?" he said, crossing his arms. "I'm beginning to think maybe you missed a few classes in secondary school."

The temperature inside rose, starting in my chest and branching out to the limbs and up my neck. All the little digs and mood swings were really grating on my nerves. Again, I found myself desperate to say something but words escaped me, so I gave him a look and walked ahead.

"Jessica—" He caught up quickly, grabbing my shoulder to turn me around. I shut my eyes tightly, willing the tears back into their ducts.

"I'm sorry," he said, hand still on my shoulder. "Don't run away from me."

Don't make things awkward, Jessie.

I pushed out a sharp breath and wiped my wet cheeks before turning to face him.

He draped an arm over me as we finished the short walk back to our riad.

Once we were back inside, he poured two beers he'd gotten from a licensed shop we'd stumbled upon just outside the touristy area. He had me wait outside in an effort to respect local norms and avoid drawing attention.

Sitting on our private terrace, we listened to the square from a distance. The awkward moment with Che was just that . . . a moment. Come and gone.

He enthusiastically told me about a blog he was reading—a British couple who'd moved to Marrakech and were documenting their experience. A lot of the places they mentioned were ones we had visited during our stay.

"You know, it could be a cool thing to try . . . move somewhere for a year. Live humbly, teach English, get involved in a completely new community."

It was the second time this trip he mentioned moving off the grid for a while. If he was seriously considering that, maybe moving to the U.S. wasn't that big of a stretch? "What would that mean for your job?" I asked.

He pulled his mouth to the side and shrugged. "I'd hand over my clients and step away. Everything would go on just the same without me. And when I came back, I'd pick up again."

"But what about the money?"

"I save. Live within my means. I'd be fine for a year, especially somewhere with a low cost of living."

I nodded, trying to picture it. How could he just walk away at his peak? From everything he'd built? To go do . . . what exactly?

"I read somewhere that the formula for happiness is quality of life minus envy," he said. "I think about that a lot."

I admired him for how intentionally he'd thought about happiness. "You're so smart." I meant it, but it came out thin.

"Smart? No. I just like to learn and think and to make an effort to understand the world. I never understood how some people . . . " He tilted his head, a strange smirk pulling at one side. "Are content not knowing things. Like, oh I don't know . . . who Che Guevara is."

What the hell?

I rolled my eyes. "Are you seriously bringing that up again? What is that supposed to mean?"

"I'm just surprised. He was an important revolutionary. And that t-shirt we saw? That image is arguably one of the most recognizable in the world."

"Well, guess what? I. Don't. Fucking. Care." My glass slammed the table harder than I meant it to. "I don't give a fuck about this guy, and I can assure you, he's *not* important." I threw up air quotes around the word important.

He went silent.

My rant continued. "I'm only human. I don't know about every topic under the sun. Sorry that I haven't explored forty countries, and you know what, Aidan? I don't want to. Sorry that I keep letting you down."

He rubbed his chin as the call to prayer from the nearby mosque filled the silence. I waited the couple of minutes until it ended, but it wasn't long enough.

"I'll try harder to hide what an idiot I am."

"Oh stop it, Jessica. That's not what I think."

"Really? Because it sure feels like it. Like you think I've been living under a rock."

"I was just surprised, that's all. I could give you a book about him if you want."

My hands slowly formed fists.

I took a deep breath. "Can we just drop it? Please?"

"Yes." The tight-lipped smile looked like it pained him. "Good idea."

We kissed, and just like that, we never again spoke of Che Guevara.

But that night, curled together on the sofa watching a movie, he got up before it ended and disappeared into the bedroom. When I followed him, he was already on his side, back to me, scrolling his phone.

He didn't acknowledge me. Didn't move when I climbed in beside him and didn't react when I touched his shoulder. I didn't ask if he was mad because the silence already answered.

He turned off the light.

I lay beside him, tears streaming silently down my face, into my hair. I tried to remember if I'd ever felt that small in an argument before but came up empty.

His phone screen lit the room for a few minutes—then went dark.

25

At the Marrakech airport, our carry-ons glided through the conveyor belt, but security barely glanced at us. After the virtually nonexistent check, we boarded the first of two flights back to Dublin without a hitch.

The layover was in Brussels. For seven hours. Three times longer than on the way over. It felt like more of a relationship test than the trip itself. I decided that at some point during our long wait, I'd ask what all the hot and cold had really been about.

Aidan went to get us coffee and breakfast while I stayed with our bags in the café. Flipping through my passport, I smiled at the stamps: Ireland, Morocco, and now Belgium. A year ago, I couldn't have pointed them out on a map. Now I not only knew where they were, but I had proof I'd been there. I was an explorer, an adventurer and now would forever have fodder for office icebreakers. A checklist began forming in my head.

I lived in Ireland for a TBD amount of time.

I drove a manual transmission through the Irish countryside and almost hit a sheep.

I watched a chicken get slaughtered in a busy medina—okay, maybe that one's not great icebreaker material.

I went to an authentic Moroccan hammam.

All were far more interesting than showing off my hyperextended arms.

I texted my parents and Lindsay an "I'm alive" update with a few carefully chosen photos—the ones that looked unmistakably Moroccan.

"I practically had to wrestle a guy for the last bacon and egg croissant. You're welcome, Missus."

I'd been craving protein after ten days of minimal meat. After seeing the chicken situation firsthand in the medina, we'd stuck mostly to lentils, chickpeas and olives.

"Speaking of wrestling . . . have you ever been in a fistfight?" I asked.

He blinked rapidly. "I'm a nearly thirty-three-year-old man. Yes, I've been in a fight."

I checked my imaginary watch. "Well, we've got six and a half hours. Spill it."

He laughed. "It wasn't chairs flying, WWE style like in films. Just one of those things that boils over fast."

I listened, eating my sandwich as if it were popcorn during an action movie.

"There was a group of us at McClennan's—some mates of mates I didn't know well. I'd just come back from Peru and was telling my friends about Machu Picchu. You know, the ancient civilization with llamas?"

"Yes, I'm familiar."

"So this guy—Jack, I think—cut me off and goes, 'Christ, mate, we get it. You travel. Big deal. Start a blog like the rest of the gap year twats.'"

"Ouch." I winced, ripping off the sharp corner of the croissant.

"Right? I hadn't even said that much. Wasn't bragging, just sharing. But it hit a nerve. I was proud of that trip, proud of what I'd seen. Proud of the physical stuff too—all the hiking we did." His jaw tightened. "With one sentence, he made me feel like some basic eejit showing off."

I could picture the whole thing unfolding. "So what'd you do?"

"I snapped. Said something snarky—can't remember what. He stood, someone tried to pull him back, and I went in. He shoved me, a pint glass smashed, sliced my arm." He pushed his sleeve, showing the scar.

"Ah, so that's where that's from. It's a battle scar."

"Something like that." He sipped his coffee. "It's stupid, but I hated feeling . . . ordinary. But now? Now I'd walk away." He reached for my hand. "Unless it involved you. If anyone ever touched you or even looked at you wrong—I'd take a thousand scars to protect you."

My heart had to be visibly dancing through my shirt.

A few moments passed before he asked, "So how many olives do you think we ate during the trip?"

I tapped my chin. "Let's see . . . every lunch and dinner came with a bowl. So . . . I'd say at least a hundred each?"

He puffed out his cheeks, eyes wide.

"Yeah. As much as I love olives, I don't want to look at another unless it's in a dirty martini."

"It's sexy you have a signature drink. Although, I think I've only seen you drink it once."

"They aren't an everyday drink. What's your signature drink?" I asked. "The only cocktail I've seen you drink was that fruity thing on our first date. Surely it can't be that?"

"Ah, the fuzzy navel." He smirked. "I picked it because I liked the name. Didn't know it'd be so sweet and come with fruit and a twisty straw."

"You ordered two more after."

"I had to. I invited you for cocktails. Couldn't exactly order a pint. I was nervous."

"You? Nervous?"

"Why do you think it took me so long to ask you out?"

"Honestly? I thought you were seeing someone else," I half teased.

"No. I couldn't get a read on you. Whether you wanted to go out. You were so focused on work, I thought maybe you wouldn't be interested. But when you sent that picture of the Coke bottle, it felt like an olive branch."

"Oh, don't mention olives," I said, frowning.

His voice softened. "So yes, I was nervous."

I felt lighter, warmer, hearing him say that. Meanwhile, I had spent half the trip reading tension as proof he didn't care.

"Were you ever nervous on this trip?" I asked.

A suspicious look. "So many questions today."

"Just giving you a taste of your own medicine."

He laughed. I liked this side of him. "Nineteen times. I was nervous nineteen times during the trip," he said with confidence.

"Go on."

"Three meals a day for six days—nervous each time about food poisoning."

"Fair."

"I was also nervous that first night in the medina. When we got separated."

That night felt like a lifetime ago. Exhaustion from the day of travel and overstimulation right before I witnessed my first chicken beheading. Then losing him in the crowd. He'd seemed completely unbothered when we reunited. Did I read it wrong? Was it all in my head?

"Gosh, I almost forgot about that," I lied.

"What do you think you'll remember most from the trip?"

"Besides the olives?" I grinned. "Probably the main square in Marrakech. The colors, the smells, the chaos. And waking up to the call to prayer. I got used to it."

He waited for more, but I wasn't going to share what I feared I'd actually remember. The off moments, the emotional whiplash. And, of course, the Che Guevara fight. It was my opportunity to mention it to him. But the moment passed.

Instead, we ate our food, drank our coffee, and checked our phones in near silence while I answered Lindsay and recorded a voice note asking what she, Jason and Cody were up to.

His eyes lifted from his screen. "So, she and her boyfriend, they're pretty serious, aye?"

"Yeah. I wouldn't be surprised if he proposes soon."

It was as if I'd announced a scandal. "What? Didn't they only start dating this year?"

"Yeah, so they've been together for seven, almost eight months. It wouldn't be unheard of. Plus she's twenty-nine, he's thirty-four with a kid. They know what they want."

Immersed in thought, he finally asked, "Have you ever been engaged?"

"No." I hesitated. "My only serious relationship was a little over four years, we met in college. I assumed we'd get married, but we never really talked about it."

It was the first time I didn't refer to Brad as a "friend" when talking to Aidan. Still, it was a half-truth. Brad had made it clear he wanted to get married, but I made it clear I wanted to be established in my career before getting engaged. Since I wasn't planning on being married until about age twenty-eight, we had time. I thought we had so much time.

So he waited to ask so he could conform to the timeline I'd laid out for myself, for us.

Yet there I was. In the Brussels Airport, days before my twenty-eighth birthday, heading back to Dublin, unmarried. The plan hadn't panned out, but I was increasingly okay with the alternative. Because it had Aidan in it.

"And what about after him?" he asked.

"Let's see . . . there were about two years between him and moving to Dublin. A few short relationships, nothing serious. I believe you know by the third month if it's working or not and to be honest, I never made it that far. I'd usually break things off closer to the three-week mark."

He tilted his head. *We'd* been together for three months. Almost four. Longer if you counted our prolonged pen pal phase.

"What about you?" I asked, unsure if I wanted to know the answer. "Ever been engaged?"

For a second, he chose his words. "No. But they all wanted it." He blew a raspberry. "At about the year to year and a half mark, they all start looking for reassurance. One even gave an ultimatum."

Ick crept in. Like Moroccan shopkeepers quoting insane prices before haggling down to a tenth of the original offer.

"If you weren't feeling it, why stay that long?"

"You're dead right," he agreed. "I should've ended things sooner. But I guess . . . I was . . . hopeful. Relationships have phases, right? I didn't want to walk away during an off patch and then miss out on something great."

It was a good answer. A great answer. Maybe it explained everything?

Aidan had been the one planning all of our dates, the trip, the gestures. He'd told me how he felt. He asked me to stay in Dublin. He said he was in "tricky" with me. He'd just said he'd get in a fight to protect me.

He went to grab something from the terminal shop. I stayed behind and opened my email. Townsend's message patiently waited for me.

After the heart-to-heart we'd had, I was ready to formalize my answer. The long layover had in fact been a relationship test.

I hit reply.

From: J.Dunhour@mcafeeconsulting.com
To: C.Townsend@mcafeeconsulting.com
Subject: Re: Checking in
Time: 10:05 a.m.

Hi Crawford,
Thank you for following up. After much consideration, I've decided not to join the Pioneer proposal team or pursue the promotion at this time. I'd like to stay in Dublin through the end of my contract and reassess from there. Thank you for your consideration.

I paused for a moment.

Aidan returned, holding a bag of Belgian chocolate.

"You didn't think I'd come to Belgium and not get any chocolate, did you?"

I smiled and finished the email.

Best,
Jessica

As my thumb hovered over the "Send" button, the red door of Aidan's parent's house flashed before me causing a warm smile.

I sent it.

26

We arrived back in Dublin late Sunday night, making Monday a rough return to reality. Thankfully, it was only a four-day work week as Lindsay and Jason were arriving early Friday morning. The timing couldn't have been better as we were ahead on the latest phase of Project Roadrunner, so the team was taking Friday off anyway. Aidan and I spent the week in our own apartments catching up on chores, work and sleep. We'd see each other when Lindsay and Jason arrived and celebrated my actual birthday in town.

I really thought I'd be settled by age twenty-eight . . . have a mortgage, a husband and a clear path to making Partner. Instead, just days before my birthday, I didn't own a home, wasn't married, and had just turned down the chance to make Associate Partner. I hadn't fully processed what it all meant, but deep down it was right. Because it was the path that led me to Aidan.

I began casually checking Daft.ie to assess the housing market and see what my savings could realistically get me in Dublin. Spoiler alert: it was a lot less space and a much older house for a lot more money. I researched whether I could even buy property before becoming an Irish citizen—which would take nearly five more years. Five years felt both comforting and terrifying.

The office felt different without Townsend. In his place was Patrick, an Irish partner, who now led the weekly status meetings and scrambled to get caught up. But it wasn't just Townsend who'd disappeared. So had my obsession for chasing his approval.

"Welcome back, Cinderella," Simon said, kissing both cheeks as we headed to the break room after the meeting. "I want all the trip deets, but first—did you get my text message? About Townsend? He bailed. Took a client in the States. Friday was his last day, and now we have this wet mop, Patrick, in his place."

"I know. He told me."

His brow arched in a way that screamed Botox was overdue.

I scanned the breakroom before whispering, "He called me the night before Morocco. National's mobilizing a team for a massive proposal . . . for Pioneer."

Simon squinted. "Why did he call you?"

"To offer me a spot on the team."

"SHUT. UP. You little minx!"

"I said no."

His jaw dropped.

"If I joined, I would have had to leave Ireland this week, maybe next. And I can't do that. Another shot to make Associate Partner will come around."

Simon stared. "Associate Partner? Wait . . . did Townsend offer you Associate Partner? Now?"

I nodded, bracing for impact. "I would've been presented to Pioneer as the Associate Partner on the account."

"Jess. You realize what that means, right?"

"I do." I smiled faintly, hoping it read as peace instead of regret.

"And what does Aidan say about all this?"

I hesitated. "You didn't tell him, did you?" He studied me, inspecting the corners of my mind with his blue eyes. "Oh my god. You're not secure in the relationship, are you? I knew it; knew he'd be like that."

I immediately felt defensive. "We're just back from a week in Morocco, for crying out loud. I'm secure and I've made my choice so let's drop it."

He nodded and turned his focus to preparing an espresso. "So . . . I'm thinking of getting a new outfit for your birthday this Saturday."

With a coffee in hand, we headed back to our desks, but his chatter about a London show with Merrick the following weekend blurred into background noise. Instead I pictured Aidan's reaction if he knew I'd passed on the promotion. Did he even know how much I wanted it?

Did I want him to know? I wanted him to know everything—except the things that might scare him away.

Raya's blonde ponytail bee-bopped in my peripherals, triggering a full-body eye roll.

"Jessica!" came the cheerful voice. She managed to make the olive tweed coat and matching skirt look trendy and not at all geriatric. "I've been out on client site for ages. How was your vacation?"

"It was good, thanks," I said, cautiously.

"Maybe we could grab lunch this week?"

In the six months that we'd been in Dublin, she never once asked me to lunch. "Uh, yeah, sure. That'd be great." I leaned in closer. "Is everything okay?"

"Everything is fantastic." She beamed like an influencer with great lighting. "I just spoke to Townsend. It was only 6 a.m. in America but he needed to talk—he asked me to join him on the Pioneer proposal! I leave Ireland next week."

Of course he'd give it to her. Didn't even try to talk me out of saying no. Just moved on. They say everyone is replaceable in the corporate world, but hot damn. It hadn't even been twenty-four hours since I turned it down.

I morphed my face from confusion to delight. "Wow, Raya, that's incredible. Congratulations." I wanted to mean it, but I couldn't find it in me.

"Thanks! And Townsend said if we win, I could make Associate Partner in a year. Can you believe it?"

Could make. In a *year*.

I would've been presented as Associate Partner now. So although he replaced me while my body was still warm, he clearly had more confidence in me. That had to count for something.

"I really can't believe it. What an amazing opportunity." I forced a smile.

"I really think I'm ready." Raya lowered her voice and leaned in. "Townsend didn't give details, but it sounded like someone pulled out for personal reasons. Probably someone who couldn't commit to the travel." She rolled her eyes. "Anyway. Right place, right time, I guess."

"It's all about the timing," I said through clenched teeth.

"But if you hear anything, tell me. I'm dying to know who it was. And I should probably thank them." She chuckled to herself.

"There's no need for that. You earned it, Raya. Seriously, congratulations."

She looked pleased, maybe even startled. "Thanks. And don't worry, Jess, your time will come. I'll put in a good word with Townsend."

I widened my eyes in thanks.

"Okay, I gotta run. So much to wrap up this week." She winked and glided off.

"What about lunch?" I called after the sassy, bouncing ponytail. The hallway was already empty.

27

At 6 a.m. on Friday, Lindsay texted updates from the cab. When I received, "Turning onto Belgrave," I ran outside.

The cab hadn't fully stopped before she leaped out and tackled me in a hug while Jason took far too long fiddling with the payment.

We jumped around like little kids on a sugar high shouting about how excited we were for the weekend and how it was going to be the best time.

Jason finally emerged, looking like a model on a yacht campaign—tall, tan, effortlessly stylish—lugging one oversized suitcase and a carry-on. I was fairly confident on which one was whose. Their hypothetical future children would be annoyingly good looking, if only Lindsay wanted any.

I showed the sleepy couple the courtyard and mentioned the rooftop that I hadn't tried before leading them into my ground floor nest.

I dramatically raised my arms in a violà fashion. "Welcome to my little flat." I never called it a flat in normal conversation but had to play up the European-ness of it all because people expect that when they visit somewhere new.

"It's fabulous," Lindsay said. "You've really made it your own—the paint, the décor. Is this a new set of curtains?"

"It's very European and tasteful. But Jessica, are you sure we shouldn't get a hotel? I'd be happy to get a room so you ladies can stay together and I don't cramp your style."

"Nonsense. I only get you guys for a few days, so I want every minute. I know we're all a little old for couch surfing, but this flowery beauty pulls out so it's basically a guest bedroom."

"It's perfect, Jess, really." She gave Jason a knowing look and he smiled back, genuine and easy. An entire conversation passed between them in a second, the way two people who really know each other can do. But did they really know each other?

I performed the Irish tea making ritual Orla had taught me, counting the circular stirs aloud while Lindsay watched wearily. They showered off the plane germs while I drew the curtains and prepared the sofa, laying eye masks on their pillows and setting two glasses of water on the mismatched coffee table. They'd nap and restart their day around 10 a.m., Dublin time.

I went to my neighborhood Insomnia for a cappuccino and some work while they rested. Since Aidan and I hadn't seen each other all week, I called him. No answer, but he followed up with a text.

Aidan: *Hey, I'm in a meeting. Everything okay?*

Me: *Yes. Just calling to say hi. Lindsay and Jason arrived. Want to meet us for drinks tonight?*

Aidan: *Maybe. I'm wrecked from this week so let's see closer to.*

I don't know what I was expecting but it was not that. But he'd be with us the next day for my birthday and again on Sunday when he'd drive the four of us to Howth for a relaxing day in the seaside town.

The brief exchange consumed my thoughts the entire walk home.

Was it unfair to expect more? Or was this what a comfortable relation-ship looked like?

Inside, Jason was chasing a giggling Lindsay until she surrendered onto the floral sofa and succumbed to tickle torture.

"We're ready to see the city and quench our thirst with a Guinness," Jason said.

They were so adorable together. But my chest tightened wondering whether or not Aidan would show up. I coached myself that it would be fine either way.

Plus, we'd see him the next day.

***

After a slow, easy day of sightseeing, we ended in a traditional pub. Warmth and cheer hit the moment we pushed through McClennan's narrow saloon doors. It was the same place where Aidan got the scar on his arm. A swoony smile tugged at my mouth remembering his words . . . *I'd take a thousand scars to protect you.*

We waded through the congestion at the entrance as Lindsay's neck craned in a one-eighty. "I still can't believe we're in Dublin!" Lindsay shouted with the enthusiasm you'd expect from a Vegas bachelorette weekend. Jason spotted a corner high-top and pounced with catlike reflexes. As we settled into our seats. I let myself savor the moment—my best friend and her boyfriend, in my neighborhood, my local pub. In Dublin.

"This is exactly how I pictured it," Lindsay said. "Dark, cozy, lively, and . . . damp."

"You get used to the damp. I've started embracing frizzy hair."

Her entire face screamed, "Ew."

I sent Aidan our location just as the drinks I ordered landed with loud clanks.

Knowing Lindsay hates beer, but would want to try a Guinness in Dublin, I pushed a half pint of the iconic beer *and* a gin and tonic in her direction.

We clanked our glasses and said, "Sláinte" which I explained meant *to your health* and not actually *cheers*. Jason closed his eyes, savoring the first sip of creamy, malty bitterness. "That," he said, wiping the foam from his lip, "is Ireland in a glass." Lindsay's eyes widened in acceptance of her small sip. I'd begun to like Guinness, but it stayed firmly in my two drink rule that I admittedly had sometimes bent. "Hey," Lindsay blurted. "Did you know Brad and his girlfriend broke up?"

My heart skipped at his name before my mind could catch up.

"Oh?" A sip of Guinness to conceal my interest.

"Yeah, I noticed he had been really quiet on social media lately so I kind of figured something happened. Then I ran into him at Target when I was getting stuff for the trip."

"Wow, they were together for what? Two years?"

She shrugged. "Something like that. He said they broke up earlier in the year, so I don't think it's fresh. But I didn't want to pry."

My chin dropped and eyes shot up. "Since when?"

"Since I came into the picture," Jason leaned in to tease. Lindsay laughed and pushed him away.

"That too, but seriously, we were close when you guys dated, and I still saw him sometimes around after the breakup, but I'm *your* friend. I lost the right to ask him about his love life when you took custody of me in the divorce."

"Fair. Well, I hope he's okay. He sent me a text when I first moved here, but that was six months ago now." I wondered if he was single when he sent it.

"He'll always love you," she said casually.

Feeling a need to change the subject, I asked them about their flight.

After they gushed about the flight attendant that hooked them up with extra drinks and recounted their taxi ride to my apartment as if it were a scene from a thriller.

Lindsay asked what my favorite things about living in Dublin were. I fished for them, trying to compare to what I'd said to Aidan in Phoenix Park the day we met. Back when I said love was a tricky word.

"Let's see . . . I'm loving not having a car. I walk, cycle or take the light rail everywhere. The trench has really earned its keep."

"Do you still remember how to drive?" she asked as a memory of Aidan pounding the center console flashed in my head.

"I don't think you lose it, but it'll probably feel weird being back on that side of the road at first."

"What's next?"

"This," I gestured around. "And Orla and Simon, who you'll meet tomorrow. Oh, and I'm a converted tea drinker—as long as it's Barry's and properly made."

"Do I hint a tiny Irish accent there?" Jason asked.

"No, no, not an accent but maybe an inflection?" I offered.

Lindsay switched to the gin and tonic. "You better lose that when you come back home."

When you come back *home.*

I'd eventually tell Lindsay about passing up the promotion. I didn't want to drop that bomb right when they arrived. She had joked about me finding an Irish farmer and staying here, but something told me she wouldn't be excited about this.

Jason crossed his arms and leaned onto the table. "And what is your return home plan? Linds mentioned your project wraps up at the end of the year?"

How diplomatic of him to dodge the real question: what will become of you and Aidan?

The three man band in the opposite, back corner announced a fifteen minute break. I could have brushed it off with "We'll see what happens" or say the project might get extended so I could avoid potential judgment, or I could tell the truth and have my best friend share in the weight of the decision and the excitement.

I set my glass down on the sticky wooden tabletop.

Lindsay blinked a few times to refocus. "What?"

"I'm going to extend my visa and stay here longer to . . . see where things go."

They both processed for a beat before confusion, and ultimately, excitement bloomed in their faces.

"I knew you'd love it here! Jess, that's amazing and does staying longer help to better position you for the Partner track? I bet your boss is so impressed," she rambled with authentic excitement.

"Umm. About the Partner track." I lifted the pint glass again. "I was offered Associate Partner . . ."

With eyes wide, she slammed both hands down, straddling the glass. "Shut up! And you didn't tell me?"

"It literally happened last week, the day before we left for Morocco."

"We need champagne. Do they sell champagne here?"

"Linds, listen to me—"

"Will you get a bottle, honey? Prosecco will work if that's all they have," she said to Jason.

"I didn't take it." It was louder than expected. Jason sat back down upon hearing there was no cause for bubbles.

"The promotion was contingent on leaving Ireland in a couple of weeks to go work on a big proposal in Atlanta. I'm not ready to leave."

"Jessie . . ."

"I know." My fingers expanded, signaling to stop.

"Jessie."

My nose tingled at the tone of her voice, the same way it did when my dad would say he was disappointed in me. "I know. I know," I managed.

"I mean, that was the whole thing . . . to get on the Partner track."

She didn't sound sarcastic, just blunt.

"I got on Townsend's radar. Six months ago, he didn't even know I existed, and now he asked me to be an Associate Partner alongside him on the biggest proposal in our firm's history."

Jason glanced between us, neutral, like someone watching a tennis match.

"I'm going to go get us another round," he said, even though we were barely halfway through the first round. The table wobbled, almost spilling beer as he left.

"And let's just say you had a change of heart—can you undo this? Can you take it back?" she asked, her tone sharper with Jason gone.

"No. They gave it to someone else. To Raya. She leaves Ireland next week."

"What did Aidan say about it? Was he supportive of you giving up your career for him?"

"Okay, first of all, I didn't give up my career for him. Second of all . . ." I hesitated a fraction too long. "He didn't say anything because I didn't tell him. I wanted it to be my decision and mine alone."

She searched my face.

"I didn't hide it," I added, even though that *was* what I'd done. "I'll tell him when it feels right, when we feel real. I don't want it to be a test or some kind of leverage."

"You need to tell him," she said. "Is he worth throwing the promotion away if you can't even tell him about this?" The question lingered like the scent of pan fried salmon. Almost backtracking, she added, "Tell me why you want to stay. Why is this the right choice?"

I imagined Simon's voice saying "Go!" after her question. It triggered an anxiety reflex just as it did when he made me convince a nonexistent audience that squirrels are "fantastic."

Is this the flight or fight reflex people talk about?

I needed to fight to defend my decision to Lindsay. And to myself.

Concealing my breath, I looked her in the eye and pleaded my case.

"Aidan makes me feel . . . he makes me feel like a whole new person and also the same person that was always there, hiding." I let out an easy breath and blinked away the tears that were forming. "He makes me want more out of life. Until now, I hadn't really wanted anything, not really. It's true I wanted this promotion, and I still do, but what I really want is . . . something *more*. It sounds stupid and cliché, but then it happened to me. Aidan happened." And another breath, this one longer. I debated taking another sip of the headless Guinness but didn't want to lose my train of thought.

"Aidan's not perfect." My head shook. "Far from it. He goes cold too often and sometimes for reasons I don't understand. He's obsessed with travel and learning new things, almost to a fault. But it's the realest thing

I've ever felt, and for the first time in my life, fighting the rat race to make Partner seems so . . . trivial."

Lindsay quietly held my gaze until it was uncomfortable. She was the one to break away first.

"Okay," she said. And with one sharp nod of her head, she agreed with all that I had laid bare. "Then you need to tell him what you did. Tonight."

Returning the firm nod, I said, "I will."

"Good." The word marked the end of the discussion and with it, Jason returned along with the band. I gulped half of the new pint in one go without toasting first. Mr. Perfect filled the awkwardness with tales of his quest in obtaining the latest round. One guy serenaded him, and another launched into a discussion about American politics as soon as he heard his accent. He bought Jason his pint, so in addition to being a handsome perfect doctor, he was also a diplomat.

Before long we were dancing in our stools and clapping to the quick sounds of the fiddle. I still couldn't recognize with any certainty which instruments were playing from sounds alone, but I was fairly confident there was a fiddle. The whole pub had joined in clapping, and many started jumping and dancing or some combination of the two. Not trusting my glass to sustain the rumbling on our handicapped table, I held it in my right and pounded the table with my left.

Every time it sounded like the song would end, they found a way to extend it. At one point, I thought it'd simply never end, and we'd stay in that moment forever.

But it did end. It always ends.

And afterward, the whole joint roared before the next song kicked off.

Jason pulled Lindsay into him for a kiss. When they pulled away, she grabbed his face and reciprocated.

Had Aidan and I ever kissed like that in public?

Stop it.

As if summoning him with thoughts, "Tiny Shorts" flashed on my phone with a picture of us and a donkey in Morocco.

He was coming. My shoulders dropped and lips raised.

"It's Aidan," I mouthed, heading outside where I'd be able to hear. He was probably trying to find parking after insisting on driving instead of taking the Luas.

"Hey, stranger," I answered, still buzzing from the song. "Are you close?"

"Hey there, Jessica. Ah, how . . . how are you? Are your friends doing okay?" Through the noise of the bar, I could still hear that his voice was stiff.

Jessica?

Your friends?

"Yeah, they're good. I'm good. Everyone's good. Are you good?"

A long pause filled the air as I stepped through the saloon doors and into the cool, damp air.

"Jessica. I... I need to talk to you."

The pit grew heavier, sinking lower and lower.

Was it his family? Did something happen at work? Was he in an accident? Shit. Was he in jail?

"Okay. What's going on?" I asked.

"Jessica. I, uh . . . I don't want to continue this relationship."

28

I'd been sucker punched.

In place of the pit was something worse.

The world around me moved in a warped blur. I reached for a sign-post. Then the spinning began—faster and faster. Trapped inside a kaleidoscope, the colorful doors of Dublin bled into one another. Then, darkness.

Was I going to pass out?

No, no, no, no, no, no, no. Breathe.

His words echoed as I slowly regained composure.

Was he really breaking up with me? *Now?* After everything? After Morocco?

With Lindsay and Jason visiting? My birthday?

Oh no.

The promotion.

No, no, no. This wasn't happening. We made plans. *He* made plans.

There had to be a mistake.

The silence was suffocating, but there were no words.

I replayed Morocco, and like muscle memory, the pit in my stomach returned.

Was there a specific moment? The lack of passion? Che?

Did I even want to know?

It was too much. Too many questions, too many emotions, too many unknowns.

"It's just that I feel . . ." He let out a heavy sigh. "I don't know, I feel . . . indifferent."

Indifferent?

Indifferent?

But *he* asked me to stay in Dublin. *He* took me to Morocco for my birthday. *He* said he was in tricky with me. *He* said he'd fight someone for me. How could it have changed so fast?

Did I imagine it? Make it out to be more than it was?

My thumb covered the microphone as I gasped for air.

How could I ask any of it without sounding desperate? Did the answers even matter?

Yes. Yes, they matter. I matter. We matter.

Mattered.

How could we be a past tense?

He exhaled again, sharp this time. "I should be excited to meet your friends and to go to your party tomorrow but . . . I don't know. I'm just not. And that's not fair to you."

The crack in my chest deepened as he explained to me the meaning of the word indifferent.

"I thought about going through with meeting them this weekend but dropping this after they left would've been much worse. I couldn't do that to you."

What the fuck?

"Jessica?" he asked, testing the connection. "Can you say something?"

What could I possibly say? Simon didn't exactly cover break ups in his lessons.

But he *had* covered what to do when things were going badly in a pitch. Keep it short. Keep it neutral. Like salting food—you can always add more later, but you can't take it back.

Townsend had said something similar on my first day in the Dublin office: the shortest answers are usually the strongest ones.

All signs pointed to short and sweet.

The inhale stung. "Well . . . I'm sad to hear this, but . . ." I willed my voice to keep from breaking. "I can't make you feel something you don't. Thanks for being honest."

I squeezed my eyes shut and covered the receiver so he wouldn't hear me sniffle. "Goodbye, Aidan."

Before I ended the call, he cut in. "Ah, Jesus, Jessica. Look—I wanted it to work, I really did. We had fun together, and I think you're a lovely girl. But you're feeling something more than I am."

My eyes widened as the sadness tipped into anger.

"Did you know before Morocco? Or was it the trip that changed things?" I asked.

"Uh . . . I-I think it started before we left. Then in Morocco, I kept going back and forth."

No shit you did.

"And then when we were at the airport, in Brussels, you said that after a few months, you might not know if something's right . . . but you know when it's not." He paused. "That was when I knew."

So I handed him the ammunition *and* the gun. What poetic fucking irony.

"Got it. Just text me whatever I owe you for my half of the trip, and I'll get it to you. Goodbye, Aidan."

"Jessica, wait—" It was *his* voice that cracked. "I want you to know . . . I feel sad. I don't feel relieved or anything."

Oh my god. Stop.

"Goodbye, Aidan."

"I hope you have fun with your friends and enjoy the rest of your time in Ireland."

The rest of my time in Ireland?

What was that supposed to look like now?

I hung up before he could hear me cry.

29

AFTER THE SHAME OF breaking the news to Lindsay and Jason, I had to endure the awkward stroll back to my apartment. They tried to console me and say all the right things. Jason insisted on wrestling with the pull out flower sofa and making the bed for them. Lindsay offered to stay in my bed with me, but I declined, preferring to sulk alone.

In bed, I rehashed every little moment between us. Could I have been funnier? More open? More interesting? Scrutinizing every conversation, every text, I searched for what I could've done or said differently.

Then I replayed the promotion call from Townsend, wondering how I could have handled *that* differently too. I was an idiot for not telling Aidan about it right away and a bigger idiot for turning it down.

Finally, I moved on to the break up call for the last round of torture.

Indifferent.

You're feeling more than I am.

It was like running on an emotional treadmill—repetitive and exhausting. I cried as quietly as I could until succumbing to a restless sleep.

I woke the next morning with the puffiness of having had bottomless dirty martinis the night before. How I wished that had been the case.

I reached for my phone, hoping for a missed call or a text from Aidan. Dread flooded in when I saw a swarm of banner messages wishing me a happy birthday. The absolute last thing in the world I wanted to do that day was celebrate.

As I scrolled, none were from Aidan, but one certainly caught my eye.

Brad: *Happy Birthday to the Stones' biggest fan! Hope it's a great one and hope you're loving Dublin.*

Brad: *P.S. am I the first official birthday wish? At least in the EST time zone?*

He remembered. And seeing it came through at 5:01 a.m. meant that he'd sent it at 12:01 a.m. his time. When we were together, we'd always make sure to be the first to wish each other a happy birthday. Each year since we broke up, he continued to do it. I did not.

There was a light tap at the door before Lindsay let herself in.

"I bring caffeine and carbs for the birthday girl," she announced like they were peace offerings. "Jason went to the little bakery on the main street. Said it was really cute but that they don't use cream here in their coffee? And a regular coffee is called an Americano?"

"Yeah, milk instead of cream," I said flatly, resisting the urge to explain that an Americano is espresso and hot water, and that the next bakery down does have filtered coffee like what she's used to. "Thanks."

"How you feeling?" She rubbed my upper back the way my dad would when I was upset.

"Heartbroken." My eyes fixated on a chipped piece of paint in the corner.

"I know. I hate that you're going through this, and on today of all days. But I'm glad I'm here."

How did that chip get there? Why weren't there others near it?

"Jess, I think we should still do dinner tonight as planned."

"No. I don't want to go anywhere." I sounded like a child, but it was true.

"Seriously, don't let this prick completely ruin your day. Don't give him that power over you. Your friends still want to celebrate you, and we don't have to mention him at all."

"I'm not going," I said, colder.

"Jess—"

"The reservations are at Sophie's under my name. Please cancel them and let Simon and Orla know. You can find them easily on social media. You and Jason go out tonight without me."

"No, I'm not doing that," she said.

"Fine, then don't. I'm still not going." I turned to the other side, facing the drawn curtains, searching for another chip in the paint on that wall.

"Come on, don't do this."

"Please get out."

"Jess, I—"

"Get out!" The words stung the moment they left my mouth.

Without another word, she left the room.

***

I don't know how long I'd been asleep when another knock at my bedroom door woke me. Why couldn't she just leave me alone? Why didn't I let them just get a hotel?

Jason stepped in, holding a glass of water, and set it on my nightstand.

"Jessica," he said, sitting on the corner of the bed. "I know we don't know each other well yet, but I'm very sorry this is happening." I sniffled quietly. "I want to tell you something if that's okay? Then I'll leave you alone."

I nodded, sniffling again.

"There was this one night, maybe a couple months after Lindz and I started dating, and I asked who her role model was. Without hesitation, she said it was you."

I bit my lip. Me? A role model to Lindsay? Why?

"Said you always do what you say you're going to do—usually even bigger and quicker than you initially planned. Said everything you do is intentional, and she wished she could be more like that." He paused. "And that everything she's gone through with her mom, you were always her safe place. Someone she could rely on."

I squeezed my eyes shut, my whole face tightening, trying to keep the tears at bay.

"Lindz canceled the reservation and notified your friends like you asked, but Jess . . . you *are* special and deserve to be celebrated on your birthday."

The mattress bounced as he stood to leave.

"Fine," I managed. At the doorway, he turned to face me. "Let's do something for my birthday. Not Sophie's—something small. And easy."

"We've got you covered." He winked. "In fact, we don't even need to leave. Get ready and come outside in an hour."

I allowed myself twenty more minutes of sulking before dragging myself out of bed. Eyedrops, face slaps, some jade roller thing I rarely used but hoped it would work some magic and make me glow. I would conceal the hurt with everything I owned from the Boots pharmacy. Unsure what I was actually dressing for, I went with a classic pairing of high-waisted jeans and a cropped black mock-neck sweater.

I didn't know what I expected when I stepped out of my room, but it wasn't emptiness.

No Simon and Orla. No Lindsay and Jason. No drinks, no music.

What the hell?

Jason said we wouldn't be leaving the apartment.

Aha. I audibly laughed. He said to come *outside* in an hour. Marching through the corridor, I burst through the main door into the chilly air outside.

Not a soul in the courtyard behind the building. Muffled music and laughter drifted from somewhere nearby. I ran to the front of the building.

Nothing.

"Jessie, look up!" someone shouted.

Lindsay's head popped over the brick edge of the rooftop.

"I've never been up there!" Leave it to Lindsay to baptize my rooftop on day two.

"Just take the stairs all the way," she called.

It was only four stories, but I was out of breath when the small group shouted, "Happy Birthday!" Orla's boyfriend Gearóid handed me a plastic flute of bubbles as his other half smacked my butt.

"We'll discuss at another time, but sweetest god, what a knobhead he is," Orla said, leaning into my shoulder.

A small, grateful smile formed. Lindsay must have told her and Simon about the break up when she called to cancel the original plans.

Green and pink balloons drifted and knocked into each other in the wind. Lindsay explained that she handled snacks and decorating. Jason had been in charge of drinks and the folding table. He'd also borrowed a cooler and folding chairs from the neighbors a few Georgian doors down. In exchange for the party gear, he invited them. Their names were

Dermot and Sarah, about mid-forties, childfree by choice and they were planning to sell within the next year to move outside the city for more space. Among the places they'd been considering were Bray and Dún Laoghaire. Hearing the places Aidan had once talked about felt like a stab in the stomach. Besides that, they were lovely, and I wished I'd made more of an effort to meet my neighbors sooner.

When I reached Simon, he held out a rectangular bag with wine and an obnoxiously bright green t-shirt that read, "Kiss me, I'm half Irish" stuffed inside.

A breathy laugh and eye roll escaped. "You saw this and thought, yes, now *that's* Jessica?" I asked.

"Just wanted to make you smile, Cinderella." He winked and pulled me in for a hug which, with my boots on, put his head against my chest. It felt like I was consoling him instead of the other way around.

"Your friend, who by the way has the most gorgeous head of red hair, said the colors would be green and pink so . . . Rosé and a tourist shirt it is."

"Thank you, Simon."

We stayed out on the rooftop a little past midnight, which of course Simon commented on. Besides Orla's "knobhead" comment, no one mentioned Aidan or the break up. But that didn't stop him from occupying every crevice of my mind for every second of the night.

30

The next morning, I again clamored for my phone at the first hint of daylight, hoping for a message from Aidan. Ideally one saying he'd made a mistake. I'd settle for a belated happy birthday message. Anything that would give me an excuse to respond.

But there were no messages. It wasn't a mistake.

I had no clue what to do with Jason and Lindsay. The old plan had been for Aidan to take the four of us to Howth. We could still take the train for a scenic day trip, but it was the last thing in the world I wanted to do. What a strange feeling—to look forward to something for so long, only to have it arrive and feel completely wrong. I hated myself for wishing Lindsay and Jason weren't there, but I wanted to be alone. Instead, I'd have to entertain. Especially after I'd neglected them the entire day before, and they repaid my rudeness by throwing me a rooftop birthday party.

I braced myself for a day of pretending to be a cheerful little tour guide and wandered into the living room. Lindsay handed me a coffee, and I asked if they wanted to go out for brunch.

"There's not enough time. Taxi's coming in forty-five minutes for you ladies," Jason said.

"Huh? A taxi? We don't need a taxi to get around the city. And what do you mean *you ladies*? What about you?" I asked.

"You two need a day to rekindle, so you have massage packages at The Merrion Spa. The taxi is just to make sure you actually make it on time."

My eyes widened. "What about you?"

"One of my old college buddies has an uncle in Blackrock. He got us a tee time at a course I've been dying to play."

"Golfing in Ireland is a huge bucket list item for him," Lindsay said, handing me a toasted bagel with butter. I recalled when she asked if Aidan would golf with Jason. Turns out I was right . . . he wouldn't. "So, everyone's happy!" she exclaimed.

My lips twitched and eyes dropped to my bagel.

"Well, you know what I mean. As happy as can be," she corrected softly. "And it will give us a chance to talk about . . . everything."

Great. I didn't want to talk about Aidan and wasn't sure if I ever would. But I felt like I owed it to her. Like being there for me mattered more to her.

"Sure," I said. "I'd like that."

***

After our massages, we sipped champagne side by side in pedicure chairs. Aidan never left my thoughts, but I forced myself to bottle it up so I wouldn't ruin the precious little time I had with Lindsay before they left the next day.

She flinched every time the nail technician touched the blisters on the balls of her feet. I recalled her mentioning her Louboutin's hadn't stretched enough but hadn't realized how much they'd torn her up.

"How ya feeling?" she asked—the inevitable question.

I sighed. "Confused. Deceived. Heartbroken. And on top of it all, I'm sick about giving up the promotion. And to Raya." I scrunched my face. "I would've been the youngest Associate Partner in the history of our office. A full two years ahead of my master plan to make it by thirty."

"You literally turned it down a week ago. I'm sure if you talk to your boss and tell him you changed your mind, he'd want you instead of Raya."

"I didn't turn down a muffin; I turned down the biggest opportunity of my career. The head of the entire company went out on a limb for me, and I rejected him."

"Okay, so maybe *that* moment passed. But you'd have to think pretty low of yourself to believe a similar, or better, opportunity won't come around again." She flinched again, asking the woman across the basin to skip the callus scrub completely. "And don't say I don't understand your job. It's a universal truth that something better always comes around."

"Yeah, you're probably right."

"Call your boss on Monday. Tell him you made a mistake, and you still want to work on the proposal, even if the promotion's off the table. Even if you have to work under this Raya person."

I couldn't answer, couldn't look at her.

"Wait. Do you want to stay in Ireland?"

We held eye contact for a beat too long. I looked away.

"Oh my god." She sat up straight in the oversized pleather chair, turning toward me. "You think you and Aidan might get back together, don't you?"

I didn't want to have this conversation. I didn't know what I wanted.

"Maybe a little of both? Maybe we could get back together? And even if not, maybe I want to stay anyway?" Of course the thought had crossed my mind. I'd even considered asking the neighbors from my birthday party how much they wanted for their place. At least then I'd get a Georgian door.

She leaned over and placed a hand on mine. "Jessie, this was inevitable. Deep down, you probably knew it all along. Remember the first day you met him at that race? You said he seemed judgy. Then he dicked you around for a month before asking you out. Simon didn't like him in the beginning. I'm not saying he didn't like you, Jess, but I think there were red flags you chose to ignore."

I scoffed.

"It shouldn't be that hard in the beginning," she continued. "Honestly? I think he gets off on making girls fall for him, playing the intellectual, then pulling away before they *really* get to know him."

"You know," I said, voice sharp and clear as crystal, "this is rich coming from the woman pretending that dating a man with a child is no big deal."

"Excuse me?"

"Come on, Lindz. You don't like kids, and you certainly don't want any of your own." Confrontation felt so foreign. My body reacted the exact same way it had when I lashed out at Aidan about Che Guevara. "You had no problem telling me to talk to Aidan about the promotion, no problem telling me to talk to my boss Monday to reverse it—as if those are easy discussions. But yet, you've been with Jason for what, seven? Eight months? When did you tell him you don't want kids?"

It was her turn to scoff and look away.

"Does he know you broke out in hives when you were alone with his son?"

Her mouth fell open like I'd betrayed her.

"At least when I kept the promotion from Aidan, I knew what I wanted. Can you say the same thing? Do you know what you want? Do you want to be Cody's stepmother? Because if you marry Jason, that's what you'll be. Forever."

The nail techs had been chatting quietly in another language but went silent as we started bickering.

"Say something," I demanded, knowing I'd crossed a line.

"Fine. I think Aidan just wasn't that into you," she deadpanned.

I blinked, confused. Processing.

When it hit me, I laughed. Hard.

She joined in and we both cackled until tears fell.

"You are such a bitch," I wheezed between breaths.

"Correction," she heaved. "A kid-hating bitch."

I thought I might pee my pants. God, it felt good to laugh.

"Okay, okay, let's be serious for one minute." I struggled through the gasps.

Pushing air through pursed lips, I tried to reset. "I'm not ready to talk to Townsend because I don't know what the plan is yet. I don't know if I want to stay in Ireland without Aidan and without Townsend. And soon, Simon will go back to London. I still have to wrap up Project Roadrunner—that's the project I came here for—but it's nearly finished. Then they'll fill my schedule with Irish clients because I did ask for a visa extension. I need to figure out what it all means for my career."

The color being painted on my toes looked darker and more brown than it had in the bottle. My plan was for more of a purply-maroon, especially since we'd just tipped into November.

"Do you like it?" my nail tech asked, finishing the first coat.

I didn't.

"Yes, thank you," I said.

"I should have explained it better," I said. "But it's a lot to process. And it's not just Aidan and my career. I miss you, I miss my family. I want to settle down but I don't even know what that means anymore."

"I'm proud of you, Jessie."

"Also, who are you with this dark polish? I've only ever seen you in nudes and dusty pinks. You're a changed woman!"

Another quiet laugh slipped out. With the second coat, the color was warming on me. "Only on my toes and because I'll be wearing boots every day. Fingers are getting this." I presented a tiny pale pink bottle.

Her toes were getting painted a brighter shade, closer to what I'd originally wanted.

"Okay," I said. "Your turn. Tell me about Cody."

There's a long sigh. "He's so sweet. He really is the best little boy, not that I have any to compare to. But the weekends Jason has him, I try to give them their space, so I don't really know him that well."

"But you love Jason?"

"With all my heart. It's real and I don't want to mess it up."

"But at some point, you need to talk about what your role will look like with Cody. Will you be 'Daddy's special friend' forever? Or do you help raise him? Cook for him, clean up after him, help with homework, bedtime, school runs—"

"Okay, yes, I get it." She placed a hand to her chest, steadying her breath.

"And if you get married . . . does he want more kids? You'll need to talk about that. Or have you already?"

Her lips pulled to the side. "Not exactly. But I will. When the time is right. Definitely not while we're on this trip." Her tone said the topic was closed.

Our toes dried on the basin, and maybe it was the second glass of champagne thinking, but I actually preferred my brownish-red color to the one I originally wanted.

31

The taxi carrying Lindsay and Jason disappeared around the corner, and with it, my reason for holding my shit together. The three days they'd spent with me felt more like three weeks—not because I was ungrateful for their visit, but because I'd been counting down the hours until I could be alone.

I thought about calling out sick. I'd never called out of work. Even as a child, the only time I missed school was when I had pneumonia. But after burning through a week of vacation days for Morocco and with the office giving us the previous Friday off, it felt like an overstep to take another day.

Determined not to be the girl who skipped work because her boyfriend broke up with her, I painted on mascara and a lip, and went in.

By the time I reached the office, Lindsay had already texted.

Lindsay: *Stone wall—1, rental car—0.*

The selfie that followed showed her making a cartoonish "uh-oh" face while Jason crouched to inspect a very visible scrape. Even their mishaps looked like adventures. Almost instantly, my smile faded, and the ache returned. The ache of reality. Loneliness.

It was 9:15 a.m. but the floor was quiet. Simon was in the London office, Orla was at the client site, and most of the Irish staff worked remote on Mondays. Perfect. I didn't want to see anyone, least of all Raya. We never did go out for lunch together, proving her "invite" was just an excuse to rub the Pioneer proposal in my face. I wasn't sure what day she was flying back to America, but hopefully she'd already left.

I hung my coat, dropped my bag, and headed for the breakroom. I filled the kettle and stood frozen waiting for it to hiss and ding to life. My mind drifted to the first time Aidan emailed me. The flutter in my chest felt fresh, as if it were happening now in real time instead of in a wishful memory.

Back at my desk, I logged into email and searched for client files. Typing nothing but the letter "M" into the search box brought up *Aidan McGovern*. My laptop hadn't gotten the memo my heart had sent. I wondered how long it would take before autofill forgot his name, the way I wanted to. I opened Spotify, swiping past the playlist we'd made together and all the others that reminded me of him. I landed on "Country Gold." He despised country music, so it was safe territory.

At the start of track three, a screeching, "Hiya there!" cut through my ear buds.

I jumped, sending one of them from my ear to the floor. Patrick—Townsend's replacement and therefore my new boss—was hovering beside my desk. The definition of average in every sense of the word—height, looks, suit.

"Sorry, I didn't see anyone when I came from making tea. Uh, good morning," I said, pasting on professionalism.

"It's a bit of a rough one out there, isn't it?" he said, hands fidgeting. "I swear, the rain this year has become absolutely dreadful, just dreadful."

Oh god. No. Please. Not meaningless weather chat with this dodo bird.

I agreed about the weather, and he managed to juice another three minutes out of precipitation patterns before finally pivoting.

"Listen," he said, clearly unsure where to put his hands, "we've got a proposal—thought of you straight away."

My ears perked. Sure, I wasn't in the headspace, but if I stayed in Dublin on a renewed visa, I'd need something in my portfolio, especially with Roadrunner winding down. Maybe this proposal from Patrick was the universe sending me a do-over.

"For Hardy's Dairy," he said brightly, fingers stretched, pausing for a reaction that wasn't coming. "They're pivoting into snacks . . . freeze dried yogurt balls and drinkable yogurt, that sort of thing. Could be a hundred grand."

I blinked slowly. Then fast. "A hundred grand . . . a month?" Surely he didn't mean the whole fee?

A full belly laugh shook out of his full belly. "That's a good one. It'll be an exciting little project, so it will."

An exciting little project? Get fucked.

If we won Pioneer, it'd be a ten-million dollar global engagement. This was marbles. No, worse than marbles. Freeze dried yogurt balls.

I smiled tightly. "Sounds interesting. Let me know how I can help."

"Brilliant! We're glad to have you staying on with us," he said, nudging his glasses up the bridge of his nose.

"Thanks."

He adjusted them again, more subtly this time, and shuffled off toward the copy room, humming merrily.

I stared at my monitor until the screen blurred. Hardy's Dairy. The name alone sounded like a joke. I considered scanning the floor for hidden cameras, but there was no way they'd find an actor good enough to play Patrick the Dweeb.

I opened my inbox, more so out of habit than an urge for productivity. A new email notification appeared.

Subject: Pioneer Project – Team Announcement

Clicking in before I could stop myself, Raya's name in the CC line slapped me silly.

Of all days to send the announcement, this was the one they chose? Now everyone knew she was chosen yet again to be the golden employee. She was in the room I'd dreamed of, working beside Townsend, within reach of the goals I'd set for myself.

An unfamiliar feral noise left my throat—half laugh, half cry. I quickly closed out of the email and pressed my palms into my eye sockets until neon shapes swirled behind my lids.

A new email notification chimed.

Patrick O'Malley has shared the file "Hardy's Dairy Ideas Collab."

The word *"Ideas"* made me laugh for real that time.

I scrolled through the deck. On the first slide: a stock photo of yogurt splashing against a countertop, surely created in Photoshop. The tagline read, "Healthy Can Be Happy!" I was no marketing expert, but the exclamation mark felt loud and obnoxious. And quite frankly, beneath me.

Pushing hard on the reply button, I typed *Got it*, deleted it, and turned on my out-of-office. If I stayed, I knew I'd cry or scream or say something I couldn't take back. I'd never taken a fake sick day, so I'd earned this one.

The elevator crawled down each floor. Although only early November, darkness already crept in by 5 p.m.

Outside, the air smelled like rain and trash bins. For the first time since Aidan's call, I stopped pretending and faced the truth. My life had gone from a possible promotion to Partner to yogurt balls in a matter of a week.

32

I CALLED OUT SICK the next day. And the next.

Without work to anchor me, the apartment had fallen into a state I didn't recognize. Dishes piled in the sink, clothes draped over every chair and a capless, half empty bottle of white wine slowly turned to vinegar on the countertop.

Time felt thick and struggled to pass. Even simple decisions like what to cook, what to order felt like chores. I stood in front of my tiny fridge, sniffing a questionable yogurt, wondering if I cared enough to check the expiration date.

Lindsay's name and face lit my screen, requesting a video call.

My chest tightened. I knew she was just checking in but wasn't sure I had the emotional bandwidth for the inevitable questions. I tapped the green button anyway.

"Jessie! We're engaged! We're engaged!" Lindsay shrieked, waving her hand at the camera so fast the diamond blurred. Her bare face glowed behind, more vibrant than any ring.

At first, the words didn't land, but then they hit all at once. Every emotion I'd been holding inside shoved itself forward. I forced my voice up an octave to match hers. "Ahh! Congratulations!"

I was happy for her. And then, just as quickly, I wasn't.

The life I'd always assumed would happen for me crept in. Marriage by my late twenties, kids a few years after. Back in my early twenties, when I met Brad, I figured we'd have those things. Not because we planned it in detail—well, I did, he was along for the ride—but because that's what you do when something feels stable. Now, none of that was in sight for me. But it was for Lindsay.

I robotically flipped through the script: the required compliments, standard questions, and the noises of excitement that are universally expected with engagement news.

"He did it last night," she said, settling into a storytelling mode. "He wanted to go for a walk before dinner, so we followed this trail behind the hotel. At one point, he veered us off the path and into the woods. We came across two horses tied to a tree and a guide who was, I swear, *maybe* fifteen."

"Oh boy," I said. If Jason had run it by me, I would've warned him about the horse incident from her childhood that cemented a lifelong phobia.

"Right? Total panic. I refused to ride alone, so we shared one. But the kid couldn't hoist Jason up, and I was already in the saddle, clinging to it for dear life. Meanwhile, he's stuck behind me, draped over the horse's ass, kicking his arms and legs like a cockroach. It was an absolute mess."

The image pulled out an involuntary laugh.

"Anyway, we got to this lookout just in time for sunset. Jason starts this romantic speech comparing the sun to love or whatever. I'm pretty sure the horse handler kid was singing an Irish song behind me. Honestly, I blacked out when I saw Jason pull out the ring. I don't remember most of what he said except that he asked me to be his sunrise and sunset for the rest of our lives."

I stepped out of frame to toss my uneaten yogurt container, rolling my eyes where she couldn't see.

"Oh my god, that's so sweet," I said.

"I just blurted out YES. He said he was so relieved because he was starting to ramble."

"It's beautiful, Linz. Really." It was. And it also hurt. "Did you guys . . . talk about what we talked about at the spa?" I asked carefully, unsure if Jason was within earshot.

"Not exactly, but it's fine, Jess. Really, it's fine." Her tone tightened, making it clear he was nearby. Conversation closed.

"I shouldn't have brought it up," I said quickly. "You're getting married!" I squealed and bounced around with excitement.

"I'm getting married!" She beamed back into bride mode. "You're the first person we've told. Well, besides the horse handler."

I smiled. "When the time difference allows, you should call your mom. She'll be thrilled." I wasn't convinced it was true but felt like it needed to be said.

"I'm in no rush to tell Eleanor," she sighed. "Don't need her list of things I'm doing wrong or how I need to start a strict workout plan immediately."

"Fair," I said. "Well, go off and do whatever newly engaged people do, and enjoy your last day in Ireland tomorrow."

She softened again. "Hey . . . how are *you?* Any word from Aidan?"

"No." A single syllable, packed with so much weight.

"And have you thought about what you're going to do? Come home? Stay? I just—" she hesitated, "I worry about you there. Alone in a weird country, after everything."

"It's not weird!" It came out too defensive. "You think it's weird here?"

"I meant it's not home," she said, laughing. "But now that I think about it, the guys wearing skinny jeans were . . . a little weird."

A small smile cracked.

She wasn't wrong. Without Aidan or Roadrunner to give me a purpose, what was I doing? The logical thing was to go home when Roadrunner wrapped up, buy a house, and try to get back on track for Associate Partner. The old plan. If it wasn't broken, don't fix it.

But logic wasn't lining up anymore.

"The only thing you need to worry about," I said, "is finding me a bridesmaid dress that doesn't make me look like Gumby." Years ago, she'd decided her wedding colors would be "Midnight Forest" and "Vintage Eggplant," more commonly known as dark green and dark purple. Her vision was for the bridal party to be in long green dresses with full-length green gloves that held dainty purple bouquets.

"You'll be my maid of honor," she said. It wasn't a question. "So you can pick out a dress that *you* like."

"Can't wait," I said, more stiff than I meant to.

Just after we hung up, an email notification appeared.

Reminder: The Paper Keys – Live in Dublin, Saturday 8 p.m.

Shit. The concert. The one date I'd actually planned for Aidan and me.

It was the perfect excuse to message him.

I opened our text thread and began typing and deleting, typing and deleting.

I could offer him the tickets? Maybe that would open a door? Maybe he'd see that he misses me? Maybe he'd want to go together? Maybe—

Another thought took over.

Maybe he'd think I was pathetic?

I tapped my nails against the back of the phone, hearing Simon's voice, "Don't follow up on a deliverable once it's been sent, Cinderella. They know where to find you."

I held down the backspace key and watched the letters vanish, one by one, faster and faster until there was nothing.

33

THE LINE OUTSIDE THE Academy spilled down Middle Abbey Street as bundled bodies shifted in the November cold. Many clutched pints from nearby pubs, which I didn't think was technically legal, but no one seemed to mind. I tightened my coat and gave Orla an uneasy smile, trying to shake the fact that it had been planned as a date night with Aidan. She tried to coax me to get food beforehand, but I'd politely declined, citing phantom "other plans". While getting ready to meet her, a perky male called, asking if we were on our way to Hawthorne & Rye, the restaurant where Aidian's sister worked and that I'd forgotten to cancel the reservations at.

Inside, the venue felt like an underground cave—no windows, minimal oxygen and walls pounding with bass. The opening act was already testing the limits of the speakers, so conversation had been downgraded to an awkward lip-reading exercise. The occasional nodding and pretending to understand one another was good for my mental state, but bad for my hearing. The bar was already packed, but we managed to get our beers quickly before squeezing through the crowd to a spot near the edge of the dance floor. The stage was framed by tracked lighting that flickered with trippy geometric patterns pulsing across the back wall.

The whole place felt reckless and loud and completely indifferent to my feelings. Exactly what I needed.

Indifference.

"This place is class," Orla screamed into my ear. After three attempts, I made out her second sentence; "Haven't been here in years," to which I simply smiled and bopped along to, sipping the beer I didn't want.

After a few songs, like an answer to a prayer, there was a break in the music while the stage switched sets for the headliner.

Her elbow nudged me gently. "Hey, how's work been? What are ye doing now that Roadrunner's wrapping up?"

"Yeah, it's fine," I said, too quickly. "Patrick gave me an early stage proposal for some sad little dairy company."

Orla squinted. "Hardy's Dairy? You're on Hardy's?" I nodded, encouraging her to continue. "They're actually on the rise—a small family owned farm, really lovely people, very profitable. My nan's sworn by their butter since I was a wee lassie. People are fiercely loyal to the brand out in the country."

"It's barely a six-figure pitch," I shrugged. "Not exactly the kind of thing you build a career on." Regret filled my lungs. Maybe it was the kind of thing careers are built on in the Irish office. Did I sound like an elitist?

Orla tilted her head. "Maybe. Maybe not. But you can still build *something* on it. If you only chase the big projects, you're not exactly proving that you can make anything work, are you?" Her words landed alongside the thud of a mic check.

"I'm not exactly feeling myself these days. But yeah, I hear you."

She squeezed my arm. "You don't have to feel it to fake it. Especially with yogurt."

I let out a weak but genuine laugh.

The lights dimmed and the crowd roared as The Paper Keys took the stage, each in skinny, black jeans which reminded me of Lindsay's comment. The lead singer had wild, black curls and wore a paper-thin, white shirt that looked like someone had pulled at the neckline. Distracted by his visible nipples, I barely noticed when they launched into their first song. I clapped along, unfamiliar with their music but grateful to be out of the house and my own head.

For a few minutes, I let it all go. Stopped rehearsing sad monologues I'd never say out loud and stopped replaying the break up call on loop. Stopped combing through every detail of the short-lived relationship, searching for a smoking gun. I let myself enjoy the music and the beer and the press of strangers around me. I was almost having a good time.

Until I looked to the right.

And saw him.

Toward the back of the venue, leaning against the rail separating the merch area from the dance floor, Aidan stood with a pint in one hand and the other stuffed in his pocket. His hair looked longer, and his usual stubble had grown into a beard. He wore a black sweater, not the navy one I used to steal, but similar enough to make my stomach lurch. A tall blonde with a bob in a cropped leather jacket stood beside him, talking to the group while he laughed along.

Of course he'd be there. I'd picked the band thinking, though not actually knowing, he'd like them. Their lyrics were poetic but oddly specific, and their vibes leaned nostalgic instead of trendy.

I froze, praying he wouldn't see me. I had no idea what I'd do if he did.

Then he shifted, and our eyes met. For just a second, I saw it . . . recognition *and* hesitation.

He looked away. Not like he was distracted, it was deliberate. He went right back to laughing with his friends, and the blonde leaned further into the conversation. He didn't look back.

"I need a drink," I said loudly.

Orla's eyes bounced between our half-full beers. "Bar queue's mental. Let's wait for the next song."

"It's fine, I wanna go now." I was already pushing through the crowd.

At the bar, I found the perfect vantage point—close enough to watch him, far enough that he wouldn't see me. He enthusiastically told a story, never once looking for me.

I ordered a gin and tonic. I didn't even like them, but beer wasn't cutting it, and it was the first thing I could think of that wasn't a dirty martini.

Aidan pulled out his phone and my heart jolted. Was he going to message me?

He flipped the screen toward a friend, and they both laughed.

I downed the sap-like drink so quickly it made my eyes water. I ordered another just as the blonde leaned in to whisper in Aidan's ear.

The sinking thought that they were more than friends or would be washed over me. I couldn't think, couldn't breathe, couldn't let him see me again. Before the bartender returned with my second drink, I slipped back into the crowd and out the side door into an alley. Cold air stung my cheeks like resurfacing after being underwater too long. I followed the wall around the corner and walked faster and faster away from the venue, away from Aidan.

With a runny nose and numb feet, I ducked into the first pub I found and ordered a gin and tonic to replace the one I'd abandoned. The now familiar taste of pine needles and chemicals numbed in a way that the cold weather could not. I ordered another.

And then another.

Even in my progressively intoxicated state, I knew ordering another from the same bartender might raise red flags, so I paid, announced I was calling it a night and strutted into the pub next door.

Halfway through my first drink there, I unlocked my phone to text Aidan. Orla's multiple texts and missed calls stopped me.

Shit.

Think. Think.

Ah-ha. In what felt like a moment of sheer genius, I typed a response, "Got sick. I'm at home, so sorry." There were minimal spelling errors and maximum heart emojis.

Proud of myself, I went back to Aidan's text thread. The last message I'd sent was telling him that Lindsay, Jason and I were at McClennan's and asking him to join us. He very much did not join us.

I typed, deleted and typed again. Playing with the phrasing and punctuation, I eventually landed on, "Was it really all nothing?"

It felt deep and profound. Like that one question might open a door that had been shut or at least give me the answers I was owed.

After staring at the line for ages, I closed out of the app without sending and ordered another disgusting drink because I was too committed to switch.

By the time the pub closed, I was properly drunk. I tried to hail a taxi instead of using an app, but when none came, I stumbled the whole way home. It felt longer than usual, and my feet were blistered by the time I turned onto my street.

Inside, I collapsed onto the bed, still fully dressed. The hem of my jeans was soaked from either beer, piss, or rain. Likely a mix of all three.

Before passing out, Aidan's smoldering eyes burned into the backs of my eyelids. Even in my drunken stupor, I knew he was right.

He really was indifferent.

34

It was nearly noon the next day when sunlight poured between the too-narrow curtains. My head throbbed, feet ached and cotton mouth had me reaching for the days old water on my nightstand. Panic set in as I tried to piece together the night before. It came back in snippets and flashes—mostly the image of Aidan staring at me before looking away, replaying over and over.

Mid-swallow of the dusty water, hope surged. Maybe he texted? To say it was good to see me and ask if I had fun. With the text notifications in double digits, I clicked into my messages frantically, only to be met with disappointment.

All of them were from Orla and Simon.

Orla: *That sounds like bullshit, but okay. Whatever.*
Orla: *Just saw Aidan. I know you didn't leave because you were sick.*
Orla: *Where are ye?*
Missed call from Orla.
Orla: *I had a taxi take me to yer flat. Where are ye cuz it's not here.*
Missed call from Orla.
Simon: *It's after midnight. Cinderella turning into a pumpkin?*

Missed call from Simon.

Simon: *Come on, love. Let us know you're okay.*

Missed call from Orla.

Missed call from Simon.

Orla: *We know yer phone is on.*

Orla: *Someone better have stolen it.*

Missed call from Simon.

Simon: *Tell me where you are, and I'll meet you. No questions asked.*

Simon: *Call us when you get in.*

I groaned and collapsed back onto the bed, covering my face. As much as I didn't want to, I eventually mustered the decency to send a group text.

Me: *Sorry guys, my phone was on silent. I'm at home nursing a hangover. See you in the office tomorrow.*

I rotted in bed for two more hours before migrating to the couch with a throw blanket and a bag of stale Doritos. I shut the living room blinds on my way, blocking out the unusually sunny November day.

After flipping through TV for an hour and with nothing but crumbs remaining in the bag, I scoured the kitchen for something else. Only Jaffa cakes and Weetabix. Both bought for Aidan and both disgusting. I settled on some crackers and a bottle of Pinot Grigio left over from my birthday gathering on the rooftop.

The sound of wine glugging into the glass harmonized with the opening theme song for *Mad Men*.

At the start of the next episode, my phone buzzed beside the half-empty bottle. For a split second, I thought it might be Aidan.

It was Simon, messaging me outside the group chat. How pathetic I was for hoping.

Simon: *Serial Mom movie day? I'll bring over dirty takeaway.*

I wasn't in the mood for pity or company, but I *was* starving. And I'd have to see him at work the next day anyway.

Me: *Fine.*

I had dozed on the sofa for what could have been ten minutes or an hour when I jolted awake to the building buzzer. Drool had dried on the side of my mouth. I wiped it away as I buzzed him in and topped off my glass. He held up a plastic takeaway bag that carried the unmistakable garlic sauce smell of Zaytoon.

He tossed a smaller bag onto the table. "Lucozade and Panadol. Breakfast, or lunch, of emotionally bruised champions."

Passing over the bag, I reached for my wine as he took stock. Oversized sweater, hair in a messy bun, an almost empty bottle of wine.

"You can't wear white after Labor Day," he said, with mock judgment. "That's a rule."

I managed a weak grin. "Suzanne Somers, this is my bad side," I replied, quoting the movie back to him. He loved slipping *Serial Mom* references into everyday conversation and although I'd never seen the movie before meeting him, I started using them too.

He plopped down beside me and gently took the wine from my hand.

"*This* is definitely your bad side," he said, circling a hand in my direction. "Drinking at home? Alone? In the afternoon? After bailing on Orla? At a concert *you* invited her to? What the shit?"

I raised my hands in surrender. "Okay, okay, I get it. I just . . . couldn't be there."

"She figured it was Aidan related."

My throat tightened at his name. "He was there. With friends and maybe even a new girlfriend, I don't know. He saw me . . . and looked right through me. Like I wasn't even there."

Simon let the words linger with the garlic sauce. He quietly broke open the Panadol and passed me a small pile of white tablets and the Lucozade.

"Four?" I asked.

"It's an adult dosage."

I choked down the pills one at a time.

"You were never invisible, Jess. He was just an asshole." He wrapped an arm around me, his head just above my shoulder. "He liked the *idea* of dating a foreigner more than the effort of a relationship."

"Maybe. But I still miss him."

"That's fair. But you know the fastest way to get over someone?"

I tipped my head back and stared at the ceiling. "Getting under someone else?" I could predict the cheesy line from him a mile away.

"That certainly doesn't hurt, but no. Throwing yourself into something new. Like oh I don't know . . . a new project maybe?"

"Like what? I blew my shot with Townsend, I blew it with Aidan. I'm just wandering. Meanwhile, all my friends have moved on. Lindsay's engaged, Merrick is your soulmate, Orla's happy, I think. Raya's perfect. And me? I have yogurt."

"Whoa, whoa, slow down," he said. "What the bloody hell are you talking about? And why are you measuring yourself against other people?"

"Human nature? Social media? My parents? Pick one." My voice cracked. "I came here to get Townsend's attention. Instead, I let a guy with a sexy accent distract me. Now I've taken three steps back."

He leaned back. "Bloody hell, how much did you drink?"

I shot him a knowing look.

"Look, love, you're not stuck. You actually have *more* options than you did before. Don't you see? You moved the goalpost when you chose to stay in Dublin for Aidan. You can keep it there, or you can move it again."

I stared at the cluttered coffee table, debating between the world's most greasy fries or the kebab. "Townsend will be back in Dublin in a couple of weeks," he continued. "You should reach out to him. Or don't. But if you want to start over, you've got to start somewhere. And if you want to stay in Ireland . . . maybe that somewhere is Hardy's Dairy?"

"Ah yes, gourmet drinkable probiotics."

"Love, it's not about the product or the size of the fee. It's the impact you make. That's the job. That's every job, really."

I exhaled long and slow before reaching for the kebab, peeling the foil carefully. Simon did the same but with an ear to ear grin.

"What? What are you keeping from me?" I squinted suspiciously, keeping my eyes on him as I bit into the mess.

"Not sure if I should tell you. Don't want to send you over the edge." I smacked into his shoulder with mine. "But you should know, as of January first, I'll be London's newest Partner."

"Shut up!" I said, mouth full. "Simon, that's amazing!" Making a fuss over his news felt more natural, unlike with Lindsay.

He waved it off. "I know it's probably not what you wanted to hear tonight, but I wanted you to hear it from me and not through the grapevine tomorrow."

"It's exactly what I wanted to hear tonight." I smiled.

"Here's what we're going to do . . . we eat this deliciousness, we watch *Serial Mom*, you go to bed early, and tomorrow, you *do* something. Dive into Hardy's, beg Townsend for another chance, apply for a completely new job, clean this disgusting flat, book a flight to Spain. Anything. But you're not going to sulk around, drinking yourself into oblivion."

He was right. I knew a pep talk wasn't going to solve everything, but I also knew I needed to start going through the motions again.

"A flight to Spain doesn't sound awful. I could walk the Camino." It was something Brad had once talked about when he was planning our trip to Spain that never happened.

Brad.

Shit. I never responded to his text on my birthday.

Simon raised his kebab in salute. "Or you could stay in a beach resort and wear head to toe linen?"

"That sounds much better."

35

THE NEXT MORNING, I woke at 6 a.m. to iron my outfit, tidy the apartment, and get an early start at the office. I did my full morning skin care routine: sunscreen, concealer, blush, and mascara. I hadn't bothered with makeup in over a week, so I felt like a new woman.

When I put everything back into the medicine cabinet, I saw it. Aidan's toothbrush and deodorant sat next to my moisturizer, waiting patiently to be used. My chest clenched at the thought of tossing them.

Not today.

I shut the mirrored door and wondered if I, too, felt indifferent toward the woman staring back at me.

Not today.

It wasn't a day for self-doubt, it was a day to break the cycle. Since I looked put together, I needed to act like it, too. At least for one day. Simon's voice echoed in my head as it so often did these days. *Do something.*

But the ghost of Aidan haunted my apartment. Gathering laundry, I found one of his t-shirts crammed behind the hamper. Sitting in the pantry were those boxes of Weetabix and Jaffa Cakes he loved. I wasn't ready to throw *any* of it out yet, wasn't ready for that kind of honesty.

As I grabbed my keys and phone, I swiped down to clear the pile of notifications that had stacked up.

And there it still was.

Brad's message.

I clicked into the thread.

Brad: *Happy Birthday to the Stones' biggest fan! Hope it's a great one and hope you're loving Dublin.*

Brad: *P.S. am I the first official birthday wish? At least in the EST time zone?*

I'd been too wrecked, too sad, too everything to respond. But now that the dark Aidan cloud had thinned just a little, I could see Brad's text for what it was.

Caring. He always cared.

Before I could overthink it, I typed back.

Me: *Thanks Brad! Really sorry for the late reply, last week was . . . rough. You were in fact the first official birthday wisher in both your time zone and mine. [smiley face emoji]*

***

Crammed into one of the smaller conference rooms, Patrick clicked to the next slide, and the Hardy's Dairy logo appeared on the screen, looking like it had been designed by a toddler with one of those oversized markers. The cartoon cow next to a lopsided butter churn was cute, but hardly the kind of branding that screamed "pick me over the competition."

He cleared his throat and slid a couple of folders to the center of the table. "So," he said, voice flat and low, "we've got a real opportunity with Hardy's Dairy." He turned to the whiteboard, sketching a crude supply chain funnel as his marker squeaked loudly, especially when he drew squares.

"They have a $100K budget for business modeling and strategic planning, that's where we come in. They've also earmarked another $100K for a separate marketing campaign with an outside agency. They haven't invested like this in over thirty years, when they first expanded outside of Kerry."

Jotting notes while Googling the company, I only found minimal information—their website, a couple of old news articles, and a seemingly defunct social media page. Whoever won the marketing account would have their work cut out for them. And on the other hand, anything would be better than what they currently had.

"Roisin Hardy is taking over for her grandfather who ran the business for the last fifty years. She wants to expand beyond the West Coast into all of Ireland. They've recently launched a few new product lines, so they need help analyzing their performance."

I tried my best not to doodle in my notebook and focus as if this were Townsend presenting—not his inferior counterpart. From what I could tell, they'd need help with data mining, a few standard forecasts and models run using a variety of assumptions. It was my bread and butter on Project Roadrunner.

Patrick capped the dry erase marker and turned to face us. "Let's pull together a clean and actionable plan . . . the full sha-bang. Like what we did for Moxi's Cider last year."

I hadn't been around for Moxi's, but I had seen their deliverables while doing population research for Roadrunner. It didn't seem transformative so there were likely opportunities for improvement.

"Any initial ideas?" Patrick lifted his chin toward the back of the room and buzzwords poured like champagne: consumer churn, bundling, value proposition. What the fuck did any of it actually mean for Hardy's?

I half listened while the tip of my pen sketched and shaded bubble letters spelling "Hardy's." I'd misjudged the spacing, so the 'y' and 's' were significantly smaller than the other letters.

A man's voice at the end of the table shouted something about "synergizing touchpoints," which made my eyes bulge as I focused harder on my notebook graffiti.

My phone buzzed in my pocket. A welcome distraction.

Brad: *Sorry it was a rough week around your birthday. I hope it's better now. If you ever need anything, let me know.*

Brad: *And if you find a pub that plays both trad AND rock, let me know about that too.*

A tiny laugh escaped me as I went back to scribbling around the bubble letters. Sweet, self-aware, slightly nerdy Brad. Like opening a window in a stuffy boardroom.

Traditional Irish music and classic rock 'n' roll. Why not? They weren't that different and probably influenced each other.

My pen froze midstroke.

Hardy's had two budgets. Two vendors. Two completely separate strategies. Why? For a company their size, that separation didn't make sense. They didn't need to deal with two firms. Their growth plan was intrinsically linked to how they marketed themselves. You couldn't model one without influencing the other.

We do both.

Suddenly, a tiny Simon perched on my shoulder, arms crossed. "What's the worst that could happen, Cinderella?" Imaginary Simon was right, even if it was a terrible idea, it couldn't be worse than the run-of-the-mill crap everyone else was throwing at the wall.

Screw it.

"What if," I said slowly, testing the words out loud, "we pitched them a unified strategy that covers both? Business modeling *and* marketing, rolled into a single, tailored growth plan." I paused to assess the room. Everyone was looking at me except for one guy in the back who'd been sleeping with his mouth open. What a legend. "I don't know the exact details yet, but I think—I know—it'd be more streamlined. And we could propose it for less than their $200K budget."

Patrick shifted awkwardly. His hands slid into his pockets, then back out, then they crossed before he finally brought a fist to his mouth as if to clear his throat. "Um . . . we're not a marketing firm, Jessica. We're a consulting firm."

"I know that. But we wouldn't run the campaign ourselves. We can design it, so it aligns with our strategy, then partner with the right firm to execute and monitor the performance."

The room went quiet. Even the annoying pen clicking had ceased.

"I know this isn't what we typically do, and I haven't fleshed out the details or run numbers yet. But I can. I will. I really think the return could be huge for us and better for Hardy's."

Patrick tried again to cross his arms. "You think you can pull this together in a few days?"

"Yes, I just need to run some numbers." It was a lie. I needed to figure out what the hell I was talking about. And *then* run some numbers. No way I could pull it off in a few days, but like Simon would say, I'll figure it out.

He hesitated, then nodded. "Go on then. Show me what it looks like by Friday. In the meantime—Callumn and Alice, you two run point on a proposal that aligns with Hardys' original request. We'll present both options to them."

I left the room feeling like I'd been plugged into an electric socket. For the first time in weeks, I felt like I was onto something. Not just checking a box or providing an expected deliverable but really contributing something meaningful. Something with purpose.

***

The next day passed in a blur. I camped out in an unused meeting room with sticky notes plastered across the whiteboard, connected by black dry erase lines. It looked like the set of a crime show where the FBI is mapping a cartel's hierarchy. And for the first time since I'd met him at the charity race, Aidan wasn't filling my every waking thought. His decision to end the relationship, and the words he chose, still cut deep, leaving me hollow. But in some small measure, it also felt as if a weight had been lifted. The pressure to keep up with his travels, to constantly be witty, to be interesting, to be . . . enough. If he'd appeared wanting to rekindle, I would have said yes in an instant, but at the same time, there was a piece of me that was glad to breathe an old breath.

I ran some milk delivery heat maps and studied Hardy's financial statements, looking for ways to expand their margins with the least amount of investment. I reviewed dairy pricing models, Googled supply chain logistics for refrigerated goods, and even dug into EU agricultural subsidies. But the piece that made me nervous was the heart of my great idea—the marketing execution, which remained a big question mark. If only I had some connections. Raya would have had connections.

Raya.

Of course. She'd mentioned her Irish roommate worked in digital marketing at a small firm. Raya had left Dublin without us ever going out for that lunch she suggested, and we weren't exactly besties, so I didn't know if she'd be willing to help me.

The phone rang twice.

"Hello, Raya speaking." I detected a tinge of annoyance buried beneath her sunny tone.

"Hey, it's Jess." I gave her a moment to place the name. "Uh, how's Pioneer going?"

She dropped to a whisper. "Oh, hey. Uh, give me one second." I could tell she was leaving a room filled with chatter. "Oh my god, the proposal team is all dudes, Atlanta is overcrowded, and the hours are insane. It's only the first week and we've been getting back to the hotel after midnight and then coming back in at eight."

"Gosh, that's suicidal."

"Tell me about it. Between all the takeout, lack of exercise and sleep, my skin is so dull. Not to mention by the time 8 p.m. rolls around, everyone starts smelling like hot dog water."

The laugh was unexpected and pushed through my nose. I thought of Simon's love of hot dogs.

"Ugh, the war room stench is the worst!"

"I'm seriously considering making little care kits for everyone with toothbrushes, gum and deodorant."

"You'll have to let me know how that goes."

I could hear her choosing her words. "So, what's up? I heard you're pitching Hardy's?"

"I am. Actually, I was calling to see if I could pick your brain on something—I have this idea to include outsourced digital marketing in our strategy pitch. Didn't you say your roommate in Ireland worked for a digital marketing company? Would she be open to talking?"

"Aoife? Yeah, she's the best. Can seriously run those campaigns in her sleep. She knows all the angles. She'd be great, plus, it'd be a huge win for her to bring in new work."

"Guess we're all just trying to impress someone at the end of the day, huh?" There's a long pause, and I'm about to ask if she's still there.

"Hey. I know about Pioneer." Another pause. "That Townsend wanted you, but you turned it down."

I exhaled. "It wasn't the right timing."

"And the way I was acting that day in the office, when he offered it to me, and I came to your desk . . ." She didn't finish. "I'm sorry."

My lips curved. "Well, if you connect me with Aoife and make this happen, I just might forgive you."

I heard her smile through the phone.

"Done."

"Oh, and Raya?" I said.

"Yeah?"

"I'm sorry too. For not making more of an effort to be friends. Truce?"

"Truce," she said.

"And we really should get lunch whenever we're in the same city again."

"I'd love that," she said, her voice warm. "Oh last thing—make sure you guys lead with intergenerational brand loyalty."

"Intergenerational?" My brain tried to connect the dots to how that applied to the conversation.

"For Hardy's. They're a legacy brand so they aren't actually selling butter, they're selling nostalgia. If you and Aoife can work that into a digital angle, it'll land."

I pursed my lips. "That's . . . a really good point. Thanks."

"Yeah, no problem. Let me know if you need anything else or ever want a sounding board."

And just like that, it felt like there was a real shot at making *something* happen with Hardy's, even without a clear plan.

But instead of feeling anxious, I did what Lindsay always said and told myself it was excitement.

And this time, I believed it.

36

Aoife spotted me before I made it through the door, waving from a table in the back. She held a cappuccino in an absurdly wide mug, the leaf artwork in the foam still intact. Her hair was twisted into a sleek, low knot, and she had that chaotic-chic look all marketing people seemed to master—layers of necklaces, an oversized blazer, bright white nails and the perfect winged eyeliner.

It was instantly clear why she and Raya had been roommates. They shared the same electric confidence, like they'd been born knowing exactly what they wanted and how to get it. Not to mention, they physically resembled one another.

"Jessica?" She stood to greet me, her hands light on my shoulders, making a guarded hug. "So nice to meet you."

"Thanks for making the time," I said, slipping into the seat across from her. "I wasn't sure how much detail Raya passed along."

Her grin widened. "Enough. You're trying to modernize a family-run dairy company that hasn't updated its logo since the seventies. Has to be Hardy's."

I laughed. "It may very well be." The proposal itself wasn't confidential, but the exact details of the services contained within it were.

So, I wanted to tread lightly. Aoife snapped her laptop shut and folded her hands in a way that showed she was in business mode. "Well if it is Hardy's, they've got the best butter in Ireland. And I just saw they launched yogurt balls? Quirky."

I made a face as if I had an opinion on yogurt balls.

"But . . ."

There it was.

"My boss is skittish about hybrid arrangement. Normally, we lead with branding—storytelling, visuals, campaign execution, data analytics. Adjust as needed. That's our flow," she said matter-of-factly.

It dripped in buzzwords that I half understood. I mean, I could safely assume what storytelling in that context meant but didn't *actually* know what all it entailed. My eyes narrowed slightly.

She continued. "But your plan is to lead with ops and finance and then have us build around it?"

"Right," I said, keeping my voice even. "We'd still rely on your creative leadership. The thought was to align the operations and marketing strategy early so the messaging reflects the business model—that we will help update—from the start. Aligning everything under one roof from the start will be more impactful."

She tapped her long, manicured nail against her mug. "You mean, it will be more profitable?"

I smiled. "That too."

"Hmmm." She leaned back, considering. "My boss will ask me who's steering the ship. We don't like being passengers in our own lane."

I hesitated, waiting for her to pounce on me at any moment. This was where Townsend or even Raya would step in with something polished and confident, shifting the dynamics back in a friendly but unflinching way.

"We're steering," I blurted, immediately wishing I'd phrased it differently. "I mean—we'd own the business plan, client relationship and budget. But you'd have full creative control on all of the campaign assets you mentioned. So you'd drive in your lane, and we'll drive in ours. We share in the success, but we alone take any falls. It's a no brainer. Plus, you'll be able to partner with us real time as we help decide where to expand and where to go lean. Instead of a company just blindly asking for help with marketing, you'll have access to our models and be able to understand the plan before it even rolls out. Two heads are better than one sort of thing."

Shit. If Aoife didn't buy in or if she couldn't convince her boss, I didn't have a backup plan. It'd be known in the office that my plan was nothing more than an idea that fizzled out as quickly as it was made. We'd have to run with the other proposal being pulled together and even if we won, I probably wouldn't be on the account. I'd be back to being homeless—at least in the work sense.

Aoife shifted in her seat. "Nice recovery."

Relief flooded my cheeks. "Thanks."

"And why wouldn't we throw our hat in the ring for the marketing proposal and get the full amount they're willing to spend on marketing? Why would we take less with your plan?"

Dammit, Raya must have told her about the two budgets and two proposals. I hoped it wasn't considered a breach of confidentiality.

I pulled out a folder and laid it between us. "I figured you might ask that, especially if Hardy's has already approached your company with a request for proposal." I couldn't tell by her look if they had or if it were in fact Raya that shared the information. It didn't matter because I came prepared. "The first page is a budget. Halfway down, you'll see a synergies section. That's the savings I'm projecting with us working together. Shared knowledge, greater efficiency. You'll have access to our databases and our interns, and we'll handle billing and negotiations. Less admin and higher profit margins for your company."

For a brief moment, she looked impressed, then caught herself.

"You can take that back to your boss," I said.

She pulled the folder close and began scanning it.

"And what are these behind the budget?" she asked, flipping the pages.

"I know you're the creative expert, but I didn't want to come empty-handed, so I brainstormed some angles based on my research."

Her gaze was as sharp as the tip of her eyeliner.

"You won't offend me if you throw it in the trash," I said.

"You came up with these? Did you use Gen AI to help?" she asked, glancing at me.

"What? No. Are you asking because they're good? Or cheesy?"

"A bit of both, to be fair now," she said, smiling. "But with household products, especially dairy, we find that a bit of cheese goes a long way. No pun intended."

I smiled, full of pride for my marketing stint. She pulled a page out of the folder. "Honestly? The 'What's in your fridge?' tagline is engagement gold. It's relatable, and we could spin that across every platform. I have the best designer—I'll have him start working on mock-ups this afternoon." She trailed off in thought. "That is, if I get the green light, of course."

"Really? That's amazing. Thank you."

"Don't thank me yet, I still need to get the boss man on board." She tapped the stack of pages against the tabletop, making them fall into alignment before sliding them into her Aspinal of London tote. "Hey, if he ever asks down the line . . . would you mind saying *I* approached *you* about this collab? I'm up for promotion and could use some credit internally."

There it was again—Raya's reflection in someone else's ambition. Or maybe my own? Were we really that different—Raya, Aoife and me? All trying to impress our bosses and climb the ladders.

"That's how I remember it," I said.

Her smile showed appreciation, and the tension in my shoulders eased.

She drained the last of her coffee as I reiterated that the pitch was in one week, so we'd need their mock-ups and a follow-up session before then.

"Oof, that's tight. I'll try to make it work, I may need to shuffle a client or two. One of my remote accounts is in Bali so he's seven hours ahead. Loves calling at random hours, but he's sound. I'll see if I can delay his strategy shift for a few weeks."

"Bali sounds amazing right now," I said, glancing out the café window. The rain fell heavier than when I arrived.

"What's the matter?" she teased. "Had enough of our Irish weather?"

"I don't know if I have or not. Still trying to decide." I smiled. "At least I'm heading home for Christmas. To Florida."

"Ah, Florida! Now *that* sounds lovely. I bet you miss it?"

"I do," I said on autopilot. I still missed Tampa and everyone there, but not the way I used to. There's a saying that home isn't a place, it's a person. But what if you don't have a person? What if you're still figuring out where you belong?

"It'll be nice to get a bit of sunshine in these winter months and to get your head out of the computer, huh?" she said.

"That's the plan."

Aoife stood, slinging her brown leather tote bag over her shoulder and pulling out an umbrella. "I'll loop you in once I get sign-off. And Jess?"

"Yeah?"

"Trust your gut. You've got good instincts; don't second guess yourself."

After she left, I sat for a few minutes watching the droplets race each other down the glass. I wondered what her client in Bali was doing at that moment. With the time zone, it was almost 5 p.m. there. Was he drinking a mango smoothie after a quick surf session? Heading to an evening yoga class? Napping in a hammock with a book open across his chest?

Or was he stuck on a work call, worried about making a deadline like the rest of us? How much of living somewhere "sexy" sounding was *actually* sexy, and how much was romanticized? I was still figuring it out with Ireland, but Bali?

It could be fun to find out.

37

TOWNSEND LEANED AGAINST THE reception desk, one hand gripping the handle of his carry-on, the other holding a paper coffee cup. His suit wasn't wrinkled, but it looked tired. The flights from the US landed at dawn, and judging by his bleary eyes and wide yawn, I could safely wager he didn't sleep on the plane.

"Dunhour," he said, voice booming with authority despite the jet lag. "Long time, no see. I've been hearing good things about Hardy's."

"Oh yeah?" I tried to sound casual, but my pulse raced.

"Very good things. Forecasting, lean distribution channels, creative strategy—you're running a one person show."

"Not quite." I gave a pointed look.

"And did I hear correctly that you leveraged a connection with a local marketing firm?" We walked to the elevator, his suitcase wheels squeaking against the tile. I rushed ahead to push the button.

"Yes. Aoife—a friend of a friend, I guess you could say." I wondered if Raya had told him anything or tried to take credit.

"That sort of initiative isn't something I've seen from you before." He grinned, clearly impressed. "You've really taken my feedback to heart. I like it."

The praise hit differently. A year ago, I would've memorized every word, replayed it repeatedly for motivation. This time it just felt . . . clinical. Like he was reciting stats from my performance file.

"It was a team effort," I said.

He waved it off. "Patrick told me you drove the whole thing. How you really took the lead and made incredible progress." The elevator dinged, and the doors slid open. "Actually," he added, as we stepped inside, "I was hoping to talk to you about something while I'm here."

My heart fluttered with cautious hope.

"In short," he said when the doors closed, "Raya's not working out on Pioneer. She's bright, polished, well-spoken. But she doesn't have your technical acumen or instincts. She's not ready to be an Associate Partner. But you are."

I felt like a gymnast who had stuck the landing—until unease washed over me. I squinted at him as the elevator rose.

"This account is going to be even bigger than we initially thought," he went on. "You could lead a project stateside, similar to what you did for Roadrunner, but on an even larger scale with higher visibility. And you could be Tampa-based if you wanted. I can't guarantee Associate Partner immediately, but within a year? Absolutely."

Was he going to take Raya off Pioneer and give it to me? Or would we have to compete for his attention again? I no longer had the energy to go neck and neck with her, especially after she'd been an unexpected supporter and sounding board on Hardy's. A month ago, I would've said *yes* before he even finished the sentence. It was everything I'd ever wanted. But the higher the elevator climbed, something shifted.

I could vividly see my life if I took him up on his offer: my first home better than the one I would have gotten with the turquoise door, better car, more tailored outfits, respect in the community. But I could also see the late nights under harsh office lighting, half eaten Styrofoam takeout containers, interns hovering with coffee orders. I could see the recycled PowerPoint slides promising "efficiency" and "optimization."

A final chime: we'd arrived on the fourth floor.

The me who arrived in Ireland would have known the grind was necessary to reach goals. The me after Aidan and after Hardy's wasn't so convinced.

We stepped into the hallway, and Townsend continued talking about Pioneer—their numbers, client hierarchy, planned transactions, but his words began to fade.

I was back in Morocco. Aidan sat across from me at the lopsided blue café table. The air was thick with mint and spices drifted in from the medina. His voice, clear as the day he said it. *What's your passion?*

My body relived the moment.

At the time, I'd taken it as an attack, an insult. I could finally see it for what it was—a mirror. A question I couldn't answer because I didn't know who I was beyond the job and the titles and the goals.

The past few weeks of work had been the first in years where I felt alive at work, but I needed to have Hardy's to compare it to. Simon was right. It's not the size of the client that matters, it's the impact.

When we reached his old office, which was now empty and mostly used for calls, I hesitated in the doorway. My mind buzzed and images overlapped. Spreadsheets and models, the turquoise door, Aidan wandering in the spice market, the red door at his parent's house, the bags of towels and bedding breaking in the rain, the sheep I almost ran over, and Brad's face when we hugged goodbye for the last time.

Townsend set his coffee on the desk and powered on his monitor. "You just going to stand there, Dunhour?"

I opened my mouth, then closed it. As he hung his suit jacket on the hook, I saw Aidan, more clearly this time. He was sitting in Townsend's chair. Legs crossed, feet on the desk and his hands laced behind his head. "This is what you want to be, Missus? This guy? Hey, what do you think his passion is?"

I blinked hard, shaking my head, and the ghost of Aidan had dissolved. But his words didn't.

I want to visit another twenty countries before I'm forty. Maybe live somewhere else. You Irish lads brought together at the Mt. Fuji summit. I'd just come back from Peru . . . Machu Picchu, you know, with the llamas?

The red Georgian door again.

His voice continued. *What if we moved here? To Morocco? Six months . . . we could teach English. Something I'll be proud of when I'm eighty.*

Was I going mad? What did they put in my Americano?

More voices layered in.

My dad, *Work hard, but don't forget to play some, too.*

And Orla, *We were talking about taking a late gap year.*

Then Lindsay, *Do you really even want this or is it just another milestone?*

Simon, steady and clear, *You're not stuck. You moved the goalpost. You have to make your moment.*

Even Brad, all those years ago, planning a trip we never took, *We could walk the Camino.*

And finally—Mom, *Maybe it's time to trust your gut?*

I couldn't tell who was speaking anymore. I squeezed my eyes shut until there was silence.

"Mr. Townsend," I said, finally. "I again appreciate the offer and the vote of confidence." A long, quiet exhale. "But again, I'm not interested."

His brow furrowed, and he rubbed his chin. "You're sure? This is a big opportunity and I thought . . . forgive me, but I-I heard that you may *not* want to stay in Ireland after all? I may have misunderstood."

"You heard correctly. We didn't work out. But separate from that, I'm not sure if Ireland is the right place for me. But I am sure that Pioneer is not."

It felt so good to say. I wished that I could go back in time and have always spoken that clearly.

He considered his next words—perhaps deciding if he should try to persuade or not. Why should he have to convince me to want to be a Partner?

I pushed off the doorframe and stood on my own. "I'll transition Hardy's. After that, I'm done."

"Ah, I'm sorry? Done? Wh—"

"Yes. I'm quitting."

"Uhh," he stammered, still unsure of how to respond. "I . . . I don't understand. I thought you were only turning down Pioneer." He stared. "What will you do?"

"I don't know," I shrugged. "I don't have a plan." A deep breath. "Maybe I'll go to Bali. Or Morocco? No, probably not Morocco. Maybe explore Ireland? Or go home? Take a gap year and figure it out?" Without a mortgage or kids, why not spend some of my savings figuring out what I want? And with beautiful scenery?

"A . . . *gap year*?" He laughed, dragging a hand through his head. "You can't be serious?"

"It's kind of the Irish way, I've learned." I laughed nervously. "And I think it's brilliant. So . . . when in Dublin, right?"

"Look, a lot has happened in a short amount of time. Why don't you take a week off and—"

"No." I raised my hand. "Mr. Townsend, thank you for all you've done. But I need to do this."

He studied me for seconds; an eternity. "Okay, then." He shrugged in defeat. "Resignation accepted."

Before turning to leave, I cleared my throat. "And for what it's worth, Raya helped me with Hardy's." It happened in a millisecond, but his eyebrows raised just a wrinkle. "She had the connection to the marketing firm, and she had insight on the direction. Which we used."

He gave a subtle nod. And I left.

"Jessie," he called. I turned back around. "Don't be a stranger."

I agreed even though I didn't know what I was agreeing to. Then, wandered back to my desk, unsure what would come next, but for the first time in years, it didn't terrify me.

38

By the time I put on my pajamas that night, the reality had set in. I'd quit. On one hand, it felt monumental. The career I'd been chasing for every waking moment for six years, the career I'd sacrificed my relationship with Brad to, was just . . . gone. On the other hand, it felt anticlimactic. There were no after work drinks, no big announcement, no looking forward to the next career. Because there wasn't one.

The apartment was quiet except for the hum of the radiator and an on-again, off-again rain pattering against the windows. I needed to mark the day, needed to let Simon, Orla and Lindsay in on the news. And my parents.

Oh shit, my parents.

What would they think? The ones who instilled in me that "Hard work pays off" and "A failure to plan is like planning to fail" and "Nothing good happens after midnight." Okay, that last one didn't have anything to do with my quitting a highly compensated job without another lined up, but it came from the same place.

I needed to tell them. I didn't want to keep it from them the way I'd kept the news of the Pioneer proposal from Aidan. I didn't want to live in a purgatory between truth and lies again.

Not yet ready to call them, I grabbed the lemon verbena disinfectant spray and cloth and began wiping down every surface. Cleaning was both a nervous habit and somehow therapeutic. In no time, everything was sparkling, so I vacuumed. Then I threw in a load of laundry, even though it wasn't Sunday, and reorganized the cupboard and pantry. Just a lunatic deep cleaning on the Tuesday night before Thanksgiving.

Mom answered first, her face jolting around the screen in the warm kitchen light as she tried to figure out how video calls worked, despite us making them countless times before. Dad sat beside her on his oversized laptop, glasses perched on his nose.

"Jessie! Are your ears ringing? We were just saying we hadn't heard from you in a week," Mom said. I decided not to point out that most adult children don't talk to their parents more than once a week. "Uh, hi." I swallowed. "I have some news." Might as well rip the bandage off.

Dad looked up, over his frames. "Good or bad?" "Depends who you ask," I said, with a nervous half laugh. "I quit."

Dad took off his glasses and set them on his laptop.

"You *what*?" Mom asked, voice sharp.

"I quit the firm," I repeated. "Townsend offered me a project back in the States—one that could've put me on track for Associate Partner. But I said no. I-I just can't do it anymore. The hours, the stress. I don't know what I'm doing anymore."

Only seconds passed, though it felt much longer. Then Dad said, "So you finally broke free from 'The Man', huh?"

"I did."

He let out a congratulatory whistle.

He was happy?

Mom's voice softened, turning logical. "But, honey, you worked so hard to get where you are."

"I know."

"So what now?" she asked.

"I don't know."

Dad smiled, the kind that made me think he'd been waiting to hear that answer for a long time. "Good. You'll figure it out, you always do."

"Thanks, Dad." I blinked back the tears preparing to fall.

When I told him I was considering visiting Spain, he mentioned distant ancestors we had from Spain and that he'd dig up the results from a DNA company he used years ago to trace it. Mom was equally supportive, and when she asked if I'd still be home for Christmas, the words hit harder than I expected.

"Yes, I'll be home," I said, smiling, "so make sure Santa gets scratch off lottery tickets for my stocking."

When the call ended, I stared at the screen.

They supported me. They always had.

Feeling strangely accomplished from the cleaning and breaking the news to my parents, I went to dial Lindsay next. But before tapping her name, I opened my chat history with Brad.

We'd exchanged a few platonic texts over the month since the break up. Not as a rebound, but as a reassuring friend. I told him about Hardy's, and he told me about his work too. He'd risen up the ranks quickly at his architecture firm, thanks to a few large commercial developments in Tampa. Earlier in the year, he'd flown to London a few times for a boutique hotel project. A tiny part of me wanted to ask if he'd be going again. Maybe I could meet him there. But I knew that'd be crossing a line.

Instead, I sent him a text.

Me: *So . . . I quit my job. Going to take some time off.*

And then I called Lindsay.

Like my parents, she answered from the kitchen. It was 5:30 p.m. in Florida. Her hair was in a messy bun and childlike monster truck sounds revved loudly in the background.

"Hey! You're catching us in the middle of dinner prep chaos," she said nervously.

"I can hear that." I laughed nervously, confused why Cody was over at dinnertime on a Tuesday when Jason usually had him on weekends. Assuming I was on speaker, I didn't ask. "I won't keep you, just wanted to check in and tell you my update—"

She cut me off. "Don't tell me you're back with Aidan?"

"Negative."

"Then . . . did you finally tell your firm to shove it?"

"Wait, how could you have known that? Did my parents call you?"

She grinned. "I tell you all the time that you're predictable. So that's a yes?"

"Yes."

She squealed. "Jessie! Holy shit. I'm so friggin' proud of you."

Her joy was contagious for about three seconds before her face fell, and she glanced off screen, mouthing something to someone—probably Jason. Cody's truck sounds faded into the distance.

"How come Cody is over on a Tuesday? Do you guys have him for Thanksgiving?"

She hesitated. "Uh . . . yes. We have him for Thanksgiving. And longer, too." Her tone went even and serious. "Cody's mom is dealing with some health stuff. I don't really know the details, neither does Jason but they . . ." Her throat bobbed. "Uh, we agreed it was best to take him for a while because she has a lot of doctor's appointments."

"Oh my god. I'm so sorry." Guilt rushed over me. I felt like an idiot for calling with my news while they were in the middle of that.

"Yeah." Her voice trembled slightly. "He'll stay here so it doesn't interrupt his pre-school routine."

"And how are you?"

"I'm fine. Just trying to process what it all means. It sounds so stupid and selfish to even say this, but—" She cleared her throat.

"The wedding?" I guessed.

A slight nod. "We're going to postpone it." She dabbed under her eyes with her pointer fingers while looking at the ceiling.

"Aw, Lindz. I'll be home in a month. For Christmas." I meant it to sound reassuring, but I wasn't sure it did. She'd been struggling with the stepmom role even when Jason only had Cody every other weekend. Having him nearly full time was going to be a seismic shift.

"Oh, and one more thing." She raised her chin and held up two fingers toward someone in the background. "You'll never guess who I ran into at Whole Foods."

I hesitated. "Who?"

"Someone still cute, still single, and apparently still in contact with you?"

I rolled my eyes with a sigh.

"Why didn't you tell me you've been talking to Brad?"

"We're not *talking*, it's not like that." My cheeks warmed. "We've just . . . checked in. Well after Aidan."

"Hey, when one door closes, another one opens, and sometimes it's one you've already been through. Or it's been through you?"

"Oh my god." I groaned. "Goodbye."

After we hung up, I let the silence fill the apartment. The rain had stopped and the radiator cycled off. I grabbed a trash bag and started tossing anything stale or unwanted—old snacks, outdated yogurt, opened wine—pausing momentarily with the Jaffa cakes and Weetabix before dropping them into the abyss. When the kitchen was complete, I moved to the bathroom cabinet. Throwing away Aidan's toothbrush and deodorant wasn't hard. The t-shirt was. Not in the same way I couldn't throw away the Rolling Stones shirt from the night I met Brad. The Stones shirt was a happy memory—a collection of them, really—folded into something that had always been mine. Aidan's shirt was never mine to begin with. It was too invaluable to return to him and too loaded to keep. There was no reason to hold onto it unless I wanted to torture myself. I held it for too long anyway, trying to inhale his scent. It wasn't cluttering my apartment, it was cluttering my head.

The smack in the trash bag landed heavier than it should have. We were over. And with that, I tied the bag, set it by the door, and took a deep breath. Why did it feel like such a big deal? We didn't even date that long and had been broken up for a month. I couldn't make sense of it.

A minute later, my phone rang.

It was Brad.

Brad? Calling me?

Shit. I was not expecting that.

I quickly cleared my throat, took a breath and answered before I could back out.

"Hey," I said, aiming for casual. "Long time, no talk."

Ugh, too cutesy casual.

"Jess?" His voice came through steady and familiar. "You really quit?"

A shaky laugh escaped. "Yeah. I really did."

"Wow." I could hear him absorbing it. "That's huge. How are you feeling? You okay?"

I sank into my old lady floral couch and pulled my knees up. The couch had grown on me. Couldn't see myself buying a botanical sofa to replace my white one back in the States, but maybe I'd get a couple of flowery throw pillows to add some pizzazz.

"Strangely, I feel . . . good. If I think about it too much, I get a little panicky, but I don't know . . . it's like I know it's the right move, even though I don't know exactly what comes next."

"Have you been deep cleaning?" he asked.

A breathy smile. "I am."

"Old habits," he said, like he could see me.

"Old habits," I repeated.

"Well, I hope this doesn't sound condescending or anything, but . . . I'm really proud of you. After all you put into the firm, it's really brave."

Brave felt strange. Forced. Like I was an imposter.

"Thanks. That means a lot."

"So . . . what's next?"

"I'm going to take some time off," I said. "A lot of people here take gap years after college, to travel before they start their careers. Maybe I'll do that?"

"Good," he said without hesitation. "You deserve that."

There was no judgment. No "must be nice" jokes. No "what about . . ."

"Where are you thinking about traveling to? Or are you going to figure it out as you go?"

"I'm thinking about checking out the architecture in Spain," I joked. "It's been on my mind ever since you . . . talked about it." I avoided naming the trip he'd planned for us right before I broke things off.

"Well, I'm glad I could play a part in your journey. No matter how small."

A pause.

I wanted to tell him that he wasn't a small part of my journey, that he was threaded through all of it. And with me the whole time in Ireland. And probably always would be. I wanted to say that I was stupid back then, that I'd made a mistake. I wanted to ask him to visit.

"I'm just waiting for my company to send me to Barcelona so I can study Gaudi in person," he said.

Fuck it.

"Well, if I do end up in Spain, maybe you could come visit?" The words poured out before I could rethink them.

Shit. Shit. Shit.

I squeezed my eyes shut so tight, I saw colors.

Why did I send those words into the universe, and why couldn't I yank them back?

And why wasn't he responding?

"Jess, I—"

"Oh god, I'm sorry," I rushed in, as if that would make it all better. "I shouldn't have said that. I-I take it back."

"You take it back?" With his tone flat, I couldn't tell if he was amused, disappointed, or something else entirely.

"I just . . . I really shouldn't have said it. It was impulsive." I covered my beet red face. Thank God we weren't on video. I needed water.

"I'm glad you said it."

Behind my hand, I smiled.

"Jess, there's nothing I'd love more than to visit you in Spain during your gap year." It sounded foreign for him to say. "I'd visit you any-where—in an alleyway or at a college hurricane party."

Tears formed, and my smile began to quiver.

"Look, I don't know exactly where you're at in terms of relationships, but I know what I want." His voice steadied. "And what I want more than anything is for you to always have all the experiences life has to offer. Go to Spain. Go everywhere. Start again, make new friends, try new foods, learn the language, the culture. You've done it once, do it again."

My throat tightened.

"But this time, do it for yourself. Not for your career. Not to prove something."

A few faint sniffles escaped as I wiped my nose with the back of my hand.

"Take this time for yourself," he added. "Don't shrink it for anyone. Or for any job. And only after you've done all that, if you still want me to visit, I'll be on the next flight."

He had knocked a wall down. I could say anything without judgment. And yet, all I could manage was, "Deal."

When the call ended, the apartment felt lighter, and so did I.

Slipping into flip-flops, I took the trash bag filled with Aidan's things out back to the bins, thinking about what Lindsay had said.

When one door closes, another one opens.

Should I open the turquoise door again?

I tossed the bag into the outside bin. The thud was loud and final. And I didn't look back.

39

RIDING THE LUAS INTO the city for the last time, I tried to commit every detail to memory. The woman's robotic recorded accent on the intercom and the vinegary smell of a chipper the second I stepped off. Most of all, I didn't want to forget the brightly colored doors along Harcourt Street that were even brighter now, decorated for Christmas.

I glanced at my phone as a text pushed through.

Brad: *Enjoy your party tonight! Since you're now FUNemployed, I expect you to stay out past midnight.*

Midsmile, I shoved the phone into my pocket and raced to smack the glowing button on the Luas door. I was already five minutes late to my own leaving drinks; missing my stop would surely add another ten.

I'd spent the previous month doing a slow and thorough transition of everything I knew from Roadrunner and everything I'd started with Hardy's. I even took my replacement to meet the client contacts I'd worked with. A two month notice period was customary in the Irish office, but since I was in between the two projects, Patrick was fine with me doing less and wrapping up just in time for Christmas.

The pub was already warm with chatter, a trad band and clinking glasses. The last time I'd been in the middle of a jolly pub, surrounded by a good time was when Lindsay and Jason visited—right before Aidan called to break up with me.

I hadn't heard from him since that phone call. Not a single text or a message passed along from his sister to Orla to me. Nothing. How could you have a relationship with someone, make plans for the future and then one day, never hear from them again? It was as if we were ghosts to each other. Maybe I wasn't even that to him?

Simon waved me toward the back, where an "Adios, Jessica" banner hung in a corner opposite the door to the bathroom. I rolled my eyes and laughed out loud at the gesture, still half believing that I was really taking a gap year in Spain. My request for an extended tourist visa had just been approved, and I'd be leaving Tampa on January first on a one-way flight to Barcelona. I'd only begun researching bilingual letting agents and emailing them my arrival date, budget, and preferences. I had an Airbnb booked for the first week with the option to extend if needed.

Before I could even take my coat off and hug Simon, Orla bounded toward me, dragging Gearóid behind her.

"This is for ye. Gotta have Guinness at your send-off," she said, handing me a fresh pint. I clinked her glass, making sure to look her in the eye—just in case the superstition about seven years of bad sex was true—and took a gulp, dipping under the creamy head to get to the actual beer.

"Now," Orla said in a loaded voice. "Not to take attention away from ye at your leaving drinks, but I wanted to tell you in person . . ."

"You're pregnant?" I deadpanned.

"Ew, no," she shot back before shoving a hand in my face, nearly knocking my pint. "We're engaged!"

I gasped and grabbed her hand with my free one. A large sapphire surrounded by two smaller pink gemstones sparkled under the warm pub lights.

My mouth hung open. "Oh my god! Congratulations!"

"*I* asked *him*," she blurted, looking like the cat that got the cream. "Simon kept planting the seed. Thought he was mad, but ah, sure, look. Here we are."

Gearóid shook his head. "She didn't *ask* me, that would imply I had a choice."

"Are you being held against your will?" I teased. "Blink three times if you need help."

"Turns out he'd already bought the ring. Had it for months and was waiting for the right time," Orla said.

"Which apparently was when you," I said, pointing at Orla, "told him it was."

She winked while Gearóid stood there with his hand on the small of her back, looking like the proudest man in Dublin.

After a pint's worth of chatter about wedding planning, I drifted into the rowdy crowd, heading toward Simon and Merrick. On my way, I ran straight into Townsend, who I didn't even know was in town and certainly wasn't expecting to see at my leaving drinks.

"There she is," he boomed over the fiddle. "The woman of the hour."

"What a nice surprise." I blinked, trying to remember why he'd be there. "Are you still winding down Roadrunner?"

"I wasn't meant to be here until Monday—just two days before everyone turns off for Christmas," he said, "but I switched my flight when I heard about this." His eyes swept the bar. "I couldn't *not* show up to send-off the woman who turned me down . . . twice."

"It wasn't you I turned down, it was the path."

"And where does the new path lead?" he asked. "Besides Spain."

"You see, it's more of a general direction than a clear path." I said with a laugh.

"Well, I hope the general direction is toward you doing more things like what you did on Hardy's. You really made an impression." His gaze sharpened. "You're more creative and collaborative than I pegged you for."

I glanced across the room at Patrick, awkwardly holding his pint glass with both hands as he talked with Claire, the office manager.

"Patrick was great, he really took a chance on my pitch."

"You have good instincts, Dunhour. And the technical capability and work ethic to back them up. That combination is rarer than you think."

I didn't know what to say, so I just smiled.

"Let me know if there's ever anything I can do. And if you ever want to come back to McAfee, especially now that we won Pioneer, just say the word."

"Well I was . . ." I stopped. "Never mind, it's silly."

"Oh come on," he protested. "You can't leave me hanging like that."

I hesitated for a beat, then decided to go for it. "When I'm . . . off in Spain, on my break . . . I was thinking of looking into what it'd take to maybe start my own . . ." I trailed off. It sounded absurd out aloud, especially to Townsend.

"Consulting company?" he finished, and my face gave me away. "I take it you'd want to focus more narrowly on due diligence, modeling and forecasting?" he went on.

"Exactly," I said, my shoulders dropping. "Work with start-ups and small companies, help them analyze product offerings and competitive advantage. Maybe bring in marketing as an option so it's all under one roof. I know it won't be easy, but it would be focusing on what I'm good at. And I'd get to stay local. After this adventure, I think I'll be ready to stay put in Tampa for a while. But anything can happen."

"I know what you mean," he said dryly. "My Marriott rewards points have to be hitting some kind of maximum allowable limit."

I shook my head with my eyes shut, unsure how he traveled as much as he did and maintained a personal life.

"I think it's a fantastic idea," he said, genuinely.

Across the room, I locked eyes with Simon, who had one arm draped across Merrick's shoulders and the other waving a nearly empty Smithwick's around as he spoke. Townsend and I drifted over to join them.

"If I move to London, we're getting a cat," Merrick said, matter-of-factly.

"Only if it's a Persian longhair," Simon negotiated, "and we name it after an *Austin Powers* character." Merrick did a quick audit of who needed another drink and slipped away to the bar.

"I suppose it's official now . . . welcome to the partnership, Partner," Townsend said, and held out his hand. Simon shook it firmly. "Cheers."

"When are you headed back to London for good?" Townsend asked.

"Next week. I'll spend Christmas with my sisters and their rug rats back in York and start with my new portfolio after the first of the year."

"Is Merrick going home with you for Christmas?" Townsend asked.

"That's the plan. Christmas in the UK, New Year in Portugal, and then he'll move to London permanently in March after finishing some things here."

I'd been so consumed by Aidan, and then by life after Aidan that even though Simon and I worked on the same project, we'd drifted.

"I hope you'll have a guest bedroom," I said. "Because no matter where I end up in Spain, it'll be a quick Ryanair flight to London."

"Right back at ya, Cinderella." He gave a familiar wink just as Merrick returned with a round of baby Guinness shots, making two trips to carry them all. The chocolate and coffee taste was sweet like dessert. It reminded me of the second round Aidan ordered on our first date at the hidden pizza place. I wondered when mundane things would stop linking back to him. When he would stop haunting me.

After I slammed the tiny glass on the table, Merrick handed me a fresh beer, and Aoife wove through the crowd to join us too. I'd thought my only friends in Dublin were Orla and Simon, and then Aidan, until he wasn't. But that wasn't true. There were many others that had left an imprint on me.

"Hardy's is loving the early campaign ideas," Aoife said. "They've already had two new distributor inquiries this week."

"I don't know what that means, but I'm guessing it's good," I said.

She laughed. "It is."

"Hey, how's Raya?" I asked. "Have you talked to her recently?"

"Not since she called me about Hardy's. I think she's been flat out on that project she went back for. Sometimes she texts me in the morning, and then I'll remember it's like 2 a.m. her time."

I shook my head slowly. Raya had the life I wanted, the one I'd been chasing. Sure, the long hours ebb and flow; it's part of the deal when you sign up for client service. And if I had made Partner, I'd tell myself it was all part of the process, and I'd believe it. But being a month out since I'd made my decision to leave, I hadn't regretted it once. In fact, I wished I'd done it sooner.

After my second pint and second baby Guinness, it was my turn to get a round. I introduced Aoife to Simon and Orla and headed to the bar. I didn't know who needed what, so I exercised good judgment and went with three Smithwick's and three Guinness. At a gut level, it felt like the right mix and if it were too much, I knew they wouldn't go to waste.

I was leaning against the counter, taking it all in when I saw him.

Aidan.

He wore the same outfit from our first date, but this time with a dark grey wool coat, unbuttoned and landing midthigh. I sucked in a sharp breath and held it as he stood in the doorway, stepping aside for a pair of cackling, middle-aged men heading out for a smoke, an unlit cigarette already hanging from one of their mouths.

He scanned the crowd until his eyes locked with mine. For a second, all of the noise and bodies blurred until they froze around us. Just like the first time he kissed me on the Ha'penny bridge, I had to remind myself to breathe.

A hint of a smile emerged, more so in his eyes than his mouth. He made his way over, stopping to hug Orla and playfully smacked Simon on the shoulder. Simon shot daggers back, which Aidan didn't see.

"Hey, you," Aidan said, voice pitched low under the band as they launched into "The Wild Rover." How could two basic words in a noisy pub take me back to when we were together—as if no time had passed?

"Hey." I tipped my head to the side. "What are you doing here?" I wasn't sure whether to smile or put up a front. The first option felt natural. The other felt like work.

"A little birdie told me you were leaving Dublin." He glanced at Orla, who immediately shot me an "I'm sorry, don't kill me" look.

"Yeah." I finally exhaled. "I fly home Wednesday for Christmas." A slight flinch crossed his face when I mentioned Christmas. I felt it too. We were supposed to spend Christmas together—buskers on Grafton Street, his relatives in Bray, *Father Ted,* Babs' awful food. That was the plan.

"And then I'm heading to Spain in the New Year."

"I heard about that." Surprise flickered across his face. "For how long?"

"A year. I think," I replied.

He couldn't mask it that time. "Wow. Impressive." I wasn't sure if the length of time was impressive or the fact that it was *me*, going alone, jobless and on purpose. Probably a bit of both.

He looked down, picking at the cuticle of his thumb. "Look, Jess . . . I know I wasn't always kind. Or patient. Especially at the end."

Heat climbed my chest. It wasn't what I expected him to lead with.

I shook my head. "Aidan, it's—"

He lifted a hand as the band hit the chorus, and the whole pub roared along:

"And it's no, nay, never."

Four claps in quick succession shook the room around us.

"No, nay, never, no more."

He raised his voice over the chanting. "It's just—we were making plans. Real plans. And I started to panic. So I pushed away."

My eyes fell to the bar, it was safer there.

"I could have handled things better. The timing. The way I did it. All of it."

The song ended to wild applause. His words about making plans rang in my head. *He* was the one making most of the plans.

"You deserved better," he said, laying his hand over mine.

After a beat, he squeezed. Once. Twice. Both too hard.

The next song started—"Whiskey in the Jar," a pub staple. The silence between us lingered. When I was ready, I offered him a soft smile and gently slid my hand away, reaching for the three pints of Guinness that had finished settling.

"Thanks for saying that," I said. "I hope you're doing okay."

His mouth pulled to one side and eyes burned through me. Like he was disappointed that was all I had to say.

"Uh, you too," he said.

The bartender added the three Smithwick's, forming a tiny army of pint glasses. I handed him a fifty euro note. He slapped down a tenner with a one euro coin on top. I stuffed the change into my pocket and gathered the first three pints into a tight triangle, ready for the transfer. Simon strolled up, and without looking at Aidan, took the other three back to the group.

I burned everything to memory—the music, the warm stuffy air, the smell of wood and malt, and . . . every curve of Aidan's face. There were so many questions I wanted to ask.

What if I'd told him about the promotion?

What if I'd called him out during the driving lesson?

What if I'd told him I loved him?

Would it have changed anything?

Deep inside, I knew the answer.

Maybe if I'd communicated better, we would've stayed together longer only for the inevitable break up to hurt worse. Or maybe we'd have ended sooner?

Either way, the ending would've been the same.

I drank him in one last time. And with the last gulp, I finagled my fingers wide around the narrow waists of the glasses.

"I really should get back to my friends. I'm kind of the main event," I said, lifting them carefully. A dollop of foam from one of the glasses slid onto my hand. "It was good to see you."

"Here, let me help you with that. Looks tricky," he said.

How can one stupid word have such an effect? I searched for a witty, slightly flirty comeback.

Instead, I said, "It's actually not."

And with that, I sank into the crowd, closing the door on Aidan.

With both hands covered in beer, I distributed the dripping glasses to Orla, Gearóid and Patrick. Merrick was vaping on the other side of the glass and Simon was in the middle of telling a story about an awkward airport security search after forgetting he had a bottle of wine and hemorrhoid cream in his carry-on. I'd already heard the story. Multiple times. Just before the punchline, my eyes veered to the bar. Aidan was gone.

***

At 2 a.m., the pub hadn't thinned but the night had. Brittle cold nipped at my cheeks as we spilled out of the comfort of the stuffy bar. They were all going to Coppers, the late night venue Orla told me I wasn't a true Dubliner until I'd experienced it, but I didn't want to go. Already out well past midnight, I said my goodbyes on the pavement, promising Orla I'd visit before her and Gearóid's wedding, and promising Simon I'd survive without his solicited and unsolicited coaching.

With my hands tucked into my coat pockets, I started home. But when the street forked, my feet carried me the long way.

Toward the river.

The Ha'penny Bridge arched ahead, its white iron glistening through a thin layer of mist. I hadn't set foot on it since that night with Aidan—the night he kissed me at the top and told me the old superstitions.

A kiss under the middle arch for everlasting love.

A coin tossed into the Liffey to keep the ghost away. Back then, I believed in the kiss. Not the ghost.

I stopped at the entrance and fished in my pocket for the one euro coin I'd gotten back in change. I didn't have a penny, but surely with inflation, a euro would suffice. Stepping onto the bridge, my boots clanked softly against the wooden boards. At the top of the arch, I held my arm over the rail—right where Aidan had backed me up against. With the coin pinched between my thumb and forefinger, I let it fall.

My crossing was paid in full.

There should be no ghosts to haunt me.

40

THE SPANISH SUN FILTERED through the canopies scattered on the street. Even as late afternoon slipped into evening, the cream-colored walls reflected enough light to keep the lane bright. Locals spoke Catalan and Spanish over their drinks, mostly wine or beer, though many still had coffee cups despite the hour. Most of the tourists—my people—had sifted back toward Las Ramblas or never made it to this part of the city.

Barcelona is known for its Gothic architecture, but I was captivated by its sounds. A street guitar always seemed to be playing somewhere in the distance, occasionally competing with the hum of scooters weaving through foot traffic. It reminded me of the vintage Rome poster in Aidan's apartment with the couple on a moped. Above, laundry fluttered from tiny balconies, and that brought me back to Morocco.

Every block or so, there was a new discovery. Quintessential Spanish tile motifs on a wall, quaint storefronts that looked like they sold home remedies, and the most adorable tapas bar with nothing but four stools at a small counter inside. I resisted the urge to make a list of all the places I wanted to visit, knowing I'd be passing them frequently once I settled into an apartment.

The day before, my rental agent, Antonio, showed me five options. After the first three, I agreed to increase my budget. My money went further than in Dublin, and it would stretch even further if I lived outside the city, but I wanted to be in the middle of everything. Two of the places I viewed were viable options; great location, fully furnished but were missing the "It" factor. As the sun set on that first day of viewings, Antonio said he had just the place and would show it to me "mañana."

I found the building he'd told me to meet him at and although I was fifteen minutes late, he was later. I'd heard about Spanish time, how everything slows down, and, so far, it was proving to be an accurate stereotype.

I pulled out my phone and snapped a picture of the bougainvillea with fuchsia flowers perfectly trained up the wall to frame the doorway of my potential future apartment building. Beside the vines, the name "Rosario" was spelled in gold-plated tiles.

Me: *Here's some door envy for you. Feeling like this may be THE ONE.*

I'd given Brad the rundown of the apartments I viewed the day prior. He'd been a steady source of support the first couple of days in Spain; I never truly felt alone.

I stared up at the Juliette balconies on the second and third floors, wondering if one of them might become mine.

My daydreaming ended abruptly when a cyclist screeched to a halt inches from plowing into me. Startled, I shouted profanities before realizing it was Antonio.

He casually dismounted, leaned the bike against the bougainvillea, and strutted toward me in shorts and t-shirt that read "TOO ZHINK", looking like any other guy on the street and not like a professional.

"Hola, Jessica." He pronounced the 'J' like a 'Y' and the 'i' pulled long—*Yes-ee-ca*. I returned the greeting and stumbled through basic pleasantries in my elementary Spanish before he switched to English.

"Let's go." He grabbed a folder and pen from the bike basket, secured in place under a bottle of water.

Through the building's entrance, we climbed the rickety staircase to the third floor, though he called it the second, like they do in Ireland. He pulled a set of keys from his pocket; an old skeleton key for the knob and a modern one for the deadbolt.

The door creaked open to a sun-drenched flat. See through linen curtains danced in the breeze above the cracked balcony sliding door. The street below was the one I'd been standing on minutes earlier. The mismatched furniture looked lived in, yet stylish, more so than what I had in Dublin. The kitchen cupboards held flatware that looked curated from flea markets. Each piece felt unique, like something I'd admire in someone else's space, but never actually buy myself. I'd always purchased the boxed sets with matching bowls, mugs and two sizes of plates.

I walked slowly throughout the narrow living space. The white tiles underfoot were simple and unpretentious, leading me into the bedroom. Cozy, with just enough space for the low profile full size bed and an antique armoire that looked like it might spring to life and talk to me like in the original *Beauty and the Beast*. The bathroom had modern upgrades including a rainfall shower head and a brand new washer-dryer unit conveniently shoved in the corner across from the toilet.

I loved it.

I loved how I felt in the space. Who I might become. Free. Adventurous. Bilingual. Collecting experiences the way the kitchen cupboard had collected mismatched treasures. Would I host new friends here? Have steamy one night stands? Spend quiet nights reading and experimenting in the kitchen? Or would I sit on the faux leather sofa and wonder if it was all a mistake, yearning for home?

Would Brad and I keep talking? Would we both be single at the end of the year?

Every possibility felt appealing in its own way, because deep down, I knew it'd all work out.

Antonio didn't say much as I strolled around. He didn't offer commentary or try to sell it to me, but as I came out of the bathroom, he said, "There is a garden."

"A garden?" I'd learned that in Ireland, a garden meant a backyard which didn't seem relevant for an apartment building.

Back on the ground floor, instead of exiting the main door, we went through a small arched door tucked behind the stairwell. It opened into a spacious courtyard filled with greenery. Some of it looked dehydrated, but I couldn't tell if that was winter or neglect. A few small iron tables—like the ones in Morocco—and a bench surrounded a fountain where an elderly woman sat with a cane resting against her leg. It was the perfect place to drink coffee or wine from one of those eclectic cups in the apartment.

Antonio and I discussed the rent for a three month lease with an option to extend. The rent was more than what my mortgage would have been for the house I almost bought in Tampa. The sensible voice in my head started shouting—renting instead of buying, burning through my savings, and not earning a paycheck for a year. Every financial rule I'd ever followed screamed that this was a mistake.

I thought of my career. How quickly I'd moved on and how little I missed it. I thought of Lindsay and my parents. I thought of Brad. I thought of my savings account north of a hundred thousand dollars—how it took six years of budgeting and sacrifice to build it for a down payment, and how on this gap year, I'd blow through half of it. I stopped at the small arched door that divided the courtyard from the stairwell. It was a beautiful door; aged oak, detailed molding and a heavy brass knocker.

Why did a courtyard door need a knocker?

It looked like the doors I'd seen in Morocco.

Morocco. Aidan.

Despite the heartbreak, I was grateful his stories of travel lit something inside me.

But I would grow from him. From the entire year in Dublin. I wanted to make it matter or at least feel like it mattered.

Antonio approached behind me. "So?" he asked. "What do you think?" Without hesitation, I told him.

"I'll take it."

Epilogue: Two Years Later

THE SEVEN-PIECE BAND PLAYED inside while I fought off beads of sweat gathering above my lip with the back of my silky, dark green glove. Even in February, the Florida heat was not for the faint of heart.

But Lindsay was divine. There wouldn't be a bad picture in the bunch.

Earlier, in the bridal suite, I'd secretly thought her curls were too tight—not that I'd ever say it, because she loved them. But now, after the ceremony and the evening humidity, they'd relaxed into the perfect beach wave. She stood across the garden of the country club in a silk gown with a soft, drooping boat neck and a plunging back. Only Lindsay would be so committed to the overall look that she'd wear long sleeves in triple digit temperatures. Then again, she claimed that her Botoxed armpits no longer sweat.

Her bouquet of purple peonies remained symmetrical no matter how she posed for the photographer. Jason hovered at her side; tall, tan and beaming as his hand drifted to the small of her back every few seconds. They looked blissfully unaware of everything but each other.

But that was not going to last.

Because Lindsay's mother was approaching.

I saw it happen before her expression changed—the tightening of Lindsay's jaw, the faint lift of her shoulders. Eleanor always evoked a response in Lindsay.

"Lindsay, darling," she began, arms wide and eyes narrow. "I still wish you'd worn your hair in an updo. With your jawline and stumpy neck, it would have added height."

Lindsay's smile didn't falter as Jason leaned in and murmured what I can only imagine were positive affirmations.

"There's still time to put it up before the reception. Shall I go fetch your friend Rosemary? The hairdresser?"

"For the fiftieth time, Mother, it's Rose Marie," Lindsay said sweetly through gritted teeth. "And she isn't a hair dresser. She's a nurse who happens to also be very good at hair and makeup."

Eleanor was unmoved. "So . . . shall I get her?"

Lindsay's eyes flicker toward me. A silent plea.

I swoop in as seamlessly as I can. "Lindz, we were hoping to get a friend group photo before the sun sets. Come on, let's gather the others." It was a lame excuse, but good enough.

As we walked away, she grabbed a flute of champagne etched with their monogram from a passing tray.

"I'm trying," she said before draining half the contents in a single gulp. "I'm trying to 'go high' and all that, but if she says one more thing, I'm going to explode." I rubbed her arm through my glove. "She's been *herself* all day. You'd think she could tone it down for one day? And she's wearing black? Is she in mourning? I guess I should just be thankful she isn't wearing white?"

I wondered whether Eleanor had been given guidance on the attire. I'd definitely seen black worn before at weddings, so maybe Eleanor didn't do it on purpose? I didn't know, but I knew better than to ask. Weddings are not a time to play referee, they're a time to pick sides.

"And the comments, the little digs, the opinions!" She threw her head back and punctuated the end of the sentence with some sort of growl. "Comments about my dress, about my weight, about how much money she spent, the strings she had to pull to have it here at the club. We got engaged over two years ago, it's plenty of time to reserve the club," she said, mocking "the club."

She wasn't wrong. Cody's mom was diagnosed with early stage breast cancer, so they held off on any wedding planning until she completed chemotherapy and was in remission. It gave plenty of time for Eleanor to reserve the date at the club where she'd been a member for over a decade.

"Don't you think you could have lost a few more pounds?" Lindsay said in a high pitch. "I mean, seriously, who says that?"

I gave her the look that said, "we both know exactly who says that."

"We're not going to change Eleanor today. It can be a post honeymoon project," I say. "Today is about you and Jason, so I think the best plan is . . ." I paused.

She nudged her chin forward. "Avoidance?"

"Precisely."

She laughed and I joined in. "I'll keep an eye out," I promised.

Jason's son, Cody, whooshed passed us in his tiny tux, steering a remote control monster truck across the wide open terrace.

"Sorry, Miss Lindsay," he said, slowing only momentarily before resuming full speed ahead.

Lindsay made a megaphone with her hands and called out, "If Gravedigger gets his muddy tires on my train, I'll have Swamp Thing make him pay!"

"You didn't bring Swamp Thing to the wedding," he teased, revealing a missing front tooth.

"You wanna bet?" She raised her arms like a swamp creature and chased after him, keeping up the charade.

I touched the small four-leaf clover necklace she'd given me and took the moment in. She had come so far—with Jason, with Cody, with herself. Watching her become a stepmom filled me with fierce pride.

Large, warm hands slid onto my shoulders as a kiss landed gently on the nape of my neck. I closed my eyes and let myself melt back, smiling even before Brad spun me around as the band inside launched into "Can't Take My Eyes Off You."

"I personally think Lindz would've made a better Dirt Crusher than a Swamp Thing," he says in my ear.

I elbow him lightly before taking off the clammy gloves.

We'd spent the last year rebuilding our lives in Tampa. Our relationship too. Brad was all in from the start, which was when he came to visit me in Spain at the end of my year there. He helped me launch my boutique consulting company, treating my wins as his own and sharing the burden of my disappointments. For six months, he spent most evenings after his own job researching state and local business laws, comparing office spaces, and building my website. I built the business plan while I was alone in Spain, but he's the one who made it a reality.

Raya, who was now back in Tampa as an Associate Partner, helped me with my marketing strategy. We finally had the lunch we'd promised each other. Fifteen months late, but better late than never.

And the real MVP of my company getting off the ground?

Crawford Townsend.

He sent several lucrative projects my way, clients I'd be unlikely to get as a brand new firm just opening its doors. He'd say that conflicts of interest kept McAfee Consulting from taking on the work. I didn't believe it for a second but was grateful anyway.

Brad's hands slid down my arms, which were wrapped around his neck. He grabbed the gloves and shoved them into his pocket for safe keeping.

"What?" he murmured, raising a brow.

"Nothing," I said. "Just really, really happy."

"Me too." He kissed my heavily painted lips. "Your maid of honor speech was excellent, five stars, no notes. I think you were made for public speaking."

"That was just the welcome toast," I corrected. "The maid of honor speech is during dinner."

"Oh god," he whispered dramatically. "There's more?"

I gave him a look. "Consider it payback for when you told me we only had two hours left on the Camino when, in fact, we had six."

He laughed—soft and familiar. The laugh I'd missed for years. The laugh I now had back. And it wasn't that it was easy for us to fall into old patterns, it was that we'd earned our way back to each other. We evolved.

"Brace yourself for Costa Rica in two weeks. I have a hike planned, but don't worry. It should only take two hours." He winked, adorable and clunky.

I wondered whether he'd propose on the hike, similar to how Jason had. Hopefully without any horses involved. I knew he had the ring—I'd accidentally seen a text from Lindsay a few weeks ago asking how the engraving inside the band turned out. I wondered which of our inside jokes he chose. Maybe something Rolling Stones related?

We'd started perusing the real estate listings. Not seriously, but just to get a pulse on the market. Between my business, our travels and apparently an upcoming wedding to plan, we weren't in a rush. But whenever we ended up with a house, one thing was for certain—I'd be painting the front door turquoise.

A server approached, asking for drink orders in Spanish. Without thinking, I answered in Spanish. Still conversationally fluent, if a bit rusty, I ordered a tinto de verano, the Spanish summer classic. When he told me they didn't have Fanta Limon, we negotiated Sprite with extra citrus slices.

Brad gave me *that* look. The one that said, "I love that this is who you are." If you could bottle up safety and security into one look, that would be it.

"I love it when you roll your R's," he said, purring one dramatically.

"I love it when you wear a tux," I countered, tugging at his lapels.

"I love being your date."

"I preemptively love the breakfast you're gonna make me tomorrow," I said.

"I preemptively love the breakfast I'm going to DoorDash tomorrow," he corrected.

"I love . . ." I tapped my chin thinking of a witty comeback.

His hand found mine. "I love you."

I was reminded again that saying "I love you" to someone shouldn't be complicated or conditional or tricky.

Not when it's to the right person.

"I love you, too," I said.

ACKNOWLEDGEMENTS

This book has been over a decade in the making. Not a consistent one, but very much a pick up and put down kind. I rewrote this story more times than I can count and the path to publication was long and sometimes frustrating, but it was also one of the most fulfilling things I've ever done. And I didn't do it alone.

First, I want to thank the people who helped shape earlier versions of this story to make it better. Nicole, thank you for your developmental insight and for pushing me to focus on conflict and stakes which gave birth to Raya. To my beta readers—Crystal, Tasha, Rianna, M.C., and Mom (Linda), thank you for reading early drafts and sharing honest feedback. I took each point to heart and hope you can see it reflected in the final product. Aspen, thank you for your thoughtful copy edits and teaching me how to properly use a comma. Although, I'll probably still add too many because I'm set in my comma-ways. Kenna, thank you for being my final set of eyes. I kept some of the informal words and decided to capitalize Partner, so any bad reviews citing those items are all on me! Brittanée, thank you for encouraging me to set stretch goals, for lending advice and most importantly—for helping to give Jess a happily ever after. Ruthie, thank you for being my official sounding board. I'm grateful for your help and brutal honesty as I navigate the world of publishing.

This is where things get "tricky." Over the past year—and really, the past decade—so many people have shown up in big and small ways. Friends, coworkers, strangers, fellow authors and book reviewers have offered encouragement, advice, their platforms, reviews, or simply listened to me ramble and brainstorm. I appreciate all of it and it all helped.

To my family—Mom and Dad, thank you for always believing in me. To my sons: one who is far too young to understand I wrote a book and the other who is far too into books with pictures to care about my "grown up book". Nonetheless, they unknowingly made me want to see this through because I'm constantly telling them "You can do hard things"—although it's usually in response to them zipping up their jackets or scaling a playground. And to my husband, who lived alongside this project: thank you for the support you gave and for putting up with the nights, weekends, and mental capacity that this dream requires.

Finally, to my readers. As I get older, I find myself increasingly aware of the passage of time, and the fact that you chose to spend precious hours of yours with my story means more to me than I can ever express.

Thank you,
T

WHEN IN
Dublin

TRACY AVERY

READERS GUIDE

DISCUSSION QUESTIONS

1. Do you think Jessica would have made the same choices at the beginning of the novel as she does at the end? What specifically changed—and what stayed the same?

2. What are some "life goals" you've set for yourself that didn't pan out? When you look back, do you wish they had worked out, or do you believe the alternative path served you better in the long run?

3. What do you think Jessica and Aidan each got out of their relationship, and what did they fail to give each other?

4. The story is told entirely from Jessica's point of view. Were there moments when you wished you could step inside Aidan's head? If so, which scenes? And what do you think we might have learned?

5. Doors appear repeatedly throughout the story: the turquoise door, the red Georgian door of Aidan's family home, the brightly colored

doors of Dublin, and the ornate doors of Morocco. What do you think these doors symbolize in Jessica's journey? Did you notice any others?

6. A theme of the story is not always saying what we think and not always getting the closure we feel we deserve. Have you experienced a relationship (romantic or otherwise) that ended with unanswered questions? Did you want those answers at the time, and how do you feel about that now?

7. Why do you think Aidan ultimately broke up with Jessica? Do you believe it was one defining moment or the accumulation of many small things? Have you had a similar experience (on either side of the relationship)?

8. How does Jessica's friendship with Lindsay function as both a mirror and a contrast to her romantic relationship?

9. Brad exists mostly in Jessica's thoughts rather than on the page. Why do you think the author chose to keep him largely off the page? How does that choice affect how you read Jessica's romantic journey?

10. In the final chapter, Jessica chooses to take a gap year in Spain. If you could step away from your current responsibilities for a year, where would you go, and what would you hope to discover or accomplish in that time?

BEHIND THE BOOK

I lived in Dublin for nearly six years, and during that time, experienced some of the highest highs and lowest lows. I made new friends that felt like family, learned how to navigate a new office culture, traveled a ton, missed home in ways that physically ached, and eventually met my now husband. It's fair to say that Dublin "made" me.

Many authors say they wrote their first book because they always loved reading or dreamed of writing. That wasn't really the case for me. Sure, I was a reader, but not in a way that translated into writing. But I became obsessed with *storytelling* and symbolism as a way to process feelings—mostly feelings around approaching thirty and not being entirely content with my place in the world.

Based on all that, you might assume this novel is somewhat autobiographical.

It isn't. And it is.

Jessie is very different from me. I *wanted* to go abroad, and for the most part, enjoyed living outside my comfort zone. I am deeply grateful for the career that brought me overseas, and I've never had a workplace rivalry. But yet, so much of what Jessie struggles with, I can so clearly relate to, either directly or indirectly. *This* is what I love about storytelling—combining little bits of real people and lived experiences with fictional ones to create characters and events capable of tapping into specific emotions and questions.

As I revised this story throughout 2025, there were a few things I hoped to accomplish.

First, I wanted to write an "American-in-Europe" story without romanticizing the move. Even in an age of FaceTime and access to global flights, relocating to another country—or even another city—is hard. It's lonely and disorienting. It can create tremendous opportunities as well as very real challenges—the biggest one in my opinion is always feeling like you either have two homes or none at all.

Second, I wanted to explore career doubt and burnout without the protagonist burning everything down. I see so many stories online about dramatic career changes with total pivots, and although that can certainly be the right choice for some, I believe that meaningful change more often comes through small decisions and subtle shifts in perspective rather than a complete one-eighty. One of my favorite things about Jessie's character arc is that after her gap year in Spain, she ultimately remains in her chosen career, but in a completely different way—on her own terms at her own boutique firm.

And finally, perhaps the hardest, I wanted to tell a love story without making it the main story. To me, there isn't a story worth telling without some element of love, but I wanted the romance to *influence* Jessie's reinvention as opposed to making it *be* her reinvention. It's a small but important distinction in how I want to tell stories. I lost more sleep than I'd like to admit wondering whether I'd disappoint romance readers by not delivering more swoony moments and tension-filled banter, but it didn't feel right for this story. In the end, I hope those who came looking for romance, got it. And those who came for self-discovery, or just wanted to take a trip to Ireland, I hope the book delivered there too.

Thank you for reading Jessie's story. I'm grateful for your time and readership.

PLAYLIST

1. *Nothing's Gonna Hurt You Baby*—Cigarettes After Sex

2. *Far Too Young to Die*—Panic! At The Disco (*)

3. *Friday I'm in Love*—The Cure (*)

4. *You've Really Got A Hold On Me*—Smokey Robinson & The Miracles (*)

5. *Electric Love*—BØRNS

6. *Try Me*—James Brown (*)

7. *These Arms of Mine*—Otis Redding (*)

8. *Cornelia Street*—Taylor Swift

9. *Dreaming of You*—The Coral (*)

10. *Like Real People Do*—Hozier

11. *Intro*—The xx

12. *Bloodflood, Pt.II*—alt-J

13. *The Night We Met*—Lord Huron

14. *Whiskey in the Jar*—The Dubliners (*)

15. *Wild Rover*—The Fisherman's Friends (*)

16. *Shake It Out*—Florence + The Machine

** Songs explicitly mentioned in the book*

Link to Playlist in Spotify

WHAT I'M WRITING NEXT

ASHMORE PLAYHOUSE SERIES

A series of interconnected standalones following the women of Sycamore Cove–an up-and-coming neighborhood in the fictional suburb of Ashmore, North Carolina. At the center of it all is the Ashmore Playhouse, where each season's musical production echoes the leading lady of the neighborhood's journey. Think *Desperate Housewives* meets *Gilmore Girls* with a theatrical twist.

BOOK 1: OFF PITCH

When a fiercely independent single mom hires a sidelined professional soccer star as a summer coach and "manny" for her two sons, she expects help . . . not to fall for him and upend her life.

Can you guess which musical takes the stage during Book 1?

Tracy grew up in Florida, has lived in Ireland and Spain, and now calls North Carolina home with her husband and two children. She studied Accounting at the University of South Florida and is a CPA when she's not reading or writing stories that mix humor with emotional depth and a touch of escapism. *When in Dublin* is her debut novel.

VISIT TRACY ONLINE

Website: TracyAvery.com
Instagram: TracyAvery.Books

FINAL NOTE

Thank you for spending time with me (and Jessie) in Dublin!

I'd be so grateful if you left an honest review wherever you share thoughts on books—Goodreads, Amazon, or both! I've included links and QR codes below. Every review helps this story find its way to more readers.

Sláinte,
Tracy

Goodreads

Amazon

www.ingramcontent.com/pod-product-compliance
Lightning Source LLC
Chambersburg PA
CBHW020909060726
47591CB00004B/1153